FREE AGENT

FREE AGENT

Jeremy Duns

VIKING

VIKING
Published by the Penguin Group
Penguin Group (USA) Inc., 375 Hudson Street,
New York, New York 10014, U.S.A.
Penguin Group (Canada), 90 Eglinton Avenue East, Suite 700,
Toronto, Ontario, Canada M4P 2Y3
(a division of Pearson Penguin Canada Inc.)
Penguin Books Ltd, 80 Strand, London WC2R 0RL, England
Penguin Ireland, 25 St. Stephen's Green, Dublin 2, Ireland
(a division of Penguin Books Ltd)
Penguin Books Australia Ltd, 250 Camberwell Road, Camberwell,
Victoria 3124, Australia
(a division of Pearson Australia Group Pty Ltd)
Penguin Books India Pvt Ltd, 11 Community Centre, Panchsheel Park,
New Delhi – 110 017, India
Penguin Group (NZ), 67 Apollo Drive, Rosedale, North Shore 0632,
New Zealand (a division of Pearson New Zealand Ltd)
Penguin Books (South Africa) (Pty) Ltd, 24 Sturdee Avenue,
Rosebank, Johannesburg 2196, South Africa

Penguin Books Ltd, Registered Offices:
80 Strand, London WC2R 0RL, England

First American edition
Published in 2009 by Viking Penguin,
a member of Penguin Group (USA) Inc.

1   3   5   7   9   10   8   6   4   2

Publisher's Note

This is a work of fiction. Names, characters, places, and incidents either are the product of the author's imagination or are used fictitiously, and any resemblance to actual persons, living or dead, business establishments, events, or locales is entirely coincidental.

ISBN 978-0-670-02101-7

Printed in the United States of America

For Johanna, Rebecca and Astrid

'Man is not the creature of circumstances; circumstances are the creatures of men. We are free agents, and man is more powerful than matter.'

From Vivian Grey by Benjamin Disraeli

I

Sunday, 23 March 1969, Hampshire

As I edged the car onto the gravel, the front door of the house swung open and Chief's steely grey eyes stared down at me. 'What the hell took you so long?' he hissed as I made my way up the steps. But before I could answer, he had turned on his heels.

I followed the sound of his slippers gently slapping against the floorboards, down the dark oak-lined corridor. I knew from years of working for him that the best thing to do when he was in this sort of mood was not to react — his gruff tone usually gave way quite quickly, and more often than not he ended our sessions treating me like the son he'd never had. So I resisted the temptation to tell him I had driven up in record time, and instead hung my coat on one of the hooks in the hallway. Then I walked into the living room and seated myself in the nearest armchair.

It had been a while since I'd last visited Chief out here, but little had changed. There were a couple of porcelain birds I didn't remember, and a new *bois clair* bookcase that looked similar to the one he had in his office. But the framed photographs on the piano, the portrait of his father above the mantelpiece and the golf bag propped against the fireplace were all still in place. A selection of books and papers were spread across a garish Turkish carpet at the foot of one of the armchairs, and a sideboard within easy reach was home to a telephone, an inkwell and what looked like a half-eaten egg sandwich. He still hadn't learned to cook since Joan's death, it seemed.

I imagined him nibbling the sandwich as he had barked down the telephone at me less than two hours earlier. He had refused to give any hints as to what he wanted to discuss, and I was naturally intrigued. What could be so urgent that it couldn't wait for tomorrow's nine o'clock meeting? One possibility that had nagged at me all the way from London was that he had somehow found out I was seeing Vanessa and was so furious he wanted to dismiss me on the spot.

I thought back over the day. Had I been careless somewhere? We had visited a small art gallery in Hampstead in the morning but there hadn't been another soul in the place apart from the owner, and after that we had spent the entire afternoon at her flat, pushing the sheets to the bottom of the bed. Then I'd headed to mine for a quick shave and change of clothes. We had arranged to meet at Ronnie Scott's at midnight: there was a hot young group from the States she wanted to see. But then the call had come through, with the request to come and see him at my 'earliest convenience'.

It wasn't convenient at all, of course. Vanessa and I rarely had a whole weekend together, and it had taken careful planning – perhaps not careful enough, though.

'Something to drink?' Chief called over his shoulder from the sideboard. 'I have some Becherovka, which I remember you used to enjoy.'

What *was* going on? A few moments ago he had been furious; now he was buttering me up. When he'd been Head of Station in Czechoslovakia in '62, we had often shared a few glasses of this local liqueur in his office.

'Good times,' I said. 'Have you kept some back since then? I can't imagine anyone stocks it in the village shop.'

He poured a few glugs of the stuff into a tumbler and passed it over. 'Barnes finds it for me,' he said.

Barnes was a Mau Mau veteran he had reluctantly taken on as a minder when he had been appointed Chief. He had resisted all entreaties for Barnes to be allowed to move into the house, claiming that the place had been his weekend retreat for years and he wasn't about to have it invaded by a stranger. So Barnes rented a cottage in the neighbouring village, and popped his head in as regularly as he could without annoying the old bugger too much. Apparently, he also made sure he never ran out of booze.

Chief settled back into his armchair and raised his glass solemnly towards me, seemingly in a toast. As I lifted mine in return, I was surprised to catch the scent of Vanessa's sex still on my fingertips. I breathed it in, and its rawness overcame me for a moment.

'One never quite gets used to it,' he said softly, 'does one?'

I looked at him blankly. 'I'm sorry, sir?'

He pointed at his glass. 'My Prague poison, Joan used to call it. Do you remember?'

He gave a short uncharacteristic laugh, which I did my best to imitate.

'Yes,' I said. 'I do remember.'

I was relieved, but also, I realized, a little disappointed that he apparently wasn't about to sack me, after all. I'd become so bloody soft I had actually been looking forward to a bit of drama.

Chief was leaning down, running his hand through the papers at his feet. Then he gave a triumphant snort and edged a manila folder out from beneath a copy of *The Sunday Telegraph*. He fished it up and placed it on his knees. It was a file from the office — a new one, by the look of it.

'Bad news, I'm afraid,' he said, handing it to me. 'Traitor country.'

*

The folder had been sent by diplomatic bag from our station in Nigeria and concerned one Vladimir Mikhailovich Slavin, a cultural attaché at the Soviet Embassy in Lagos. He had turned up at our High Commission there on Friday evening and announced that he wanted to defect.

It was a slim folder: as well as a transcript of the interview with Slavin in Russian and an English translation of the same, it contained a page of notes by the Chief of Station, Manning, and two grainy, passport-sized photographs that had been taken at some point in the previous two years as part of the station's routine surveillance of foreign diplomatic staff. It had a very restricted distribution: just Chief and Heads of Section.

It took me a good ten minutes to get through it. I found that I desperately wanted a cigarette, but as there was nothing more certain to get Chief's dander up than that, I made do with drumming my hands on the arm of the chair.

'High stakes,' he muttered, tapping his glass with his fingers.

That was an understatement. Slavin claimed to be a colonel in the KGB and was asking to be smuggled out of Nigeria to a new home in England. In return, he was promising to reveal information about a British agent who had been recruited by Moscow in 1945.

Since Burgess and Maclean had fled to Moscow in '51, several Soviet agents had been uncovered in the Service, Five and elsewhere. Philby had been the biggest blow – he had been tipped by many for the top. In the six years since his disappearance, the Service had become almost paralysed by the fear that other traitors remained undetected. I'd lost count of the number of officers whose pasts had been put under the microscope; I had even faced questioning myself.

'Has Henry seen this yet, sir?' I asked. Henry Pritchard headed up Africa Section; as Slavin was in Nigeria, he would be heavily involved.

Chief nodded. 'I had it hand-delivered to the homes of all Heads of Section a few hours ago, apart from Edmund, who's still away – his went to Smale instead. Because you and Henry

5

will be taking the lead on this, I attached invitations to your copies asking you to come round this evening. Station 12 told me you'd been out when they called round, which is why I rang you up myself.'

Station 12 was the messenger service. 'I see,' I said. 'Sorry about that — I was at a concert for most of the afternoon. Was Henry not in either, then?'

He shook his head briskly. 'No, he got it. I scheduled him for a bit later, though, because I wanted to talk it through with you first. See what you made of it.'

I stood up and walked over to the fireplace, trying to think of a suitable answer.

'Could Slavin be a plant?' I asked, but when I turned round I saw he was already shaking his head. It surprised me he felt so certain: several recent defectors were suspected of being Trojan horses, sent over by Moscow to make outrageous allegations so the Service would chase its own tail.

'It's something Slavin said in his interview,' he explained, seeing my confusion. '"In 1945, we recruited a British agent . . ."' He waved at the dossier impatiently. I walked back to my armchair, picked up the papers and scanned them until I found the place.

'". . . We recruited a British agent in Germany and gave him the code-name *Radnya*."' I thought for a moment, trying to see what he was getting at. 'Radnya is Russian for "kindred", or "related". They go in for clever code-names, don't they — perhaps this means he's related to the Cambridge gang? Recruited later, but part of the same network?'

He shook his head. 'Nothing to do with the code-name. Have a look at that part in the original, and see if you can spot anything.'

I sat down again and searched for the line in the Cyrillic. 'What am I looking for?'

'I think that sentence has been mistranslated.'

'Deliberately, sir?' Had he called me out to deepest Hampshire for a rant about the quality of staff in the colonies?

'I'm not sure,' he said. 'It's possible, but I think it's more likely to have been a slip-up. I wanted to hear your view. It's the phrase "*tajnaya sekretnaya sluzhba*". How would you translate that?'

'Secret service,' I said. 'Only . . .'

He leaned forward slightly. 'Yes?'

'Only *tajnaya* and *sekretnaya* both mean secret. A literal translation would be more like "secret secret service" . . .'

'Exactly!' He beamed at me. 'I suspect the translator thought that a British agent would by definition have been working for intelligence, so he dropped it. But that is precisely the point. What Slavin seems to have been suggesting is that this chap was a member of a *secret* intelligence agency. And as all intelligence is, by definition, secret, what could that mean?'

'I'm afraid I don't know, sir,' I said. I had a feeling he was about to share his own theory. Sure enough, he immediately leaned forward and pinched the knees of his pinstripe trousers, revealing two strips of pale skin above his woollen socks.

'Back in '45,' he said, 'I was chief of the British army's headquarters in Lübeck. A couple of months after the war ended,

I was walking out of the mess and ran straight into an old friend from my days in Cairo: your father, Lawrence.'

'Father? You've never mentioned this before.'

He coughed into his hand abruptly, which I knew meant he was extremely anxious. 'No,' he said. 'And I'm sorry about that. I know how hard it's been for you, but I could never find a way to . . . It's very delicate, you see.'

My father had last been seen in the bar of White's in May 1945, just a few days after victory in Europe. Nobody had ever discovered what had happened to him.

'Did you talk?' I asked, and Chief raised his head and looked me in the eye.

'Yes, we talked. He seemed extremely agitated. He asked me to take a walk outside with him, whereupon he told me that he was on a vitally important job – extremely hush-hush. He didn't divulge any more details, but said that the entire operation had been compromised by a Russian nurse who was working in the Red Cross hospital in Lübeck.'

'He wanted your help?'

'Yes,' he said after a few moments. 'He asked if I could take some men round to the hospital under cover of darkness, detain the nurse, and have her transported to the War Office's interrogation centre over in Bad Nenndorf.'

'That's quite a favour to ask,' I said. 'Did you oblige?'

Chief carefully placed his glass on the nearest side table. 'Well, I tried. He provided me with a dossier containing her photograph and particulars – her name was Maleva – and I assembled a small team immediately. We took a jeep round to her quarters that same night. Unfortunately, when we arrived we discovered that she was already dead.'

I paused for a moment to take this in.

'Suicide?'

He shook his head. 'Shot through the chest. Quite messy. Of course, I got my men out of there as fast as I could. British officers kidnapping a Russian nurse would have been bad enough, but if we'd been caught with murder on our hands there would have been all manner of problems.' He looked down at his drink a little mournfully. 'And that was that. I never saw Larry again. I've often wondered whether I was the last person to see him.'

'I'm glad you told me,' I said. 'And it sounds like this operation he was on may be the key to his disappearance. But I don't quite see how it relates to the situation in Nigeria.'

'Oh,' he said. 'Didn't I mention? The nurse Slavin's claiming recruited the double – it's this same damned Maleva woman!'

I stared at him uncomprehendingly. 'But how can that be?' I asked. 'I mean, if she was shot in the chest . . .'

'I know,' he said. 'And it had me stumped for a bit. But SOE had a section for camouflage and make-up techniques – perhaps the Russians had similar expertise.'

'Perhaps,' I said. 'But what about her pulse? Presumably she wasn't just lying there with her eyes closed, holding her breath.'

Chief took another sip of liqueur. 'That had me stumped for longer. In the end I rang Bill Merriweather and asked him how he would have done it.' Merriweather was our man at Porton Down, the Ministry of Defence's chemical laboratory

— back in '56, he'd developed a nerve gas to use on Nasser. It would have worked, too. 'He told me about a discovery someone on his team made a few years ago. Using a very strong tranquillizer called haloperidol, they found a way to stimulate what he referred to as "a temporary state of death". The Russians have apparently been using the stuff on uncooperative prisoners for years, but if it's administered correctly, it can induce catalepsy, which looks like death even to a trained eye. Bill thought there might be other drugs that could produce the same effect.'

'I see,' I said, although it all sounded a little fantastic. 'But I don't understand why you think this is the same woman Slavin is referring to. He doesn't mention what name she was going under in 1945 . . .' I picked up the folder again and found the place on the page. '"During and after the war, Irina Grigorieva, currently the assistant third secretary at the embassy here in Lagos, worked as a nurse in the British Zone of Germany. There she fell in love with a British officer, according to her the one true love of her life. She succeeded in recruiting this man into the NKVD . . ." It doesn't say which hospital she worked at, and there must have been dozens in the Zone. Lagos Station's photograph of her is also a little blurred — what makes you so sure she's this Maleva?'

'Instinct,' he said. 'Instinct and experience. I've spent half the afternoon examining her photograph — I can't be one hundred per cent certain it's her until I check its counterpart in Registry tomorrow morning, but I'm fairly close to that. It has to be her.'

He was looking at me expectantly. And that was when I saw what had been staring me in the face since he had answered the door. Why he'd called me out here tonight instead of leaving it until tomorrow morning. Why he was drinking more than usual. And why I had to act now.

'You needn't worry, sir,' I said.

His broad face reddened immediately, and I knew I'd hit the mark. 'Worry? What makes you think I should do that?'

'You're quite right about the interview,' I said. 'Whoever translated it got it wrong. In the original Russian, Slavin quite clearly states that the double was recruited while involved in some sort of black operation in Germany at the end of the war. It sounds like he might have been part of Father's junket and become entangled with this woman. Did Father give you any idea how many people he had out there with him, if any?'

Chief shook his head. 'He didn't tell me anything at all about the operation – just that it was vital it continued.'

'All right. Still, the fact that you were openly working at British headquarters clearly rules you out as the double. I'll explain the whole thing to Henry as soon as he gets here. When was it you said he was coming over, again?'

'Henry? Nine.'

I glanced at my watch. It had just gone half eight. Pritchard might even be early, knowing him.

Chief was taking a congratulatory draught of Becherovka: he was in the clear now. He must have read the file this morning and panicked – not that another traitor on his watch would lead to calls for him to resign, but that his being stationed in the British Zone in '45 might bring him under suspicion of actually *being* the traitor. His position as Head of the Service was no guarantee of protection: Five's Deputy Head had almost lost his mind after being investigated by other officers in '66. Even a Chief could be brought down. He had probably spotted the omission in the translation some time during the afternoon. It exonerated him, but he knew it would cut more ice if someone else pointed it out. Of the officers who would be hunting the double agent, I was the only one with good enough Russian to spot it – outside Soviet Section, 'Tolstoy' and 'Turgenev' were about all anyone could muster. Additionally, I would have good reason to protect him, as he was a family friend and my father had apparently asked for his help. So he had called me in to get his story straight before tomorrow's meeting. 'It can't possibly be Chief,' I'd tell them. 'There's been a translation cock-up.' Good old Paul.

'Of course,' I said, 'Henry won't be the only one who will need convincing.'

He looked up, alarmed. 'What do you mean?'

'Osborne and Farraday,' I said.

'Yes, yes, of course. I see that. But can't you explain it to them, too?'

'I thought you'd already discussed it with them,' I said lightly, raising my glass. It was empty, and I made sure he noticed.

'What? No, not yet.' He stood up and walked over to the drinks cabinet. 'I thought it best to sound you and Henry out first.'

'Very wise,' I said, lifting my glass. He poured a generous

measure, and as he stepped away I took out the Luger, gaged the safety, aimed between his eyes and fired in al the same moment. The kick pushed me into the armchair and I felt one of the springs dig into my back as the crystal shattered on the floor and his body slumped to the ground and the liqueur began to seep into the carpet.

It was very quiet then. I could hear the wind whipping against the trees outside and a joist creaking somewhere in the house. My head was pounding, the blood careering around it. There had been a moment, a fraction of a moment before I had fired, when he had stared into my face and I'd thought he might have understood what was about to happen to him – that he had realized who I was.

I replaced the Luger and stood up. Pritchard was due to arrive in twenty-eight minutes, and I had to clear up the mess and be well away before then.

I set to work.

II

Sunday, 8 July 1945, British Zone, Germany

I reached the farmhouse about an hour before dawn and hammered on the door. After several minutes it opened, and a tall, lean figure with piercing blue eyes peered out at me.

'*Kann ich Ihnen helfen?*' he said, in an unmistakably English accent. He looked exactly the same as he had the last time I'd seen him.

'You're English,' I said, searching his face for a reaction but getting none. 'That *is* good news. I'm afraid I'm lost. I'm looking for the British headquarters at Lübeck.'

'You *are* lost,' he said, placing his emphasis equally carefully. 'It's a good distance from here. Come in and I can show you on a map.'

It was typical of Father: the war in Europe had been over for two months and there wasn't a soul for miles around, but he had still insisted on keeping to nonsensical recognition codes with his own son until we were inside the house. As soon as we were, he shook my hand and asked if I had had a safe journey. Barely pausing to listen to my reply, he led me through to a cramped, low-ceilinged room and told me to take a seat. He didn't ask about Finland, or Mother, or anything else. He had business to attend to.

The area looked as though it had once been a sitting room, judging by the elaborate floral pattern on the wallpaper and armchairs, but it was now inescapably the domain of a military operation, with most of the space given to a row of card tables that had been pushed together and covered in maps and papers. The room was lit by candles – there was no electricity in the house, and wouldn't be for several weeks.

Against one of the walls was a dilapidated-looking wardrobe, next to which stood a ramrod-straight officer-type. Despite a neat beard and severe spectacles, he looked only a few years older than me. I guessed that this was Henry Pritchard, a Scot who had been Father's second-in-command on several operations early in the war. Father confirmed this, and Pritchard extended a bony hand to shake mine, but said nothing.

Father seated himself in one of the armchairs and I did the same. Pritchard remained standing.

'The first thing I wish to make clear,' Father said, 'is that this job is completely off the books. And I mean completely. Only one living soul outside this room knows what we are doing here, and that's the Prime Minister. Nothing is on paper, nor will it ever be. This goes with us to the grave, or we shall have done more damage than we are trying to rectify. In the hands of our enemies, this information could create the next war. I gave the PM my word, and I intend to stick to it. Do you understand?'

I glanced over at Pritchard to see if it was some sort of a prank. His face was set like stone. Father didn't go in for pranks, I reminded myself.

'I visited him in London a couple of weeks ago,' Father continued. 'It wasn't easy to pull off, but I called in some favours. He gave me ten minutes to outline what I had in mind. He didn't like it at first. Said it would get out, one way or another, and that that would put us in a terrible position.' He smiled, the first time I'd seen him do so since arriving. 'He asked me to leave the building and never come back, actually.'

'What changed his mind?'

He nodded at Pritchard, who turned to the wardrobe and unlocked it. Inside, someone had placed a shelf where the coat-hangers would normally have been, and on it were several stiff-backed folders. Pritchard took one of these out and handed it to me.

It contained a sheaf of documents telling of the execution of two British commandos at a German concentration camp in November 1943. There were photographs of the corpses and eyewitness accounts, all of which pointed to one man as having ordered the deaths. Bodhan Shashkevich was a Ukrainian who had joined the Einsatzkommando, an SS unit whose special responsibility was the hunting and killing of women and children. The British commandos had interrupted some of his fun and games, but had been made to pay.

I looked back at the wardrobe, and at the other folders in it. 'Why do you need me?' I asked. 'This isn't my field.'

Father smiled tersely. 'Since May, SAS have been building up dossiers on suspected war crimes committed against their men and other British commandos. Last month a team moved into a villa at Gaggenau, over in the French Zone, and started trying to track down the perpetrators in order to bring them to trial. Henry is part of that team.' He nodded at the younger man, who smiled at me: for some reason, I wished he hadn't.

'Henry contacted me while he was on leave in London last month,' Father continued. 'He was concerned that some of the guilty parties could evade justice even if they were to be brought before a court. In cases where our men were out of uniform, their lawyers are bound to argue that the conventions did not apply. As a result, they may escape with light sentences, perhaps as little as five or ten years. Worse, some may not even come to trial at all: under the terms of Yalta, most Ukrainians, for example, are being sent back to the Soviet Union. Many of them will be killed on arrival, but the likes of Shashkevich survived the war against strong odds – if they have enough money or other influence, they may yet slip through the net.'

He stood up and walked over to the window. It looked onto a small garden, surrounded by a high wall. He turned back to face me.

'Henry showed me six files, concerning the very worst offenders. As soon as I read them, I realized it was an intolerable situation: many of the victims were British officers, and we should do everything in our power to see they receive justice. I set about trying to get in contact with the PM, and when he gave the go-ahead, came out and secured these premises. Henry has helped prepare a lot of ground for the job I have in mind – unfortunately, his leave ends on Wednesday, and his absence from Gaggenau would be too conspicuous if he did not return. You, however, are off everyone's radar, and that, to answer your question, is why you're here. We will be working very much along the same lines as the team at Gaggenau, with one major distinction: we will not be bringing any of these men to trial. We will have very limited access to supplies, fuel and transport, but Henry has put together papers identifying both of us as members of a British war crimes investigation team, and those should be accepted everywhere apart from the Soviet Zone. Once Henry leaves, though, we are on our own. Do you have any questions?'

I wondered if the two of them had lost their minds and begun weaving fantasies; many were these days. But they didn't look mad: that was the frightening thing.

Although barely in my twenties, I was already an old hand at the spy game, having been attached to several cloak-and-dagger units over the course of the war. This was something else entirely – an execution squad, pure and simple – and the war in this part of the world was meant to be over. But as I looked into Father's grim face flickering in the candlelight, I knew I had no choice in the matter, and shook my head meekly.

'Good,' he said. 'We start tomorrow – Henry's located Shashkevich.'

*

It was a beautiful morning. The air was crisp and clean, and the fields seemed almost to be glowing as the sunlight travelled across them. Somehow it made what we were about to do even worse. Father had briefed me on the day's job, but he hadn't told me how I would feel: as we cut our way through the countryside, a chasm of despair opened up in my stomach and I became terrified I would have to ask him to stop driving so I could vomit. For the first time in my life, I felt like a child playing at soldiers.

When we reached the camp, the guard on duty hardly glanced at our papers, waving us through at the sight of our jeep. In the central reception hall, Pritchard showed our papers again and we were led through to an area of stone cell blocks. A young Ami corporal marched us down a dimly lit corridor, unlocked one of the doors, saluted us, and marched away again without a word.

Shashkevich was seated on the bed, shivering under a rough grey blanket despite the morning sun filtering through the small window set high in one wall. He was still a large man, but the imperious-looking officer of the photographs in his dossier had been all but extinguished. His eyes were now deeply sunken and his skin pitted and sallow. He looked up at us, confusion spreading across his face as he registered our uniforms and berets. He wasn't shivering, I realized then, but rocking back and forth and mumbling something to himself in his own language. Whether he was reciting a prayer, a list of everyone he had ever met to keep his mind active or the defence he planned to use when he reached court I do not know.

Father told him to get up in Russian, and the fear turned to defiance.

'Who are you?' he said.

'Get up,' Father repeated, gesturing with his Luger.

After he and Pritchard had cuffed him, I held the door open as they marched him into the hallway and out to the jeep.

We headed out towards Frankfurt, taking small lanes to avoid the delays on the crater-heavy *autobahn*. It was mid-morning now, and the lines of refugees tramping across the fields, either on their way to DP camps or simply foraging for food, had grown. On the outskirts of the city, we took a turning into deep woods and kept going.

I breathed in the fresh air and tried to fix the moment in my mind: the birdsong, the smell of the trees, the strange emptiness of the sunlit ruined land. The engine stopped. We walked into the middle of a clearing and Father handed me the Luger. I released the safety and pressed the muzzle against the back of Shashkevich's pale neck. The coldness of it woke him up, and the fear came over him in a rush. His hands started shaking violently and I had to clutch him towards me to restrain him. I called out to him in a voice that sounded surer than the one in my head to stop moving or I would shoot. It was an absurd thing to say, because by now he knew I was going to shoot him anyway, and something in me realized this, but I suddenly couldn't stomach the position I was in, shooting him from so close. Without even considering it, I let go of him and stepped away, at the same time jerking one of his arms towards me so that he swivelled around as though it were a ballet. It all took place very fast, and contrary to everything we had planned – we hadn't considered the possibility he might lose control. Shashkevich's hair was plastered to his forehead with sweat and his eyes were staring out of his skull like a maniac's. I thought hard of the photographs I had seen in the dossier and squeezed the trigger.

'Pockets,' said Pritchard after. 'Don't forget his pockets.'

I leaned down and ripped away some papers and trinkets, then handed them to Father and staggered off into the trees.

*

Pritchard returned to Gaggenau a couple of days later, leaving Father and me to work together. We had five more men to find, and it didn't appear that any of them were in custody. We began following the clues contained within the dossiers, re-reading the testimonies and tracing possible escape routes on large-scale maps in the makeshift operations room set up in the house. The pace was furious, and we worked all day, every day, and often through the night. We visited scores of rundown barns and cellars all over the Zone, and I grew accustomed to the look in the eyes of children as we questioned their parents and grandparents. On one occasion, a young boy tried to rush us as we entered a disused stable where he and his family were hiding, and Father very nearly shot him. I began to know what it felt like to be part of an occupying power, and it frightened me. Sometimes I would lie awake in my bed in the attic of the farmhouse and watch the spiders making webs in the beams, thinking back to before the war and dreaming of a future when it would finally be over for me.

Father had no such doubts about the mission, of course. It was his crusade: there was a light shining in his eyes and a spring in his step. He was meting out justice. Although we never spoke of much aside from the work, I was initially pleased that he had felt the need for my assistance, and did all I could to show him I was worthy of his trust. He never mentioned Shashkevich again, and in time I forgot that I had almost botched it and was pleased that I had at least contributed to getting rid of one of them.

It took me several weeks to realize the true nature of my role in the operation. As well as helping him in the field, it was also my job to polish our boots, care for our uniforms and, once we had got the electricity back, cook from the stores in the larder. He never thanked me for any of it, and it slowly dawned on me that this was the primary reason he had wanted me with him. It was his operation, but he needed someone to deal with the household chores and offer support – I was effectively his batman. I felt like I was twelve years old again, lugging his gear around Brooklands. Did he not know what I'd been through in Finland? Hell on earth! Only to be followed by weeks underground in Iceland. And for what? I'd thought he had finally realized that I was now an officer, and a highly capable one at that – but he still saw me as a boy.

My resentment was muted by fear, however: I couldn't shake the feeling that it was a dirty job. With the war over, there were no longer any hard and fast conventions to follow – or if there were, we certainly weren't following them. I remembered the righteous anger that had overtaken us all the previous year when we'd heard about Hitler's Commando Order, which said that we could be shot without trial. In avenging the men killed under that order, weren't we committing the same crime?

By the end of August, four of the targets were dead. But the final name on the list was the one Father wanted most: Gustav Meier. He was an SS officer, and there was compelling evidence that he had raped and tortured the families of suspected members of the Resistance in France, including children. We hunted for him throughout September, but with no luck. Father was acutely aware that the chances of finding him were fading with every day that passed: he might have jumped on a boat to Argentina by now. But in the last week of September, there was a breakthrough. Father returned from a long excursion and barged into my room. 'I've found him!' he shouted. 'I've found the bastard!'

He had discovered from the papers of one of Meier's colleagues that he had relatives living near Hamburg, right across the road from a British army barracks. We had conducted surveillance on the area for several days, but to no avail. But Father had returned for another look and had chanced to spot Meier as he had driven through the nearest village. He was working as a gardener, and further enquiries revealed he had been living with the family under an assumed name.

Father had come back to the farmhouse for a very particular reason. On the two previous targets, he had found pea-sized suicide capsules hidden in their clothing, similar to the potassium cyanide 'L-pills' SOE gave its agents. Himmler had bitten into one when he had been captured in June, and Father was determined not to allow any of our targets to take the same way out: he didn't want them to have that control, and I suppose also felt they deserved to know that vengeance was being served on them. Some reports had claimed that Himmler had been equipped with *two* capsules – one in his clothing and one that he had kept in his mouth. Although they were rubber-cased to avoid accidents – they could be swallowed with no harm done – there was clearly a danger that in a tussle someone might bite down without meaning to. Father wanted very much to deal with Meier on his own terms, so to be doubly sure no accidents happened, he needed another pair of hands: mine.

That evening, he came up with a plan. It involved me dressing up as a displaced person and him as a policeman. We would approach Meier and I would accuse him of some crime – a petty theft. Meier would naturally protest and, taking the opportunity of surprise, I would pretend to fly into a rage and pounce on him: in the resulting mêlée, either Father or I would retrieve any capsules he had on his person. As soon as this was done, Father would 'arrest' Meier, and it wouldn't be until we were some distance away that he would realize what had happened.

After going over it several times, we set out for Hamburg the next afternoon. We found Meier soon enough, working in one of the gardens as he had been the previous day. We approached him in our respective garbs and I claimed that the tools he was using were mine, stolen from me the previous week. But either Father's plan wasn't as clever as we'd thought or my acting was poor, because he saw through it at once and made a dash for it across the garden and into a nearby field. We had no choice but to go after him, but when I caught up and leapt on top of him, I found that he didn't have any capsules on him – but he did have a knife. Where he had hidden it, I don't know, because he had been dressed in very little in the afternoon sunshine, but I felt it go in, and it was the last thing I remembered when I woke in the sanatorium.

*

I have very little recollection of the first few days after the stabbing: I was blacked out for most of it. I do remember being forced to drink endless amounts of a tepid broth that seemed to stick in my throat. And I was occasionally lucid enough when being given a bath or being taken to the bathroom to feel enough residual shame at the indignity of being exposed to strangers that I lashed out at a few people who, after all, were only trying to help me.

One of those was Anna, but I only became aware of her once I had fully regained consciousness and was already a fair way along the road to recovery. She had explained how I had been brought there by a British officer one afternoon with a great gash under my kidneys, and had given me the letter from Father, still sealed in its envelope. The letter enraged me, because he had couched his abandonment of me in a mixture of military jargon and euphemisms: I was now 'on the bench for the remainder of the game' – that sort of thing. As an emergency measure, he left encoded directions for a dead drop near an abandoned well a few miles from the hospital. He said he would check this each day as long as he was in the area, which should be a few weeks more. But the main message was clear: recover, return to England, and forget I'd ever been to Germany.

I disliked Anna at first – or rather, I disliked myself for finding her attractive. Although not long out of boyhood, I was no stranger to the opposite sex, and had had my share of flings along the way. But none of the girls I'd known were anything like this. She was twenty-six, a Georgian with dark, rather flamboyant looks, but there was an unforced grace to her manner that set her apart. After five years of blood and battle, this fit, efficient woman, with her tanned arms, long lashes and perfectly set features seemed almost like a goddess to me. She seemed to belong to another world, where everything was bright and calm, and I wanted to jump through the looking glass and join her in it – but what hope had I of that? I knew that her beauty and job would mean she had probably long become tired of being mooned over, especially by patients, so I resolved not to fall for her, while, of course, at the same time hoping that my aloofness would make me more attractive than more obvious suitors.

My resolution barely lasted a couple of weeks, partly because my wound was so messy that it required almost constant attention, and I was isolated in my own room. While she administered medicine and changed my linen, I had discovered she spoke excellent English. After a few tentative exchanges, I dared to ask if she would mind arranging for me to have some books from the mess library. This she did, and I soon discovered she was very well-read, so after that we began to discuss literature: she was shocked I had never read any of the Russian greats, and proceeded to feed me all the English translations she could find.

I soon found that she was also passionate about the state of the world – when I asked her what she thought the future held for the new Europe, she openly condemned the British for pursuing what she saw as an openly anti-Communist policy so soon after the Soviet Union had, as she saw it, almost single-handedly defeated the Nazis. 'It's not you, Paul,' she would smile, 'but your government is really doing some despicable things. I thought we were allies.'

I tried to steer us away from such topics at first, but she was clever and eloquent – and I was happy just to be able to talk to her. We wrangled good-naturedly, with her usually taking the line that Marxism was the only way ahead and me desperately trying to remember all the reasons I'd been taught that that was wrong. But I couldn't catch her out: her answers were always lucid and thought-provoking. She was very good at sticking to abstract concepts. Whenever I brought up problems, such as the Moscow show trials and executions, she would fix me with her calmest gaze, concede that humans had misunderstood and abused the ideology, then solemnly insist that the world would only be bettered when class and states had been completely abolished and the dictatorship of the proletariat had taken their place. She used the language of Communist ideology with such a straightforward faith in Peace and Brotherhood that most of the time I acquiesced, simply not to appear a cynical beast and thereby lose her friendship. But when I felt particularly bloody-minded and pursued her on such points, her apparent innocence and naivety vanished and she would counter-attack, questioning British policy in India, for example, or picking out some other apposite situation to prove her point. I realized with growing surprise and admiration that her view of the world had rather more consistency and logic to it than my own, and over time had to concede that, in many areas, I was far more naive and ill-informed than she.

But politics was only one subject of our many conversations that autumn. Anna taught me about Russia, but also about herself. She was a born storyteller, giving vivid and moving accounts of her upbringing and her experiences in the war: she had been with the Red Cross all the way through it, which was why she was now working in the British Zone, rather than the Soviet one. Our friendship soon developed into one of those intimate affairs where you stay up all night talking; we ranged over every subject imaginable, skipping from one to the other like pebbles skimming across a lake. She would often visit me for an hour or so between her shifts on the wards, and it was on one of these occasions that I first kissed her.

Love is a fast worker, especially first love, and so it was that, barely three months after being admitted into the sanatorium, I found myself in bed contemplating proposing marriage to my nurse. I could scarcely imagine how Father would react at the news! The instructions in his letter had been clear: I should not visit the farmhouse again unless it was an emergency, but I was past caring — and well enough to leave the hospital. I had been well enough for a couple of weeks, in fact, but had been loath to leave for fear of letting go of Anna. Now I knew she loved me, I made up my mind to propose to her and, if she agreed, journey out to see Father and tell him the news before taking her back to England.

All my dreams evaporated later that evening, however, when she came to visit me after her usual rounds. I was sitting up smoking a cigarette and I sensed the change in her the moment she entered the room.

'What's wrong?'

'Paul,' she said, looking up at me with a strange panic flooding her eyes. 'I am so sorry.'

I gestured for her to take a seat next to me. 'Why? What's happened?' She was usually so controlled.

She walked into the room and closed the door, but didn't move any nearer to the bed. 'I have lied to you,' she said simply.

'What have you lied about?' A cold feeling had begun creeping through me.

She looked down at her hands. 'My name is not Anna Maleva,' she said quietly. 'My real name is Anna-Sonia Kuplin, and I am an agent of the *Narodny Komissariat Vnutrennikh Del*. Two months ago, I was instructed by my superior, a man in the DP camp at Burgdorf, to seduce you and recruit you to our cause.'

She seemed to be talking at me through a fog or a dream.

I looked at my hands and was surprised to see they were shaking. I couldn't seem to stop them. 'Why?' I asked, eventually. 'Why . . . were you asked to recruit me?'

She walked over to the bed and stood by the edge of it. 'My superior wants to know about all my patients, but he was particularly interested in you,' she said. 'He knew of your father, and of his hatred for Communism. Your experience in intelligence and your youth were also seen as . . . attractive qualities.' She grimaced at this, but made herself continue. 'I was told to work on the bitterness you feel against your father to persuade you to join us.'

The blood was rushing around my head, and my chest was heaving.

'So all of this . . .' I said, gesturing futilely at the room where we had spent so much of our time together in the previous weeks, where we had made love, even. 'All of this was because you wanted me to *spy* for you?'

'It was also thought that once I revealed the true nature of your work here, you would be more interested in hearing our proposals.'

'What work?' I said, rage suddenly sweeping over me. I leaned over and grabbed her by the wrists, then thrust my face into hers. 'You can't possibly know what my bloody work involves, you . . . you little Russian whore!' I brought up my hand to slap her, then stopped myself. She hadn't flinched.

'I know more about it than you,' she said quietly, her eyes facing the floor. 'You have been deceived by your father. He was a prominent member of several British fascist groups before the war, and is now part of a secret movement intent on waging a new war against the Soviet Union. The men you were hunting down and murdering were not Nazi war criminals, but Soviet agents.'

She looked up at me for a moment, desperately trying to hold my gaze. But it was too late. There was nothing there for me any more: she wasn't my Anna. I had an almost overwhelming desire to take the pillow from the bed and place it over her face so she wouldn't be able to utter any more lies. 'So that was meant to be enough to turn me, was it?' I said, finally. 'A few fireside chats about politics and a half-baked story about a fascist conspiracy and you thought I'd sign up for Uncle Joe's brand of storm-troopers? How *dare* you accuse me of such a thing? And did you really expect me to believe that our side's made up of blood-thirsty savages and you're all pure as the driven—'

'Oh, Paul,' she said. 'Don't make me tell you it is true.'

'It is not true,' I said coldly. 'And you are the one who has been deceived. I read the orders given by these men. I read the witness reports.'

She had recovered something of her old composure now, and was prepared to fight back. 'Such documents can be easily forged, as you must know. Would anyone else be able to confirm that your mission was legitimate, or did your father perhaps tell you it had been deemed too secret to go through the usual channels?' She looked up, saw the confirmation in my eyes, and continued. 'The first couple of men would have been bona fide, to persuade you. But after that, did you see all the files of the men you killed?'

I didn't answer.

'Meier,' she said. 'Did you read the file on him?'

'Yes, Anna, and he was a rapist! He raped children. How can you do this?'

'I can't!' she said, and her eyes began to well with tears. 'Don't you see? I told my superior to go to hell. I love you, Paul, more than I ever thought it was possible to love someone, and I want us to start again. To forget this.' She stood up and walked towards me. 'I thought at first not to tell you, just to ask that we leave this place, with no explanations. But I don't want any secrets between us, Paul, none at all. Don't you see? I *had* to tell you.' She let her arms open, beckoning me. 'Please.'

I looked at her and part of me wanted more than anything to take a step forward. But that, I knew somewhere deep in the core of me, was weakness, and the kind of immature sentimentality that had led me into this situation. Without looking at her, I told her to leave. She refused at first, continuing to plead with me to listen to her. But I had detached myself, and after a few minutes she saw it. She ran from the room, and I listened dispassionately to the sound of her sobs echoing down the corridor. Then, taking great care not to lean on my wound, I manoeuvred my way down from the bed and started dressing.

*

It was my first taste of fresh air in a long while, but I hardly noticed it. I stopped thinking about Anna's betrayal of me and started focusing on what it meant. She knew about Sacrosanct

— and, presumably, so did her handler in Burgdorf. Father had said in his letter that he would continue the operation for a few more weeks. If he had done so from the same location, as seemed likely, he could be in great danger.

As I started heading for the house, a terrible thought occurred to me. Anna's allegation that Father had mounted a rogue operation and was running around murdering Russians was clearly fantasy, but she had still known a great deal about the operation: the name Meier, for instance. Only two other people had access to that information: Pritchard and Father — and Pritchard had left months earlier. Perhaps Father had risked venturing into the Soviet Zone, and been taken into custody. Under interrogation, he could have revealed Pritchard's and my involvement, and even our locations. Pritchard was surrounded by commandos in the French Zone, so they wouldn't pursue him, but I was alone, and injured. Anna had been assigned as my nurse a few days after I had entered the sanatorium — perhaps the idea for her to recruit me had stemmed from knowledge they had gained from questioning Father.

It all seemed horrifyingly plausible: I couldn't think how else she could have known about the operation. And if I was right, Father was almost certainly dead, and they would soon be hunting me. They would probably be waiting for me at the farmhouse, in fact.

I slowed down, and started walking in the other direction. Father's letter to me had still been firmly sealed, and I guessed Anna had not dared open it for fear of losing my trust early on. The drop, then. I headed for it at once, and left a message that Anna Maleva, a nurse in the Red Cross hospital in Lübeck, was an NKVD agent, and knew about Sacrosanct.

*

A few hours later, I was holed up in a cabin halfway up the mountains, shivering in a wooden cot in the dark. Father had come across the place one day when we had been tramping across the Zone looking for clues. It had been used before the war by local mountaineers as a resting stop on their way to higher climes. Later, the Hitler Youth had taken it over for their excursions, and there were still signs of their occupation, from the insignia above the entrance to graffiti they had carved on the walls: the same sort of obscene phrases and drawings teenage boys make all over the world, for the most part, but disturbing nonetheless. I had immediately thought of the place, because it was well away from the main paths and still within easy walking distance of the nearest town if I needed food. There were no amenities for cooking, or anything else, and it was a lot less comfortable now than it had been during July, when we had come across it. But it was shelter.

I had placed my clothes in one of the cots for padding and tried to sleep as soon as I had reached it. But it was no use. Although still seething over Anna's betrayal, I couldn't shake the feeling that I had missed something in her allegations against Father, something in the tone of them. As daylight began to seep through the wooden slats of the walls, I finally realized what it was: despite trying to resist it, part of me could not help recognizing the ring of truth. He *had* been a fascist before the war, and was ardently, even fanatically, anti-Communist. And even if the Ukrainians had been guilty of the most horrendous crimes, we had nevertheless murdered them – did it make any difference in what cause? But the thing that kept pushing to the front of my mind was Father's obsession for protecting the operation at all costs: his insistence that nobody could ever learn of it.

Had I just signed Anna's death warrant?

As soon as I thought it, I knew I had to reach her again. We would do just as she had said: leave here and start again. I had an image of her in her nurse's smock in a clinic somewhere in England. She loved me – how could I let her go?

*

After eating a handful of wild berries to give me energy for the journey, I walked back to the outskirts of Sankt Gertrud, then ran the remainder of the way to the sanatorium. The other nurses seemed perturbed at seeing me, and after I had managed to push past some of them into the ward area I saw why. One of the doctors was talking to a group of men in uniform. *Russian* uniform. As one of the men saluted, he turned away and I saw the stretcher. Blankets had been placed over her body, but her head was still exposed and the features beneath the yellowish grey complexion and closed lids were unmistakable. One of the nurses told me in a hushed voice that she had been found in her quarters a few hours earlier, and that her body was being taken to the Russian Zone, and then back to Georgia. Apparently the soldiers were looking to trace a visitor she had had the previous evening: a man wearing the uniform of a British officer.

Father had received my message loud and clear, and had acted to eliminate the threat: nobody could know about Sacrosanct. I turned before any of the soldiers spotted me and started running for the farmhouse.

⋆

As I finally crested the hill two hours later, I saw the outline of the jeep and made a desperate effort to increase my pace. He was still here! I pushed open the front door and almost fell into the living room. 'Where are you, you bastard?' I screamed. 'Where the hell are you?' But there was no reply, to that or the other abuse that I hurled at him, and I found out why when I reached his bedroom. He was lying at the foot of the bed, still in his uniform. No pills — he hated the easy option. He'd done it the same way he had meted it out, with a bullet to the temple from his Luger. The left side of his face had been completely destroyed, and the wall behind him was splattered with blood. There was no note, so I could only guess as to why one more murder had woken his conscience. Perhaps she had begged for her life, or told him about her love for me.

It didn't matter any more. He didn't matter. I took him out to the garden and buried him. The wind was fierce — winter would be here soon. I had only one thought in me. I had to get to Burgdorf and find Anna's handler.

I had a proposition to make him.

III

Sunday, 23 March 1969, Hampshire

As I crouched down to take a closer look at Chief's body, there was a noise somewhere behind me and my hand flew to the Luger. But it was just the bleating of the telephone from the sideboard.

I let out my breath and placed the gun back in my jacket. I had taken it from beside Father's body twenty-four years ago, and kept it as my personal weapon all this time. Now I had learned that he had apparently not used it to take his own life, or Anna's: he himself had been murdered, as part of a squalid little conspiracy to lure me into serving Mother Russia. The British officer who had been seen visiting Anna's quarters hadn't been him, but Chief. And the soldiers carrying Anna off in a jeep would have been NKVD — they had probably driven round to the farmhouse minutes later. Had Anna been the one to pull the trigger, or had she still been in her coma? It didn't matter: she'd been part of it.

Now I had murdered Chief. I had had no choice. He had spotted something crucial in the Russian transcript of Slavin's interview: that the double had been involved in *secret* secret work — some kind of deep operation. He'd known that Father had been involved in just such an operation, because Father had told him, but he hadn't known who else had been involved: me. However, Pritchard, the only other surviving participant of Sacrosanct, did know that. If Chief had lived another half hour, he would have told Pritchard about the translation error and the rest, and Pritchard would have realized at once that I was Radnya.

I had had to kill him, but it had only bought me a little time, because I had no idea what else Slavin might know about me. Defections usually involved delicate negotiations, and Slavin would know not to use all his bargaining chips too early. He was due to be interviewed again at the High Commission in Lagos on Tuesday morning, where the deal would no doubt be done to exfiltrate him to London. They could also try to get hold of Anna — she wasn't offering to defect, but they knew she had recruited the agent. I had to reach both of them before anyone else did, otherwise . . . Otherwise what? I would either be jailed or hanged. But what was the alternative? The masters I had served for over half my life had killed Father: how could I continue to serve them now? I knew I couldn't.

The phone stopped ringing, bringing me back into the room with a jolt. Who had called? I knew from previous visits that Barnes usually rang just before Chief sat down to dinner, so it was unlikely to have been him. Pritchard, to say he couldn't come? It made no difference — I had to act on the basis that either of them might arrive at any moment. But I couldn't kill either: while I might still manage to make it look like Chief had disappeared, nobody would believe that the Head of Africa Section or his personal minder had also happened to go missing at the same time. I would have to make other plans.

Still, there was only one road leading into the property, so I couldn't leave until Pritchard had been and gone, or I'd risk meeting him on the way out. But I had to hide the car — if he saw that, I was done for.

I took the key from the front door and walked out, locking it behind me. The moon's dull glow illuminated the car. It was a sports model, and I remembered with horror that it had no boot. Still, it was futile blaming myself — it wasn't as if I could have considered where to store Chief's body when I'd bought the thing.

I didn't have time to waste on it now — something would have to come to me while I worked on other problems. As I turned the ignition key, I added another to the list. I was used to starting her up in London; out here in the sticks, the noise was deafening. I could drive out of here at 150 miles an hour, but the decibel level would bring Barnes running, if not everyone in the county.

Very gently, I took her deep into the shrubbery that backed onto the riverbank. Then I ran back up to the front door to examine the result. She was completely hidden behind a hedge, lying under the canopy of one of the larger beeches, but there were now marks across the gravel where I'd turned. I hoped it wouldn't be noticeable to a new arrival coming up the driveway.

I unlocked the door, went in, and locked it again from the inside. Then I drew the curtains and switched the lights off in the living room and hallway. After rummaging around under the kitchen sink, I came up with a torch, a dishcloth, a pair of rubber gloves and some gardening bags. I took an empty bag, soaked the cloth, put on the gloves, picked up the torch and went back to the living room, where Chief lay on the floor, his eyes staring up at me.

I closed the lids, and tilted his head so I could inspect the damage. I'd used a full metal jacket, so the exit wound was small. Thankfully, the little spillage there had been had fallen on the spread of papers that had been under his chair. I placed these in the bag, and then got to work cleaning the wound thoroughly – I didn't want remnants of matter brushing against the carpet when I moved him.

Then there was the bullet itself: it was embedded in the wall behind where Chief had been standing, to the right of the Georgian fireplace. I managed to jimmy it out and cleared the resulting dust with the other corner of the dishcloth. Now I had to find a way to hide the mark. The bookcase would have done the trick, but I didn't have time to move it, and anyone who had visited Chief in recent weeks would spot such a large modification to the room's layout anyway. On the other hand, anything I could easily shift would be moved by an investigating team later on, if it came to that.

I settled on the piano, which stood about a hand's width to the right of the mark. It was on a carpet, one of Chief's finest Afghans. I got down on my knees and pulled it, a fraction of an inch at a time, towards the cornice. After a few minutes, I had it in place. I left it a couple of inches short of the wall to make it less obvious, but the mark couldn't be seen unless you were right above it.

I continued my tour of the room, searching for anything either of us had touched. I threw both tumblers and the Becherovka bottle into the bag, along with the ashtray, the unfinished egg sandwich and the Slavin file. As I executed the moves – pick this up, clean that, check this – another part of me circled over the scene and wondered how I was capable of it. Why I was doing it. What I had become. But the machine in me drove on . . .

I climbed the staircase and negotiated my way along the narrow corridor to Chief's bedroom. From a quick sweep with the torch, it looked cramped and rather untidy. I took a few summer suits from the wardrobe and stuffed them into my bag with a couple of lightweight shirts, underwear, socks, and a couple of pairs of shoes.

The bag was now full to the brim, so I left it at that and carried my haul back down the stairs. I took my coat from the hook in the hallway, put it on, and headed into the living room to collect Chief. I took him in a fireman's lift. He was heavier than I expected, and I could still smell the Becherovka on him. I picked up the bag with my spare hand and half-staggered to the hallway, taking care not to move too fast – the batteries in the torch were going and the last thing I needed now was to break a vase.

By the time I'd reached the front door, my shoulders were

starting to ache. I rested for a moment, then switched hands on the bag so I could open the door. I nearly cricked my neck doing it, but I eventually managed to squeeze through.

I locked the door a final time, pocketed the key, and stumbled down the stairs onto the drive. By moving the car, I'd ensured a longer walk for myself. I focused on the thought that had Pritchard arrived before I'd moved it, I would have had to kill him, too. And, as I had already reasoned, I couldn't stage disappearances for both of them.

It had started to rain: just a drizzle, but the wind was gusting it around. I got a sudden whiff of urine, and held my breath for a few seconds. There were some large beeches with plenty of shadow, and I headed for them. I had to stop several times, but then, somehow, I was there. I let Chief slide to my feet. I could see by the moon now, so I let the torch fall into the bag, then counted to ten before picking him up again, ready to attack the final few steps to the car.

Crunch.

Wheels on gravel. I froze. Then, in one movement, I stepped back a pace, deeper into the undergrowth.

A moment later, headlights flooded the drive.

I dropped the bag and laid Chief on the ground by my feet, then turned up the lapels of my coat and buttoned them across so that nothing of my shirt or jacket could be seen. It wasn't the best camouflage routine I'd ever executed, but it might make all the difference.

The car sidled up alongside Chief's Bentley. The driver craned his neck out of the window to check whether he was near the verge. I could make out a few features: silver hair, glasses, and a neat little beard.

Pritchard.

*

I stood in the undergrowth and watched as he stepped out of his car. He was wearing a close-fitting red coat, white breeches, and leather boots. I remembered he liked hunting — he must have come straight from the chase. He walked round to the rear door and opened it. A dog leapt out: a black, white and tan dog with a long muzzle. The sound of its bark came like a shot, travelling across the drive and negotiating its way through the branches until it reached my ears, sending my brain a simple, stark message: I was done for.

They started for the house, Pritchard striding as though he were measuring out a distance, the hound zigzagging manically around its master. As they passed, I caught the expression on Pritchard's face. Perhaps it was a trick of the moonlight, or one of those odd extrapolations induced by proximity to extreme danger, but I could have sworn he was smiling.

This baffled me. What did he think he had been called here to discuss? Chief had said he hadn't yet discussed the Slavin file with any of the others. At least, I thought he'd said that. If I'd misunderstood, I had no option but to kill Pritchard now. I thought of the old Service proverb: three people can keep a secret, as long as two of them are dead.

But killing Pritchard would mean an immediate murder inquiry.

As he took the stairs to the front door, I weighed the odds. It seemed clear that I should stay my hand and simply wait for him to leave, but the uncertainty of it nagged at me. It would have helped if I could have convinced myself I'd imagined his gleeful expression.

Then another thought occurred to me: could it simply be that, far from resenting having his Sunday evening interrupted — as I had, and as most people would — Pritchard *relished* the prospect of a late-night rendezvous with Chief? Was he simply aroused by the scent of intrigue? I didn't have many dealings with Pritchard these days — I tried to avoid him as much as I could — but thinking back to the safe house in Sankt Gertrud, I decided it was quite possible.

He was ringing the doorbell now, rather forcefully — the car and the barking would normally have been enough to bring Chief to the door, so perhaps he was already wondering why they hadn't.

'Hallo? Anybody there?' After he had called out a few times, he checked the door was locked, found it was, and so walked round to the window and tried to peer in, the dog following at his heels.

The wind suddenly became stronger, whipping the branches to and fro, and I stopped one with my arm before it took out one of my eyes. The gust had also hit the bag, spilling its contents over the ground. There was the unmistakable clank of glass, and the dog swivelled its head to locate the source of the disturbance.

Keep still.

Keep very, very still.

The dog started barking.

Pritchard chucked it under the neck. 'What's the matter, Fizz?'

Barking in my direction. There, master, the traitor and the corpse. In the undergrowth.

'What is it?'

Barking ferociously, pointing its head, trying to get its message across. Pritchard peered out at the drive.

'Find!' he shouted suddenly, and let go of the leash. The dog bounded down the steps and headed straight for me at a terrifying pace. Pritchard set off after it.

Keep still, and stay calm, I told myself. Foxhounds are trained to hunt foxes, not men, so it would not be looking for my scent, nor Chief's.

It was just a few feet away now. I could hear its rapid panting and see the wet glint of its snout foraging through the leaves. Pritchard came stamping up behind, talking all the while in a tender, singsong voice: 'What's eating you, you silly fool; what's wrong, eh?'

Foxes, not men, I repeated in my head, foxes, not men, trying to blank out the cramp, the fear, the ache in my jaw from the rain.

'There are no foxes here, you daft old thing.'

And then I could almost hear him thinking it: no, but there might be something else. And now he started to sniff the air, too, and my mantra no longer helped me.

Because Pritchard *was* trained to hunt men.

I breathed through my nostrils, as slowly and evenly as possible, and prayed that the rain and the mud and the foliage would mask any scents emanating from me, the bag, or Chief. I closed my eyes. He might pick out my whites from even the tiniest of movements, or see the reflection of the moon in my pupils. I shut down my brain and retreated inside myself, urging every fibre of my being to blend into the tree, the wind, the night, so that Pritchard would not register my presence.

I don't know how long I stood like that. Perhaps several minutes, perhaps only seconds. Then I heard a footfall and I broke back into full consciousness. He had moved into the hedge, a step closer to me. Could he sense me? If he came any nearer, he would *see* me. I wondered how quickly I would be able to draw the Luger. It shouldn't be a problem: I was younger, fitter and stronger than Pritchard, and he wouldn't be expecting it. Fizz wouldn't like it, but I could handle a few bites, if necessary.

Two steps more and I would have to kill him. I had killed Chief so that Pritchard would not suspect me of being the traitor. But if he discovered me now, with Chief and the debris from his murder beneath my feet, it wouldn't have helped me much.

The debris beneath my feet. I opened my eyes a fraction and looked down. I could see the Becherovka label, and a small greyish lump. Chief's sandwich.

Pritchard had his back to me now, turning to see where Fizz had gone. Taking care not to brush against any branches, I crouched down very slowly and picked up the sandwich. The rain had transformed it into a knot of mush. With my hand still an inch or so above the ground, I flicked the thing with my wrist, as though I were skipping a stone, in the direction of the riverbank.

Fizz barked at the rustle in the leaves, and ran over to see what it was.

Pritchard waited a few seconds, and then followed.

I stepped back another pace, deeper into shadow, and looked up to count the stars to calm myself. I couldn't make out much through the spitting rain, though, so I soon gave up and tried to peek over towards where I'd thrown the sandwich.

Where were they?

And then I saw Fizz emerging from the undergrowth a few feet down. The dog had a bird in its mouth, and Pritchard was laughing and calling it a stupid beast and then he took it by the scruff of the neck and they set off back up the drive.

Pritchard walked round the house and rapped on the windows again, then went back to try the front door again. He was puzzled and frustrated now, but finally he marched back to the car, the buttons of his coat clinking as he walked, stroking Fizz's ears with one hand.

The sound of the engine faded. I waited a few minutes, still breathing at the same slow pace, until I was sure he was not returning. Then I set about putting everything back into the bag. I picked it and Chief's body up again, and made my way through the bracken to the car.

*

There was some space for him behind the seats. Not much, but it might be enough. I put the bag on the passenger seat and set to work. First, I tried to squeeze him in with his knees folded to his chin. When that didn't work, I used a series of swift downward strikes until his legs broke at the knee. That helped me push him to the floor, at which point I heard a thin sharp crack, which must have been his spine. An image suddenly flashed into my mind of the look on his face when he'd seen the gun. I forced it away. It wasn't Chief I was doing this to — it was just a lump of flesh that would soon become part of the soil, as we all did at some point . . . And as I would too sooner rather than later if I didn't focus.

I took off my coat and draped it over him, partly so he wouldn't be seen on the road, more to hide his unmoving stare. Then I walked around the car, stretching my legs, feeling the rain on my forehead, trying to rid my mind of bullets and broken bones and formulate a workable strategy to get me out of this hole. I had a rendezvous with Vanessa at midnight. Miss it, and I'd have some awkward questions to answer later on. Make it, and it would avert suspicion, although the idea made me queasy inside. The last person I wanted to see now was Vanessa — let alone use her as an alibi. I snapped out of it. I wasn't about to be hanged because of an attack of qualms.

I climbed into the front seat and put the key in the ignition. The house was in my rear-view mirror, dark and deserted under the sliver of moon. I had a sudden memory of school: holidays when I'd stayed behind, the gloom of empty dormitories in the dark.

I started her up, and began to move off slowly.

*

Winding through the empty lanes at about twenty miles an hour with the lights dimmed, the urge to push the pedal and leave it all behind was almost overpowering. But I couldn't yet risk it. I didn't want to wake people up.

I'd gone about ten miles when I came to a call box. I parked on the verge, went in, and put in a collection of sixpences. Nothing happened. I cursed and was just about to hang up when I got through.

'Yes?' said a gruff voice.

'Something is going to fall like rain,' I said. 'And it won't be flowers.'

'Pardon?'

Oh, Christ.

'Something is going to fall like rain – and it won't be flowers.'

There was a long pause, and then a resigned 'Righty-ho' and he hung up. It's only when you're forced to rely on emergency measures that you see all the holes in them: a straight-faced 'Please pass the message on to Sasha that I need to meet at location four in two hours' would have sounded a deal less suspicious to anyone listening in. And what the hell had Auden been going on about? I wondered. Why would flowers fall like rain? Wouldn't rain be the more likely turn of events?

The spy games concluded, I climbed back in the car and set off again. I carried on weaving through the lanes until I reached the turn-off to the A32, and then put my foot down. It had already gone half ten, and it was going to be very tight getting everything done and still making Ronnie Scott's before midnight. I tuned the radio to some rock music on one of the pirate stations. I could barely hear it at this speed, but all I wanted was some noise. As the car tunnelled through the night, I wanted something chaotic to churn beneath it all, to keep me conscious that the soft years were over.

There was no way back.

＊

I wound the window down to let some air in.

He was already there, which was a good sign. A no-show would have left me with all sorts of difficulties. I had given myself two hours from placing the call, but that was the absolute minimum: standard procedure was four hours, with an intricate set of checks and double-backs I'd developed over the years, but that clearly hadn't been possible tonight. This was an emergency, and I was working to a very tight deadline — Vanessa would be arriving soon, checking her coat, ordering a Cointreau — and it had been tempting to take a few more shortcuts on the security. I comforted myself with the fact that it was a Sunday night, which was probably the safest time of the week. I finished my cigarette, then got out of the car and walked across the street.

＊

There were fewer people than I'd hoped for: some old men playing mah-jong; a couple of dockers. I breathed in the smell of fried rice, pork and incense. This was location four, the New Friends restaurant, one of the last surviving vestiges of the old Chinatown. A waitress with impossibly thick eyelashes drifted towards me, but I nodded in the direction of the man hunched over a table in the corner, and she moved off again.

He was pushing the remains of a chow mein around his plate and nursing a cup of tea. His postage stamps, our usual cover for conversation, were already neatly laid out on the table.

I seated myself beside him. I'd last seen him six months ago. His beard was a little greyer, his paunch a little wider.

'Hello, Sasha,' I said.

'Hello, Paul. I hope this is good.'

He was irritated at being called out to an emergency meeting: he'd grown accustomed to routine, as had I, and had started to believe he had a right to lead a normal life.

I pushed the barrel of the Luger into his thigh.

'Not here,' I said. 'Not enough cover.'

He quickly shuffled his stamps together, left some money on the table, and followed me out to the car.

*

The streets were mainly one-way, and there were long gaps between the lamps. But I knew where I was going. I circled round the back of the restaurant and found the Horseferry Road turning.

I looked across at him. He wasn't doing a good job of hiding his fear: he couldn't keep his eyes still and rivulets of sweat licked his forehead. I put the gun away. I didn't want him to give the answers he thought I was looking for – I'd had enough of that.

'What happened?' he said.

'*Radnya.*'

It was the name Moscow had known me by for over twenty years, the name he had sat and encoded after every one of our meetings. The name I hadn't known before tonight.

He swore in Russian.

'Who?' he said. 'How?'

Who had betrayed me? How had I learned of their betrayal?

'Anna.' It answered both questions.

This time I got a different reaction: shock, and a seemingly overwhelming sadness. Apparently I'd underestimated his emotional range.

'I think you should explain,' he said, which was lovely. I composed myself as I dipped the headlights for an oncoming car.

'How long have you known she was alive?'

He looked down. Always, then.

'I never lied to you, Paul. You must—'

'Don't *Paul* me,' I said, and I felt the anger rise. 'No, you never lied, old friend. Just omitted a few things.'

'You're forgetting,' he said, and his voice wavered as I took a corner at high speed. 'We are both only pawns in this game.'

That made me laugh. My life falling apart, and he was feeding me B-film lines. Judging by the expression on his face, I was sounding a touch hysterical, so I carried on, out of spite. I felt sorry for him, too, of course: his longest-serving agent losing his nerve so spectacularly. But there it was – the taste of betrayal fresh in my mouth, and I felt sick with it and desperate to lash out. Perhaps I would use the gun again tonight. He deserved to die more than Chief. He had known of the plot — he had not only failed to tell me about it, but had continued to feed it to me.

'We're not pawns,' I told him. 'I told you at our very first meeting that I didn't want any more games — I had enough of that with Yuri. If you had told me the truth then, I would have accepted it.'

'No,' he said, regaining his composure. 'You wouldn't have. That, too, is horseshit.'

I ignored him. He wasn't answering my questions, and I needed answers to them, now.

'Why?' I asked him, my knuckles straining against the steering wheel. 'Why this way?'

'It shouldn't matter how you were recruited.'

A few hours previously I would have agreed with him, if we'd been discussing some other poor fool who had been lured in like this: yes, a clever little honey trap, very nice, the means justify the ends, and all that crap. Very nice — in theory. 'It matters to *me*,' I said, barely able to control my fury. 'The murder of my father *matters to me*, Sasha.'

'I am sorry,' he said after a moment. 'But you must understand that he would have been seen as a dangerous enemy.'

Yes, I understood, all right: eliminate a prime anti-Communist, and recruit his own son off the back of it. My code-name even gloated over the fact.

'How did it work?' I asked. 'How many people were involved? I want to know the details.'

'I don't have them,' he said. 'I was shown your file before I left Moscow, but the matter of your recruitment had only a very brief description.'

'Indulge me,' I said. 'I suspect it was fuller than the one I got.'

He turned to me, the shadows on his face shifting shape as we passed in and out of the fields of each streetlamp. 'You were admitted to a Red Cross hospital, where the agent you knew as Anna cared for you. Investigations established that you were the son of a leading British intelligence officer with links to fascist groups before the war.'

I kept glancing over at him, because I needed to match the meaning of his words with the way he said them. If he sounded a false note — if he was lying — I needed to know. I couldn't yet tell.

'So a plan was drawn up.'

'Yes. Anna was to persuade you of the rightness of our cause using her particular talents—'

'That's one way of putting it,' I said. 'Who killed my father?' I asked. 'Who pulled the trigger?'

'That I do not know, Paul.'

Narrow Street. I veered into it and Sasha lurched into the dashboard as we flattened a few cobblestones. Was this the truth — or more omission?

'And Anna disappeared.'

He shrugged. 'There was nothing else about her in the file. Perhaps you can tell me what you have learned?'

I debriefed quickly, leaving nothing out but embellishing nothing either. He didn't say anything, didn't react at all, even when I'd finished. He seemed to be more interested in the

54

activity on the river: there were a couple of tankers moving silently about their business.

'Did you hear me?' I asked.

'Yes,' he said. 'You did the right thing.'

'The *only* thing,' I corrected. 'There wasn't anything right about it.'

He turned away from the river to look at me, and smiled thinly. He placed his palm on my shoulder, a pastiche of avuncular affection. 'I understand your distress,' he said, and it was all I could do to stop myself reaching for the gun again. 'That is something I can't help you with. You must look in your soul and examine the reasons things were done in this way. In time—'

'What do you know about Slavin?' I asked him. I didn't *have* any time – that was the bloody point.

'Slavin?'

'Yes,' I said. 'You remember – the KGB officer whose defection is threatening my life.'

'Only what you have just told me: that he is attached to the Soviet Embassy in Lagos. Considering the strategic importance of Africa, and Nigeria in particular, I imagine he is regarded highly by Moscow. But that is all I know, I'm afraid – that and I count my blessings that my services are required here, surrounded by beauty and art, whereas Comrade Slavin has the ill fortune of being posted to one of the world's most inhospitable cities during wartime.'

I looked over at the dirty black river and wondered about Sasha's definition of beauty.

'Forgive me if I don't share your sympathy for him,' I said.

'Oh, don't be so self-pitying, Paul! You have enjoyed more than your share of luck tonight. You weren't spotted by Henry Pritchard, for example. Although, of course,' he added, 'you will now have to be especially wary of him.'

Yes. Yes, I would. *'The control, at one remove from the action, may be able to offer the agent fresh insight into problems he faces in the field.'* It was from the Service manual, but I imagined Moscow had some similar gibberish printed up. I resisted the urge to tell him that it had already occurred to me that I might now have to be especially wary of Pritchard.

'Still, I don't think there's any need for you to worry yourself unduly,' Sasha was saying. 'Slavin will be dispatched tomorrow.' He gave a short chuckle.

I told him that nobody was going to lay a finger on Slavin, and after he had recovered from the savagery with which I had spat this out, he politely asked me why not. He even managed a sliver of bewildered amusement in his tone – I didn't like that. I wanted him scared.

'Volkov,' I said. 'It'll look too much like it.'

Konstantin Volkov had walked into the British Consulate-General in Istanbul in 1945 and asked to defect. He'd had information that would have blown Philby, but Philby had wangled his way into getting the job to fly out to interrogate him, and he'd taken enough time doing it for his handler to send some goons in to take the Russian and his wife back to Moscow. This was now known, thanks in part to Philby himself, who had published a slippery little volume of memoirs revealing just enough to push my colleagues into further paroxysms of paranoia. If Slavin suddenly disappeared, it would be clear he had been silenced by the double, and as the only men who knew about Slavin's allegations were Lagos Station and Heads of Section, that would narrow the field considerably. I had to get out to Nigeria as soon as possible, because I couldn't run the risk of someone else interrogating Slavin before me. But if anything happened to him, either while I was there or on my way out there, it would narrow the field to just one.

'You're safe,' said Sasha. 'Didn't you come through with flying colours last time? Nobody would ever seriously suspect you.' He patted the leather upholstery pointedly. 'Your cover is impeccable.'

'You're making me blush,' I said. 'But my last experience of being questioned was notably different, I think, don't you? I hadn't, for example, just killed the Head of the Service. If Slavin is mysteriously shipped off in bandages moments before I arrive in Lagos, I'll either spend the rest of my life in Pentonville or end up dangling from the end of a rope.'

'Let us be perfectly clear, Paul. What is it you are asking of me?'

'Keep your thugs away. Let me deal with Slavin.'

He took a sharp intake of breath, and gave a quick shake of his head. 'It is far too dangerous.'

'Reassuring to hear that you care, but I'll be the judge of that.'

'It's impossible.'

'It's non-negotiable.'

He gave me a long look. 'They won't let me.'

'Then don't tell them.' I leaned a little on the last word —

his incessant passing of the buck was beginning to irritate me.

'I can't do that. There is another option, you know—'

I gave him a cool look. 'The flat in Moscow? Pissing away the rest of my life on cheap vodka like Philby and the others? No thanks.'

'I'm afraid I can't help you. I wish I could, I really do, but it's not in my power—'

I took the next corner, up a ramp to a space in front of someone's lock-up, 'Millwall FC' scrawled across it in blue spray paint. I pulled the brake and drew the Luger, then faced my comrade down the barrel.

He'd shut up now.

I leaned forward and placed the nose against his forehead.

'It's in your own interest,' I said. 'If they take me into the rubber room – which I can guarantee you they will if anyone touches Slavin before I get there – I'll give them everything I have on you before I bite down on the capsule.'

His expression remained blank – he didn't think I had enough on him for it to matter.

'They mightn't find you, of course,' I said. 'You mightn't even be here by then.'

'What do you mean?'

'If I come under suspicion, Moscow will almost certainly recall you.'

It had a more benign ring to it than 'dispatched', but it amounted to the same thing. His breaths had started coming short and fast now, and I thought I could see the logic gradually penetrate.

'All right,' he said, finally. 'You're on your own.'

'When's your next report?'

Hesitation. I twitched my finger a fraction.

'The second, barring emergencies.' He managed a smile, and I liked him a little for it. It brought to mind the Sasha I had known and worked with for so long.

But, then, that Sasha was a liar.

The second: that was ten days away. We drove on in silence for a few minutes, and then I pulled up at a yard filled with blackened barges. A sign on a wall proclaimed that 'DOGS LOVE VIMS'. The dirt in the air from the coal-loading wharf upstream was everywhere, impregnating the lamp-posts and the buildings, and the smell of tar and water was suddenly pungent. 'Your chief's body,' Sasha said suddenly, as I drew to a halt. 'You didn't say what you had done with it.'

I'd been wondering how long it would take him. I nodded at my coat behind his head. He glanced back over his shoulder and swore violently in Russian. 'You're going to dump him in the river.'

'No,' I said. 'We are.'

*

I parked the car close to the edge and we carried the body down, wrapped in the blanket. I took the arms, Sasha the feet, and we shuffled along to the end of the lock, stopping every couple of minutes – he kept complaining that it was tricky to keep a firm hold. Finally we were there, and we lowered Chief onto the moist gravel.

Sasha clapped his hands together, looking for a moment as though he would make a comment about the recent cold snap. I prayed he wouldn't – I didn't want to lose control altogether.

I began scouring the ground for stones and suggested he do the same. When I had a handful that were large enough, I stuffed them into Chief's pockets.

We carried on doing this for a few minutes, not saying anything. I think Sasha was afraid to – in silence, it was easier to pretend we were doing something else, so he busied himself with selecting the best stones for the job, delegating their placement to me. It was as though he were a child building a sandcastle, searching for decoration for one of the turrets.

When Chief was pretty much laden, I took his house-keys from my coat and placed them in his top pocket. No harm in being tidy. I signalled to Sasha. Chief's face and hands already looked grey in the yard's sulphurous light. Had I not pulled the trigger, he'd have been stirring his cup of cocoa and shuffling into bed about now – having just heard all about my involvement in Father's mission from Pritchard, and had me arrested for treason as a result.

I stopped looking at him and told Sasha to do the same; it wasn't making things easier. We lifted him again, shimmied to the edge and started swinging him until we had a reasonable rhythm and some height. Then I counted to three, and we heaved forward and let him go.

*

I was enveloped in a fog of cigarette smoke as I walked into Ronnie Scott's. Once I'd made my way through it, I saw that the support band was still on – three earnest young men sweating for their art in matching orange brocade suits – and the place was packed.

I usually savoured the atmosphere, but tonight I had to find Vanessa, and fast. I was close to half an hour late and I wasn't sure what kind of mood she would be in – our afternoon of lovemaking might have left her feeling the snub even more.

We hadn't visited the club since the previous summer, and it had expanded in the meantime, but I remembered that she liked to sit as close to the stage as possible, so I bypassed the bar and made for the candlelit tables up front. There was no sign of her. I scanned the crowd desperately: a handsome Indian gent in a pinstripe suit and white turban; a party of young women, all sporting the same outlandish hairdo; an elderly man enraptured by the band, playing along on an imaginary piano – every face in London, it seemed, but one. Perhaps she was in the lavatory, or had left a message with one of the waitresses. I was walking towards the bar, when I felt a tug at my sleeve.

'So there you are,' she whispered in my ear. 'I was about to give up hope!'

Her hair was down and her body poured into the turquoise shantung dress I'd bought her at Dior a few weeks earlier on a spree. She'd embellished it with a cream organza shawl and a necklace of ivory bones that showed off her tan. Her eyes were a little hooded, and one shoulder sloped oddly: she was either drunk, or high, or both.

I felt the tension leave me. 'I'm sorry, darling,' I said, raising my voice so I could be heard over a saxophone solo. She laughed gaily and offered me her hand. I took it and she led me away from the stage, towards her table.

'Yes, well, I'm sorry, too. Where on earth have you been? Killing Russians again?'

I forced a smile. 'Not quite. But something came up.'

'It's all right,' she said. 'I've been quite happy, really. I bumped into one of Daddy's friends and he's been entertaining me in your absence — such a charming man, and so knowledgeable. I believe he's also in your game?'

The tall, slender figure was seated at her table between a half-finished bottle of chilled Riesling and a plate of chicken curry, his jacket resting on his knees and his eyes fixed on me.

'Why, hello, Paul,' said Pritchard, with a wintry smile. 'Fancy seeing you here.'

IV

Monday, 24 March 1969, London

I woke to see the word 'BECHEROVKA' swimming in front of my eyes. My first thought was that I was still at Chief's house, but then the ringing in my ears and the coating on my teeth brought it all back.

Pritchard had left the club soon after my arrival. He hadn't mentioned that he had been at Chief's, though in a way I'd found that more troubling. But strangely enough, despite the fright he'd given me, I had almost been sorry to see him go, as I hadn't had much to say to Vanessa. I'd hung on at the club with her for another hour, wearing a death's-head grin and sweating inside my coat as the music spiralled out of control, before finally feigning tiredness and suggesting we leave.

I'd hailed her a cab — the longer I spent with her, the worse it would be. She hadn't been pleased, of course, but she'd taken it reasonably well and hadn't asked any questions. I had told her I'd call her in the morning, then I'd hopped in the car and driven back to South Kensington.

After parking near the flat, I had taken the bag from behind the back seat and thrown it into the bins behind an Italian restaurant. On impulse, I'd fished out the bottle of Becherovka and taken it up to the flat with me, hiding it under my jacket so the porter wouldn't see.

I'd slept very little, spending most of the night going through what had happened and getting to the bottom of the bottle. Now, as the dawn light fell on overturned chairs and shattered glass, I stripped and forced myself to work through the old fitness regimen. By the end of it, I was dripping in sweat and my mind was focused on the morning ahead. I had three objectives. Visit Station 12 and pick up my copy of the Slavin dossier – I didn't want to have to explain why I hadn't already received it. See if Chief's file on Anna was in Registry – as a Head of Section I had full clearance, although one didn't usually ask to see material related to Chief without a very good reason. I had several. But above all, I had to make sure I was sent out to Nigeria. I had no idea what else Slavin might have up his sleeve, and I needed to hear it before anyone else.

Resolved, I took a bath, shaved, and put on a fresh suit. After a scratch breakfast, I packed an old canvas hold-all with a few clothes and took the lift downstairs. I left a message for George to give the car the full treatment, outside and in. Then I hailed a cab and asked the driver to take me to Lambeth.

*

'Gentlemen!' William Osborne's stentorian tones put a sudden stop to the murmuring around the table. 'I think it's time we settled down and got this show on the road, as our American friends like to say.'

He gave a slightly unconvincing chortle, and his waistcoat expanded in the process. Unblessed by the breeding or charm that had smoothed the waters for others, Osborne had clawed his way to becoming Head of Western Hemisphere Section by virtue of his prodigious intellect. A highly capable adminis-trator, he had been widely expected to take over as Deputy Chief last year, but the job had instead gone to John Farraday, a smooth Foreign Office nob with no previous experience of the spy game but a penchant for hosting lavish dinner parties. Osborne had managed to isolate him within weeks, and nobody was in any doubt who really ran things when Chief was away. But he didn't have the title, yet – and it was by no means a certainty that he'd get it.

This meeting was held every Monday morning at this time, and was known as 'the Round Table', although none of us were knights and the table was, in fact, rectangular. Farraday had just arrived and taken his place in his usual corner; he was now busily checking that his cuffs were protruding from his jacket sleeves by half an inch. Seated immediately to his right, and directly facing me, was Pritchard. In a crisp, narrow-cut pinstripe suit and woven silk tie, he didn't look in the least as though he'd been sipping Riesling in a Soho jazz club less than nine hours ago.

After the war, Pritchard had joined MI5, where he had

eventually become Head of E Branch: Colonial Affairs. When it had finally become clear to the Whitehall mandarins that it was suicidal to have intelligence officers posted in former colonies with no official links to the Service, which was responsible for all other overseas territories, E Branch had been taken over, and Pritchard had moved with it. Coming from Five, and being a Scot to boot, had initially made him a deeply suspected outsider, especially as many of the Service's old guard had been forcibly retired at the same time he joined. However, he was also a decorated war hero, independently wealthy, and staunchly right-wing, and within a few months of his joining the Service he had been taken up as a kind of mascot by its rank and file: their man on the board. While in Five, Pritchard had been converted to the Americans' idea that British intelligence was still penetrated by the KGB, and he'd devoted a great deal of time and energy to examining old files and case histories in the hope of catching another mole. He'd brought this zeal with him to the Service, and it had made him a lot of high-ranking friends. Chief and Osborne had initially been all in favour of Pritchard's 'hunting expeditions', as his periodic attempts to uproot traitors were known, but now felt that he and his clique were stoking an atmosphere of paranoia and distrust. I tended to agree.

Naturally, I had watched Pritchard's entry into the Service and subsequent rise in popularity within it with considerable unease – the tall bearded ghost I had met in a farmhouse in Germany in 1945 was, for obvious reasons, the last person on earth I wanted to work alongside, especially as he now seemed on a drive to find moles inside the Service. I had been appointed Head of Section at an unusually tender age, partly due to Father's near-mythical status within the Service and partly due to Chief's patronage. Now Pritchard had caught up with me, and although Africa was one of the smaller Sections, there was already talk of him in the corridors as a potential Deputy Chief, or even Chief, somewhere down the line.

Also seated around the table were Godsal, who headed up Middle East Section, Quiney, responsible for Western Europe, and Smale, who was standing in for Far East as Innes was on leave. They all looked harmless enough, with their schoolmasters' faces and woollen suits, but I was under no illusions: they could be lethal. One ill-timed gesture, one misplaced word, and they would pounce. Technically, treason still warranted the death penalty. If I were exposed, I had no doubt they'd apply every technicality in the book. So: tread carefully. I needed things to go my way.

Osborne pushed a garishly cuff-linked sleeve to one side to examine his wristwatch. 'I was hoping Chief would be able to start us off,' he said, 'but he doesn't seem to have arrived yet.' His piggy little eyes, buried behind thick black frames, darted downwards, as if he thought Chief might be about to emerge from beneath the table.

'Strange,' I murmured under my breath.

'Did you say something, Paul?'

'Sorry,' I said, looking up sheepishly. 'It's just that . . . No. Never mind, carry on.'

'What is it?'

'Well . . . it just struck me that it's very unlike Chief. He's usually in well before nine on Mondays, isn't he?'

Osborne inspected a fingernail, then nibbled at it viciously. 'Has he called in?' he asked Smale, who was performing his usual duties as the head of Chief's secretariat in parallel with his new role. Smale shook his head.

'Perhaps traffic's bad,' I said. 'God knows this place is hard enough to get to from the centre of town.'

Osborne nodded: the old buildings had been a short walk from his flat.

'It is a little peculiar,' said Pritchard suddenly, the traces of his Morningside accent amplified by the room's acoustics. 'He called me in to see him last night but wasn't there by the time I arrived.'

'Oh?' said Osborne, turning his head. 'What did he want to see you about?'

'The Slavin file — at any rate, his message was attached to that.'

'What time did you get the message?' asked Osborne.

'Around seven. I'd just come back from Enfield and left straight away, but the house was deserted when I arrived.'

'Perhaps he'd fallen asleep,' I suggested.

'I don't think so. I checked pretty thoroughly.'

Yes, I thought — you did.

'I was worried something might have happened,' Pritchard continued, 'but I couldn't for the life of me remember the way to Barnes's cottage and didn't want to call in a Full Alert without ample reason. I suddenly remembered Chief sometimes spends weekends in London with his daughter, Vanessa. I called her flat, and her roommate — a charming young Australian girl — told me she'd just left for a club in Soho, so I thought I'd drive in to see if Chief was with her — or if she knew where he'd got to.'

'And did she?' asked Godsal.

'No. She also thought he was out at Swanwick and was equally mystified. But I bumped into Paul there.'

The table's eyes turned to me.

'Caught red-handed,' I said, grinning sheepishly. 'I've a soft spot for jazz.'

'Oh,' said Pritchard, 'is that what it was?' Then, pointedly: 'She seemed quite taken with you.'

I did my best to blush.

'Perhaps we should give him a call,' said Osborne, rescuing me. 'Perhaps he's simply slept in.' He nodded at Smale quickly, before anyone could dwell too much on the unlikely image of Chief failing to set his alarm clock, and Smale walked briskly across the room and picked up a telephone sitting on one of the filing cabinets. As he dialled, I imagined the ring echoing in the empty house. To fill the silence, people conspicuously shuffled pieces of paper, fiddled with pen tops and suddenly realized they had lost their glasses cases, until Smale eventually replaced the receiver and shook his head, and we all went back to staring at him.

'Call Barnes,' said Osborne, and waved his hand to indicate he should do it elsewhere.

Smale nodded and slithered out of the door. And that was

that: the ball was rolling. Within a couple of hours, a team of specialists would begin prowling through Chief's living room with dogs and cameras and ink pads. Looking for evidence, looking for blood. I'd carried out last night's work in a kind of concentrated trance. Now I was gripped by panic as the reality of it came back to me, and a series of possible lapses leapt through my mind. Had I swept every inch of the carpet? Covered the bullet-mark adequately? I had a sudden flash of Chief's dark, frozen eyes staring up at me from the floor – could I really have removed all trace of that horror?

Osborne clapped his great hands together. 'I think we should start. I know some of you have to prepare for the Anguilla meeting later. There is only one item on today's agenda – the Slavin dossier, which I trust you have all now read. All other matters will be covered in our next meeting.' He turned to Pritchard. 'Perhaps you could start us off, Henry?'

'By all means.' Pritchard walked over to the door and dimmed the lights, then fiddled with the projector in the centre of the table. After some clicks and whirrs, a magnified photograph suddenly appeared on the wall facing us. A man with stooped shoulders and a widow's peak was bending down to examine a wooden mask at a street market, a quizzical smile on his lips.

'Meet Colonel Vladimir Mikhailovich Slavin of the KGB,' said Pritchard. 'Unmarried. No children. Walked into the High Commission in Lagos on Friday and asked for a British passport in exchange for information about a double agent. In an interview with Geoffrey Manning, the Head of Station, Slavin claimed that Moscow had recruited this agent in Germany in

1945, and that he was given the code-name Radnya.' He peered at the table over his half-moon spectacles. 'Needless to say, if true, this would be a monumental disaster. Twenty-four years is a very long time for a double agent to remain undetected, and Christ knows what damage he could have caused.'

With a click, another photograph filled the top half of the wall. This was of a woman, three-quarters in profile, her hair swept back, no make-up. She looked older, of course – but it was her. I focused on her eyes, trying to read anything in them, but she was squinting in the harsh light and it wasn't possible. An ancient line of poetry I'd last heard recited in a dusty class-room suddenly flashed through my mind, unbidden: *With them that walk against me, is my sun . . .*

'This is the other figure we're looking at. Irina Grigorieva, a third secretary at the Soviet Embassy in Lagos. According to Slavin, she recruited Radnya after falling in love with him. *Cherchez la femme.*' He allowed a brief interval for polite laughter. Once a couple of people had obliged, he continued: 'Both of these pictures, incidentally, were taken by the Station's watchers within the last couple of years, so we can take it that this is more or less how they look today.' He walked back to the door and turned the lights back up.

'Do we know what their duties involve?' asked Farraday.

'I had a look at our records this morning, and we have Slavin down as arriving in Nigeria in '65, under cover as a political attaché. Before that, he was in similar positions in Kinshasa and Accra, which makes him something of an Africa expert in Russian terms. Our educated guess is that his job is to formulate policy in the region – and, of course, to keep an eye on what everyone else is getting up to.'

'Everyone else meaning us?' asked Farraday. He seemed to be following the discussion, for a change.

Pritchard nodded. 'Among others. I presume everyone here's au fait with the situation in Nigeria?' He took some smart buff folders out of his briefcase and handed them round the table – the covers boasted the grand title 'THE NIGERIAN CIVIL WAR: A SUMMARY AND ASSESSMENT OF THE CONFLICT TO DATE'. 'This is a draft of a paper we'll be sending the Cabinet next week,' he said. 'I think you'll find we've covered a lot of ground.' Leafing through it, I could see he wasn't exaggerating: there was a section on the country's history, a detailed chronology of all the major events of the war so far, profiles of the leading personalities on both sides . . . I felt a pang of professional jealousy.

'I think you all know the basics,' Pritchard went on airily. 'But in case you've got sick of following it on the news, I'll quickly summarize the salient facts. Nigeria is our largest former colony. When it gained independence in '60, it was the great hope of Africa – a shining new democracy of thirty-five million people, with enormous potential both as a trading partner and as a political force for good in the continent. But independence was swiftly followed by chaos and violence. Pogroms against the Ibo tribe in the east eventually led to that region seceding from the rest of the country and renaming itself the Republic of Biafra. That sparked a civil war. So far, so Africa. From our point of view, however, it's been a complete mess, unfortunately compounded by our government's handling of the situation.

We initially refused to take sides in the war, sitting resolutely on the fence. Then, in August '67, the Nigerians — "the Federal side" — took delivery of several Czech Delphin L-29 jet-fighters from Moscow. That sent us into a panic: nobody wants the Russians to be in control of one of Africa's largest nations once the war ends. As a result, we've now painted ourselves into a corner, and are effectively competing with Moscow to provide more and more arms to the Nigerians, in the hope of gaining favour with them after the war.'

'And what does Nigeria have to offer us?' asked Farraday innocently.

'Oil,' I said.

Pritchard flashed me a contemptuous look. 'You shouldn't believe everything you read in the papers, Paul.' It was a nice little dig — I was known for my contacts in Fleet Street. 'Contrary to public perception, the Biafrans never had *all* of Nigeria's oil.'

'They had rather a lot of it, though. Rather a lot of it that we would prefer remained in our hands. No?'

He leaned forward, glowering across the table. 'There's much more at stake here than oil. This is about the four hundred million pounds we've invested in the country — and the stability of the whole region. If Nigeria falls to Communism, the rest of the continent could follow.'

'The "domino" theory? I thought that was a Yank idea.'

He refused to be goaded. 'Even the Yanks are occasionally right.'

'And who are they supporting in this thing?' said Farraday. 'The Americans, I mean.'

Pritchard turned to him. 'Well, so far they've been officially neutral, but broadly on our side. They've left us pretty much alone, though — too busy trying to find ways out of Vietnam and beating the Russians to the moon. That may change now, though, as Nixon made a lot of noise about the Biafrans' plight during his election campaign. The Prime Minister has made much of the fact that he hasn't committed British troops in Vietnam, but the Americans aren't ecstatic about that arrangement and their good will may soon run dry. I don't think they are going to start supporting the Biafrans — yet. However, there are plenty of *other* powers already supporting them. France has been supplying them with arms through the Ivory Coast and Gabon in increasingly large quantities in the last few months. De Gaulle would like to protect francophone influence on the continent and sees the plight of "*les pauvres biafriens*" as a way to win back popularity after the mess of the student riots last year. He also wants access to Biafran oil, of course. Then there's China, who are apparently lending the rebels their support simply to show up the Soviets as imperialist lapdogs for allying themselves with us and the Americans. It's hard to gauge what impact these skirmishes they're having with the Russians along their border might have, but it could mean that they step up their involvement in this conflict as well. Also supporting the Biafrans are the Israelis, who seem to believe that they're stopping the next Holocaust, and Haiti, who we have reports recognized the rebel regime this weekend — we're not quite sure what their reasons are. Finally, South Africa, Rhodesia and Portugal are all selling the rebels arms simply because they're happy to help one gang of wogs continue to butcher another.'

The room went quiet while everyone took this in.

'And the Biafrans, knowing all this, continue to buy arms from these parties?' Farraday asked.

'They have little choice.'

'Poor bastards.'

'Poor us, rather,' Pritchard replied. 'As a result of support from this motley crew, the Biafrans have managed to hang on by the skin of their teeth for nearly two years. We only agreed to supply arms to the Nigerians on the calculation that the whole affair would be over in a couple of *weeks*. The British public's disapproval of our involvement is now at an all-time high, partly because of "kwashiorkor". That's this disease the children get when they've not enough protein. It fills their stomachs with fluid — you'll have seen the footage, I expect. The Biafrans are now calling it "Harold Wilson Syndrome" and putting that on their death certificates, because they blame him in particular and the British government in general for not allowing enough food and aid through. We also have reports of the PM's name being used as a swear-word in Biafra.'

'Well, it's been that over here for a while!' said Quiney, eliciting a few quiet chuckles around the table.

Pritchard smiled. 'Yes, even his own party seems to be turning against him now. That's largely down to his stance on Biafra, and the pictures that are coming out of it. Liberal do-gooders don't seem so worried when the starving *look* like they're starving, but when they develop pot bellies it shocks them so much they feel compelled to organize jamborees and start marching on Trafalgar Square. Last week, *The Times* ran a series of articles claiming that the Nigerian pilots are deliberately bombing Biafran civilians. In response to increasing calls for him to resign, the PM announced he will fly out to Lagos this Thursday, supposedly to find out the facts of the war for himself and report back to Parliament.'

Of course. I'd seen it in the papers, but hadn't realized it was so soon. I asked if there was any ulterior motive to the trip, such as peace negotiations.

'Partly,' said Pritchard, 'although everyone's started playing that down in the last day or two. There was a similar plan last year for him to go out as a kind of super-mediator, but it was vetoed by the Nigerians, who are very touchy on the issue of outside interference. Ojukwu, the Biafrans' leader, has made it clear he will only meet Wilson within the borders he currently controls. Agreeing to that would enrage the Nigerians, though, because it would look like we were giving Biafra recognition – that's how the Biafrans would play it, anyway. Because of the pressure here, the government needs to be seen to be doing *something*, but our Nigerian sources say there's little expect-ation Wilson's visit will help matters beyond possibly improving the PR situation. But even that might backfire – he was going to go out there with some spades and agricultural tools until someone pointed out it might be reported he was smuggling in arms.'

'And the Biafrans?' said Farraday. 'What do our sources there tell us?'

'We don't have any reliable Biafran sources at the moment,' Pritchard replied, an edge to his voice. 'I visited Nigeria in December, and Lagos is still a little haphazard.' The colonial Stations had all been under Pritchard's control when he had been in Five, but they had been next to useless without the Service's input. Now they were finally under Service control, but it was clearly taking him longer than he liked to move things on.

'Are we informing the Prime Minister's office of the situation?' asked Godsal.

'No,' said Osborne. 'Nothing is to leave this room. That includes the PM's office, the FO, the Americans, and even our friends in Five.' He glanced at Pritchard. 'Especially our friends in Five. They might conclude that the PM is Radnya.'

Osborne had made a late play for the mantle of head jester. Some of the far right-wing officers in Five – a few of them Pritchard's cronies – had convinced themselves that Wilson was a Russian agent. I'd even asked Sasha about it. He wasn't. It was just another whispering campaign against him. The previous spring, there had even been rumours that Cecil King, owner of the *Daily Mirror*, had been plotting to overthrow the government with the support of Lord Mountbatten, Prince Philip's uncle. Nothing had come of it, of course.

Osborne waited for the tittering to die down before turning back to Pritchard. 'Isn't it a little convenient that a defector has turned up on the eve of this trip?'

'Slavin may be a plant, you mean?' Pritchard asked. I had asked Chief the same thing.

Osborne reached for the carafe in the centre of the table. Very deliberately, he poured some water into his glass, his eyes firmly on his task.

'It would be a pretty little trap,' he said coolly. 'Don't you think? Get us all running around for another traitor.'

Pritchard gave one of his soft smiles. 'But which is it, William? Either the Russians are so fiendishly clever that they've managed to keep one of their agents running in this organization for over twenty years or they're so fiendishly clever that they're sending us false defectors to claim that they have.'

Osborne sipped his water.

'Neither's an especially appetizing prospect,' Pritchard went on mercilessly, 'but considering that we have already discovered – at quite some cost – that we *were*, in fact, penetrated by the KGB, very successfully, it doesn't seem unreasonable to investigate the possibility that others remain in our ranks, undetected.'

'Hear, hear,' I said.

The two of them looked at me in surprise – my usual line, of course, was that it was divisive and paranoid to search for phantom Philbies among us.

'Look at the interview,' I said. 'If it's a ploy, it's not a very clever one. Slavin specifically states that Radnya was a British intelligence officer recruited in Germany at the end of the war. It can't be too hard to draw up a list of everyone we had involved in secret work in that area at that time. If we gave them all polygraph tests, we'd soon find out if Slavin's telling the truth.'

There was no response for a few seconds, and I wondered if

I'd misjudged it. I got worried when Pritchard cleared his throat, but Osborne beat him to it.

'I'm not sure we're *quite* at the stage of deciding how to go about investigating this, Paul,' he said, blinking furiously as he pushed his spectacles up the bridge of his nose. He could usually rely on me to head off Pritchard's demands for more mole-hunts, so it was natural he'd be peeved. 'At any rate, I think it would, in fact, be rather difficult to draw up a list of everyone we had involved in intelligence in Germany in 1945. There were hundreds of people engaged on that sort of work. We also have no idea where the double is now — if he's become the Director-General of the BBC or Home Secretary, a request for a polygraph would need a lot of evidence to justify it.'

I nodded, conceding defeat, but he'd made the point I'd been angling for: there were hundreds of possible suspects.

'Can I just ask a silly question?' said Farraday, and everyone busied himself trying to look puzzled by such an idea. 'If this chap's not a plant and there really is another double, can someone give me a simple explanation as to why? I mean, why they want to betray us. I can't really understand it — surely they read the news? How can they keep believing they're on the right side with tanks rolling into Prague and so on? Or did they all fall in love with Russian dolly-birds who turned them onto it?'

'Not all of them go for dolly-birds,' put in Pritchard archly. It was like *Hancock's Half Hour*.

'But seriously,' continued Farraday, turning to me, 'Paul, has your department done any sort of thinking about this, about what makes these people tick? Perhaps it will help us find this one – we could look at family backgrounds or what-have-you.'

They were looking at me intently so I took it they actually expected an answer. 'The only certain thing,' I said, after I had taken out a pack of Players and lit one, 'is that every double agent is different. The most common reasons for betraying one's country, as far as we can establish, are ideological conviction, disaffection with authority, pride – they get a perverse kick out of deceiving everyone around them – blackmail, and good old-fashioned pieces of silver.' I could have added a new one: hopeless credulity.

I took a drag of the cigarette. 'As to how a person can continue to serve a cause in the face of events that compromise its principles, which would appear to be the case with Philby and his friends, well, nothing's ever black and white, is it? After all, we all believe we're on the side of good, despite the fact that Henry has just given us a lot of information about how our government is contributing to the deaths of thousands of innocent people in a war in Africa because we don't want anyone else to get their hands on the oil there.' I put up a hand to stop Pritchard from interrupting. 'I know, it's not just about oil, and I'm simplifying, but hopefully you can still see my point. If you happen to think we're doing the wrong thing in Biafra – and most people in the country do – it doesn't mean you're suddenly going to abandon everything else you believe to be good about the way we do things and start working for the Russians.'

'But the Russians are supplying arms, too,' said Farraday, and a couple of others nodded.

'All right,' I said with a sigh. 'Bad example. Suez. Kenya. Aden. Take your pick of situations we've made a mess of one way or another in the last couple of decades. How do we continue to do our jobs in the face of this knowledge? We look at the wider picture, of course. I imagine it works much the same for the other side. And from what we know of the KGB's methods, I doubt it's all that easy to supply them with secret material for years and then one day announce an attack of conscience and ask if you can swap sides again, without them getting rather peeved, and perhaps sending a man with a silencer after you. The longer in, I suspect, the harder it would be to extricate oneself. And this chap seems to have been in for rather a long time.'

I paused. How could I possibly explain to these people, even in abstract terms, the ups and downs of my journey with Communism, from my tentative steps with Anna to my convert's zeal after her death – or staged death, as it now appeared – through to agonizing doubts and resulting confrontations with Yuri, and later Sasha, over everything from documents I didn't want to hand over to, yes, tanks rolling into Prague. I decided I couldn't, so I concentrated on my cigarette and waited to see if they had any more idiotic questions. But they didn't – they all seemed to have gone rather quiet.

'Thank you, Paul,' said Osborne. 'Most illuminating, and some food for thought for us all. I'm not sure what it is you think we did wrong in Kenya, exactly, but perhaps that's for another day.' He gave a slight nod to Farraday to indicate he was closing the issue. 'Perhaps you can tell us more about this woman who seems to be involved – Grigorieva? Do you have anything on her?'

'Actually,' I said, 'there is something.' I took my briefcase from the floor and placed it on the table. 'I had a look around Registry this morning and found this in "Germany 1945". I think it confirms that Slavin is very unlikely to be a plant.'

I'd read all of Father's files several times – I'd had to, for cover. But Sacrosanct had been off the books, so they hadn't contained anything about that. I hadn't known he had asked Chief to take Anna into custody, though, or that Chief had written a report about the incident. Along with his other military records, it had been carried over to his Service file, and once I'd found the relevant bundle it had been easy to locate. I sprang the briefcase open, took out the photostats I'd made, and passed them round.

'As you can see, this is extracted from the monthly reports that Chief wrote in September 1945, when he was head of the British army headquarters in Lübeck in Germany. If you turn to the top of the third page' – I waited for people to do so – 'you'll see the entry headed "Anna Maleva". Chief – or Brigadier Colin Templeton, as he then was – relates how he had been tipped off by SOE officer Lawrence Dark – my father – that Maleva, a nurse in the Red Cross hospital in Lübeck, was in fact a KGB agent. Chief took a small team to her quarters to detain her on the night of the 28th, but when they arrived she was dead, shot through the chest.'

A police car raced through the street below, its siren blaring, and I let it pass before continuing.

'Now, if you turn to page four of the dossier, you will find a photograph of Maleva, given to Chief by Major Dark for the purposes of identification. The photostat hasn't come out too well, so let's look at the original.' I walked over to the projector and placed it in the slot. I dimmed the lights, and the picture appeared on the wall.

The photograph had not aged well in the file. The edges were turning brown, and there were black spots across her forehead and her eyes. It had been taken outside the hospital: she was in her uniform, smoking a cigarette. I had naively thought that Father had simply abandoned me, but he had been keeping an eye on the hospital all along.

I pressed the lever to turn back, and the picture of Anna in Lagos filled the wall again. I flicked it forward and back a couple of times and then stopped. 'As you can see, it would appear that Maleva was not, in fact, killed in 1945, but is currently working in the Soviet Embassy in Lagos under the name Grigorieva.'

There was silence for a few moments. In my peripheral vision, I could see that Pritchard had his head down and was reading the file. I was taking a huge risk bringing this to the table, because I was revealing a direct link between Slavin's allegations and my father's work in Germany. As Pritchard knew what that work had been, and that I had been involved in it, he would naturally now suspect me. But there were no records on that operation – he could suspect me all he wanted, but if he couldn't prove it I didn't care. And I was fairly confident that he wouldn't be overly keen to confess to his part in an assassination squad, even after all these years.

'She was quite a looker, wasn't she?' Godsal was saying. 'The mouth's a touch thin, but still . . . she'd probably have got me to sign the Five Year Plan.' Nobody laughed. Godsal, I should note, has a face like a deranged horse.

'What would the Russians have had to gain by faking her death?' asked Farraday.

'I don't know,' I said. 'Perhaps Chief will be able to tell us more about the situation when he gets here.'

As if on cue, there was a knock on the door. All eyes swivelled as Smale entered.

'Well?' said Osborne.

'No sign of him,' said Smale: he must have been wondering why everyone in the room was staring at him so intently. Osborne nodded for him to carry on. 'Barnes went over and called me back. Says he seems to have packed his bags and left in the middle of the night. Didn't cancel his milk or papers.'

'Packed his bags?' asked Pritchard, his voice rising. 'Are you sure of that?'

'Well, it *looks* that way,' Smale backtracked. 'He said there appeared to be some clothes missing. Jackets, suits, that sort of—'

'What about his car?'

'That's still there. But the railway station's a ten-minute walk, with trains to London every hour.'

'Did Barnes talk to him last night?' asked Osborne.

'Yes – he made his final call at half past seven and says Chief answered as usual, with nothing to report. He was just getting ready to go over for his morning pass-by when I rang.'

Osborne harrumphed. 'Well, if Chief doesn't see sense now and let the chap have the spare bedroom, I don't know what we do. This system clearly doesn't work.' He turned back to Smale. 'What about neighbours? Has Barnes had a chance to ask around yet?'

'Most people are at work. But he said one local claims to have heard a car around nine last night.'

'What time did you leave, again?' I asked Pritchard.

'Around then,' he said, meeting my gaze. Yes, he suspected me, all right.

Osborne took his glasses off, decided they were dirty, and rubbed them on his tie, smudging them even more. He nodded at Smale, who scurried over to the trolley and put the kettle on.

Farraday was looking at Osborne. 'Chief received the Slavin dossier as soon as it arrived?' he asked.

Osborne glanced up, red indents from his frames either side of his nose. 'Yes – he was sent it yesterday morning. Why?'

'Well, because within twenty-four hours of receiving it, he's disappeared, that's why!' said Farraday.

I asked him what he was implying.

'Oh, I'm sorry, Paul,' he said, turning to me. 'I know you're close to the old man. But there *is* a link with this Grigorieva–Maleva – you've just told us so yourself. Mighty suspicious, isn't it?'

'I'm sure there's a simple explanation,' I said.

But Farraday was on a roll. 'What could that be, though?' he pressed. 'According to this file you've dug up, which Chief himself wrote,' — he stabbed a long finger at the initials at the top of the page — 'she died in 1945. Either he's lying or the dame in the photo ain't her.' His attempt at hard-boiled American vernacular was painful, and thankfully he dropped it at once. 'But it does look rather a lot like it *is* her, doesn't it?'

The kettle whistled and everyone suddenly busied himself with passing cups and saucers around. Chief's empty chair suddenly looked very bare.

'I don't believe it,' said Godsal. 'It's unthinkable! I mean . . . I mean . . .' He searched for a way to get it across. 'We're talking about *Chief*, for God's sake!'

'The same Chief,' said Farraday, 'who conspicuously failed to catch Philby and fluffed the Cairncross business. And like them and the rest of the rotten bunch, he's a Cambridge man.'

Pritchard smiled at him generously. 'So's half the Service, John.'

'I'm not,' said Farraday. 'I was at Oxford. You were, too, weren't you, Paul?' I nodded. 'And you, William?'

Osborne pushed his glasses onto his nose prissily. 'Manchester. Look, we don't know where Chief is at the moment. But I don't think we can jump to the conclusion that he's a double agent simply because he's missed our regular Monday meeting.'

'I'm not concluding anything,' said Farraday. 'But surely we would all agree that no one — not even Chief — can be above suspicion in a case like this. That, after all, is how traitors survive.'

Osborne drummed his fingers against his glass, and we all watched him. 'With all due respect,' he said, finally, 'I've known Chief for a great many years and he has never given me a moment to doubt his integrity or patriotism. If the man has been acting, he's the best bloody double that ever existed.'

He'd meant it to be a throwaway comment, but as the silence stretched out, it took on an unintended resonance, and he began twiddling his thumbs.

'As I see it,' said Farraday, splaying his fingers out on the table as though he were about to start playing a piano concerto, 'there are only two options. Either Slavin's a KGB plant designed to get us running around for a traitor who doesn't exist or he's real and the traitor *does* exist. Chief has seemingly disappeared, and Paul has found the file on this woman who he says was killed but apparently wasn't, and whom Slavin just happens to mention as his source for the entire house of cards. Now if—'

'If I could just stop you there,' Osborne cut in, and his usual Billy Bunter tone had been replaced by overt aggression. 'I must insist that we wait for Chief to be present before we start flinging accusations around.'

'As you wish,' said Farraday. 'But this may be the last chance we have for an open discussion on this. Once Chief gets here — presuming he hasn't done a flit to Moscow — any such talk will be next to impossible on account of his position.'

'Nobody seems to have taken his position into much consideration,' said Pritchard. 'It's surely far more likely that the

Russians or someone else have taken advantage of his abysmal security set-up and snatched him. I would suggest we give Barnes some support to search the area properly, and put out an alert to all ports just in case.'

'Should we circulate the names of Chief's known aliases?' asked Quiney. 'Or is that too delicate?'

'Far too delicate,' said Osborne, before Farraday could open his mouth.

'Perhaps your Section could look into the Slavin dossier,' Pritchard said to Quiney. 'See if your contacts in Germany can get a list of all the patients admitted to this Red Cross hospital in 1945.' He was talking to Quiney, but he was looking at me.

'Yes,' I said, meeting his gaze. 'Good idea. Perhaps you could also collate all the files of British military operations in the area at the time. I seem to remember there was some sort of a base in Gaggenau.'

Pritchard's mouth locked tight. I'd put forward a way of implicating him, but it was precisely what the other version of me, the patriotic British agent who had never gone near any Russian nurses, would have done. I'd have suspected Pritchard for the same reason he now suspected me: I knew he had been in the British Zone in '45.

'I'll do my best,' said Quiney. 'Though I can't imagine many of those records have been kept.' Good old Quiney – you could always rely on him not to do anything in a pinch.

'I would like to go out to Lagos and interview Slavin,' I said. 'It's been five days since he approached us, so time is of the essence – his colleagues could realize he's thinking of defecting at any moment and then we'd have lost any chance to find out what's really going on here. Henry has already as much as admitted that Lagos Station isn't up to the job, and I have a personal interest in making sure a thorough job is done. This operation of my father's occurred after he was last seen in London, so it obviously could provide an explanation for whatever happened to him.' I avoided looking at Pritchard, because he knew I was lying at this point.

'Perhaps Chief killed him,' murmured Farraday, at which Osborne's eyes nearly popped out of his head.

'*Killed* him?' he said. 'Please, John, let's try to keep the discussion sane. Chief's hardly a killer.'

'You have a point,' Farraday replied, nudging the photostat forward on the table. 'He last didn't kill someone twenty-four years ago, to be precise.'

Another silence descended, and people started shifting in their seats. This was a new side to Farraday, and no one knew what might be coming next.

'Paul has made an interesting proposal,' said Pritchard, in that fastidious tone of his. 'But let's consider it. I agree that Lagos Station isn't capable of dealing with something of this importance, and that it's vital someone go out there at once to do so. Because, of course, if the traitor's not Chief, then the real Radnya may be among us.' He paused to let that sink in, and then continued. 'But while I'm sure we all sympathize with your desire to discover the true cause of your father's disappearance,' — he looked into my eyes at this point, and I tried not to react — 'I'm not sure a matter of this magnitude

should be influenced by individual officers' personal concerns
– however troubling they may be.' He dropped a sugar cube
into his tea and dipped his spoon in to stir it.

'Chief's an old friend of the family,' I said. 'If he's a traitor, or
involved in my father's disappearance, I bloody well want to know.'

'We all want to know,' said Pritchard. 'But have you ever
even been to Nigeria? Or Africa at all, for that matter? It's not
quite *la dolce vita*, you know.'

It was another crack: my last posting had been in Rome. I
didn't rise to it, just asked him if he had any experience of
handling Soviet defectors. 'You don't even speak Russian,' I
pointed out.

He laughed it off. 'There are people in Lagos who can translate,' he said. 'Someone translated Slavin's interview, didn't they?'

Not very well, I wanted to tell him. But I didn't have the
chance to formulate another response, because there was a
cough from the head of the table. It was Farraday.

'Gentlemen,' he said. 'Let us not bicker, please. I have come
to my decision.' Osborne started turning puce and made to
interrupt. Farraday shushed him and smiled, pleased that he
was exerting control and, finally, rather enjoying this espionage
business. 'Paul,' he said, 'you and Chief are very close – not
just as colleagues but as friends. So I understand that this is
something near to you. Believe me. And I quite see how the
matter of your father's disappearance is something you would
want to clear up.' He leaned back in his chair and spoke to a
point on the ceiling, just left of the ventilator shaft. 'But I agree
with Henry: I think it's probably best if he deals with this one.'

Then his head dropped down again and he smiled innocently at Smale. 'Any chance of putting some more water on?'

★

My office was cold and cramped. I turned the radiators on full
blast and lit a cigarette.

Not good news. Not good news at all. I began pacing the
carpeted cell. After several dozen crossings and two Players, I
came to a conclusion: I'd have to go it alone – without back-up,
without sanction, and probably with Pritchard in the same field.

The first thing to do was to write a note: something for them
to get their teeth into, something that would appeal to their
Boy's Own view of the world. When I'd prepared a few suitably
indignant lines, I dug out the Service's Operations Manual from
a drawer and looked up which vaccines and certificates were
needed for Nigeria. These turned out to be yellow fever and
smallpox, so I took out the forms and spent the next ten minutes
carefully filling them in, making sure the dates were well within
the prescribed time. Nigeria being a former British colony, no
visas were needed. Then I placed two calls: one to a travel agent
in Holborn, and the second to a number in Fleet Street, where
I asked to be put through to someone in the newsroom.

'Dobson,' he answered. He sounded tired and a little angry.
Not especially propitious.

'Joe!' I said, putting all the chumminess I could muster into
my voice. 'It's Paul. Paul Dark.'

'Paul, me old china!' he said, more jovially. He liked to play
up the old cockney wag act, even though his father was a

barrister in St John's Wood. 'Long time, no hear. Got a scoop for me?'

It was a joke, of sorts – I wasn't a journalist, and he was reminding me of the absurd nature of our relationship – but at the same time he was being serious. He wanted to know if I did, indeed, have a scoop.

'I can get you one,' I said, 'if you return a favour.'

He laughed. 'You owe *me* a few, don't you, mate?' After a moment or two, he bit: 'All right. What can you get me, and what's the favour?'

'Something big is about to happen in Nigeria,' I said. 'I need to be there.'

'Nigeria? Since when was that your field? You been shifted to the Africa desk and not told me?'

'No, nothing like that,' I said. 'I just need accreditation – that's all.'

'Paul, old son, you do know there's a civil war on there?' I said I did, and he harrumphed. 'We've got three stringers out there already. I don't see how I could justify another. It's not like BOAC will just fly you into the jungle . . .'

'I don't want to fly into the jungle. I want to fly to Lagos.'

I listened to the sound of prolonged wheezing. 'Nice try, but April Fool's ain't 'til next week. There's bugger all fighting in Lagos – even I know that much.'

'Yes, but that's where the story is. Trust me.'

He laughed again. 'The PM's visit, you mean? Nobody's flogging that one. Unless you can give me a clue—'

'I've got everything else,' I said, trying to keep the desperation from my voice. 'I just need you to have me listed with the Nigerians that I'm one of yours — in case nobody buys my press pass, you see.'

'Robert Kane?'

It was the pseudonym we'd used for several stories I had sent his way. I'd had the documents made up months ago, as I did for all my cover names — now I was going to have to bring 'Kane' to life.

A sudden noise erupted in the background — the grinding of a machine. 'Hang on a tick,' said Dobson. The line went quiet and I chewed my nails. Outside my door, the secretaries chatted about boyfriends and pop stars' weddings, and further down the corridor Pritchard was in a briefing room, quietly going about making arrangements that might see the end of my days.

'Sorry about that,' said Dobson when he came back on the line. 'Bit of a balls-up on the press.' He took a deep breath, and I took it with him. 'All right, mate, I'll give it a go. For old times, as they say.' It was good of him — we didn't have any old times to speak of, unless you counted a few furtive meet-ings in the back room of the City Golf Club. I wanted to kiss him. 'All being well, I should be able to have you on the list by the end of the week.'

The kiss could wait.

'Can't you make it sooner?'

'Bloody hell!' he laughed. 'Give you lot an inch, you want a flipping hectare. Come on, then — let me have it. When were you planning on getting into Lagos?'

'Tonight,' I said.

V

Monday, 24 March 1969, Lagos, Nigeria

The heat hit me as soon I stepped onto the ladder – it was like someone throwing one of the airline's hot towels over my face. I walked towards the terminal building, shimmering in the evening haze. Along the tarmac, a large group of soldiers was silently unloading crates of ammunition.

Twelve hours previously I had rushed home to the flat to collect the Kane passport from the safe and then taken a cab to Heathrow – only for the flight to be delayed. My frustration had been slightly mollified by discovering the latest issue of *Newsweek* at a stand in the departure hall. As well as the dozen or so pages covering the trials of the Robert Kennedy and Martin Luther King assassins, there was an in-depth article on the civil war in Nigeria, including an interview with Ojukwu, the Biafrans' commander-in-chief. I read through it and Pritchard's briefing dossier over a cocktail in the airport bar. After committing as much of both documents to memory as

I could, I went to the lavatory and spent ten minutes tearing the dossier to shreds and feeding it into the bowl.

The flight itself had been calm, and I had managed to sleep after we had refuelled in Rome. It was now 22.00 local time — the same as in London. But even if Pritchard moved very fast, he wouldn't be able to arrive until tomorrow morning at the earliest. My departure would almost certainly have prompted another meeting, which would mean more tea and banter until they reached a decision on how to proceed. He would already be inoculated against yellow fever and smallpox, so he wouldn't need to forge the documents as I'd done, but he would still have to complete his B-200, get it stamped and cleared — another meeting to debate what the procedure for that was in the absence of Chief and before the acting Chief had had his position confirmed — and then have his diplomatic cover arranged, flight booked by the secretariat, and so on. My flight was the last to arrive tonight, so I reckoned I had at least until dawn to try to swing things in my favour.

Before anything else, I had to get to Slavin and find out what more he knew, and how he knew it. The obvious move would be to track him down as soon as I got out of the airport, and kill him. But murder was a last resort: his death or disappearance would automatically bring me under suspicion with London, as I had run out here without asking their permission. There was also the question of Anna — I wanted to find her, too, and that would be much harder if Pritchard were actively hunting my hide.

The arrivals terminal was heavy with sweat and frustration.

A solitary fan turned high above us at an agonizing pace, while passengers stood around an unmanned desk waiting for their luggage to be brought from the plane. Thankfully, I just had my one bag, so I walked straight through to the passport control area.

There it was even worse. The queues were enormous, interlocking and unmoving. I picked one of the lines at random and joined it. As on the plane, there were a handful of white people – aid workers and diplomats, I guessed – but the rest were Nigerian. All around me, conversations were being held, sometimes in local dialects but mainly in pidgin English, which Pritchard's dossier had told me was the lingua franca. I spent a few minutes tuning in, managing to pick out words here and there, accustoming myself to the tones in which it was used. It seemed an exuberant, rich language, a world away from the Pritchards and Osbornes of the world. The clothing was a mixture of African and Western, but there was exuberance in that, too. Businessmen in Western-style suits clutched important-looking briefcases, while matronly women in multi-coloured loose-fitting dresses sported thin Cartier watches. Soldiers wandered between the lines, looking over passengers and prodding their rifles into bags. They were young and arrogant, and just the look of them brought the reality of the situation home more than the endless statistics and prolix phrases of Pritchard's report. Something about them chilled the bones.

They seemed just as interested in me. Within less than ten minutes of my entering the hall, a pattern of surveillance had closed in around me: two by the gates, one by the toilets, and a small, neat-looking man in a beret operating them with nods from next to the telephones. There was nothing I could do about it. I was a journalist, and any move I made would only make things worse. They had probably marked me out because I was a white man they didn't recognize – the aid workers they would know. It was normal. Relax.

It was getting on eleven by the time I made it to the front of the queue. The clerk had a long, narrow face and thick glasses. Behind him was draped the country's flag – vertical strips of green, white and green. He picked up my passport and started to leaf through it slowly. I wasn't worried – the document had been made in precisely the same way as if it had been genuine. He stopped at the back page.

'Press?' he said.

'Yes.'

He looked troubled at this. He leaned down and took some papers from a drawer, then placed them in front of him and started reading, tracing the miniature lines of text with a finger. I had a mounting sense of unease. Had Dobson let me down? Surely my accreditation had come through?

The clerk suddenly glanced up at me, a pained expression on his face.

'What's wrong?' I asked. 'What's the—'

He was looking behind me. I turned. There were four of them. Quite a party. Broad chests and muscle visible under their uniforms, and patterns of scars down their cheeks. It was no use struggling – there'd be more of them elsewhere in the building, and I wouldn't have a hope. They'd shoot me in the leg, or send a car to get me. And then I'd have a real job explaining my behaviour.

'You come this way,' one of them said, and pushed a rifle into my back.

Do nothing. They just want money, beer, cigarettes. Pay them, get out of here, and get to work.

Do nothing.

*

They took me down a narrow, unlit staircase and shoved me into a sparse, harshly lit room.

'Wait here.'

They slammed the door and I listened to their footsteps recede. I looked around the room: it contained two hard-backed chairs, a low table, and some brochures advertising the International Year of African Tourism.

After ten minutes spent reading the brochures, the door opened and the small man in the beret walked in, followed by several of his men. His uniform was immaculate, his beret trimmed with gold braid. In one hand, he gripped a riding crop.

'Good evening,' he said. 'I am Colonel Bernard Alebayo of the Third Marine Commando Division. Who are you?'

I took out my passport and offered it to him. He took it, but didn't open it. 'Your full name, please.'

'Robert David Peter Kane,' I said.

'That is more like it. Thank you. Cooperate with me and we will get along.' He smiled genially. He looked very young. 'Are you in Nigeria for business or pleasure?'

I examined his face. He appeared to be serious.

'Business,' I said.

'And what is your profession, Mister Kane?'

'If you look at my passport—'

'I am not interested in your passport at this particular moment,' he said, smiling sweetly again. 'I want to hear it from the horse's mouth, as it were.' He spoke English quickly and precisely, accentuating each word in an almost sing-song fashion.

I'd known who he was before he introduced himself: he'd been all over Pritchard's dossier. Alebayo, 'The Panther', was the Nigerian army's most famous commander. Trained at Sandhurst — like most of the military leaders on both sides of this war — he had a reputation for brutality and unpredictability. He was known to despise do-gooders, politicians and journalists.

'I'm a journalist,' I said.

He stroked his chin.

'For which newspaper?'

I told him.

'Ah,' he said. 'The famous *Times* of London.' He walked around the table, his boots squeaking. 'Of course, we have our own *Times* here.' He swivelled and faced me. 'Not perhaps as large a publication, or as renowned globally, but, nevertheless, quite respectable on a national level.' He looked down at his reflection in his boots for a moment. 'Yes, quite respectable.'

I murmured interest as best I could, and wondered where on earth this was heading.

Alebayo opened my passport, held it away from him as though it were contaminated, and squinted at my photograph.

'Do you know Mister Winston Churchill?' he asked, suddenly.

'My colleague, or his grandfather?'

'Are your articles as facetious as your speech, Mister Kane? Your colleague.'

'Yes,' I said, 'I know him. I wouldn't say we were friends—'

'Well, then,' he interrupted, 'as your newspaper has sent you to "cover" events here, you have presumably been "boning up" on what Mister Churchill has already written about this country in your newspaper? Yes?'

'Of course.' It had been Churchill who had alleged that the Federal pilots were targeting Biafra's civilian population. His articles had caused such an outcry that Parliament had held another emergency debate on the war — the same debate in which Wilson had announced his trip.

'Your colleague appears to believe we are savages, Mister Kane,' said Alebayo. 'Cold-blooded killers, devoid of any moral sense.'

He suddenly held back his head and laughed, and his soldiers joined in, until he whipped the table with his crop, and the laughter abruptly stopped. It was like a very bad opera production.

'Can you imagine it, Mister Kane? The cheek of the grandson of Winston Churchill to write such a thing! Has he forgotten Dresden?'

'I don't know,' I said. 'You'll have to ask him.' The analogy didn't seem fair, somehow, but I wasn't going to get into it.

He leaned in again. 'Do you intend to file the same species of report as your colleague?'

'I don't think so,' I said. 'Lagos is four hundred miles from the fighting.'

'Quite so,' he said. 'You are a sharp one, my friend.' He was pacing around, confusing the flies buzzing about his face. 'So what will you be writing about? Expatriate dinner parties? Our local cuisine? What are your editor's orders?'

'Colour stories,' I said.

He bristled. 'I am so sorry, I didn't quite hear. Could you please repeat yourself?'

I reminded myself to choose my words rather more carefully. 'A picture of life in the capital of a country at war. What the feeling is in the corridors of power, how negotiations are going, that sort of—'

'Are those what you call "colour stories"?' he said.

I nodded.

'I could tell you a few others. But perhaps your readership wouldn't be interested in hearing the reverse side of the coin.'

'We're interested in the truth,' I said, and he laughed again.

'Let me be honest with you, Mister Kane. I do not like journalists. In fact, more often than not, I find them repellent – vultures circling around others' misery, looking for something to misconstrue.' He said the word beautifully, savouring its syllables. He was watching me very keenly. 'Are you certain you are a journalist? You don't look much like one.'

'What do I look like?' I asked.

'I'm not sure.' He used one hand to squeeze my right bicep

through my shirt. 'But this arm has lifted more than a Parker pen in its time, I think. Perhaps you are a mercenary? I could use a few decent mercenaries at this particular moment. Were you ever in the army, Mister Kane?'

'Where's this going?' I said, cranking up my indignant civilian act. 'I demand to see someone from the British—'

'Were you ever in the *army*, Mister Kane?'

'Yes,' I said. 'A long time ago. But, look, I'm an accredited member of the press, I have all the necessary visas — why am I being detained?'

'Because I don't like the look of you,' he said. 'Your newspaper already has several correspondents in Nigeria, and I find it hard to believe it would suddenly have a need for "colour stories" hundreds of miles away from where anything of real colour is happening. So I want to know more.' He leaned in to look at me, his nostrils flaring.

'The British prime minister is visiting,' I said. 'On Thursday. I'm to report on that, too.'

'Ah, yes,' he said. 'Of course. Our dear and esteemed Mister Harold Wilson. I had heard mention of that. How fortunate for us all that he has decided to pay a visit. How newsworthy.' He tilted his head and looked at me as though I were a Picasso he suspected had been hung upside down. 'Do you know what the rebels call your prime minister, Mister Kane?'

'No,' I said, wearily. I was losing so much time it didn't bear thinking about.

'"Herod",' he said, grinning. 'Or sometimes "Herod Weasel".' He walked behind my back now, his heels clicking loudly. 'You maintain you are a journalist!' he suddenly shouted into my ear, making me jump. 'And yet your press accreditation only came through *tonight*. Please explain, Mister Kane!' He whipped the crop against the desk again, almost as though he felt he had to.

So that was it. I hadn't thought they'd be quite so hot on it.

'A colleague at the front was due to cover the trip,' I said, as calmly as I could. 'He cabled yesterday to say he was ill and wouldn't be able to make it back to Lagos in time, so my editor decided to send me out on the first available flight instead. That's why I've only just been accredited.'

Alebayo was silent for a moment.

'Are you perhaps a spy, Mister Kane?' he said, quietly.

I looked up at him. 'A spy?'

'Yes. A secret agent like your Double Oh Seven, saving the world from villains and foes . . . Amusing that you British have taken so long to realize that you no longer have an empire.'

'Isn't this approach unwise?' I said. 'My readers will be most interested to know how the Federal army treats the citizens of valued allies.'

'I think *I* will decide what is wise here – not you. There have been plenty of misleading reports about me in your newspapers already. I cannot imagine another will do any further harm. That is, if you ever succeed in filing a report on this little meeting.' He turned to the largest of his thugs. 'Is the transport ready?' The thug nodded. 'Good.' He turned back to me. 'Perhaps a visit to one of our prisons would provide some good material for your editor? Some "colour"?'

'This is outrageous!' I said, and now my indignation was only half-acted. 'Call my office in London! Call the British High Commission! I demand—'

'Please, Mister Kane, save your tantrums. They will not do you any good here.' He stood a little straighter and adjusted his beret. 'I must now return to Port Harcourt, where I have many things to attend to. There is the small matter of a war to win. But you will be well looked after by my boys here, I promise. And they may even discover what it is you came here for . . .'

There was a sudden banging at the door, and Alebayo glanced sharply in its direction. He nodded at one of the thugs, who walked over and opened it. Framed in the light was a large white man with a crumpled red face, wearing what looked to be a pair of pyjamas.

'Let this man go, Bernard!' he said in a booming English voice.

*

'Geoffrey!' said Alebayo through gritted teeth. 'How delightful to see you again.' He strode over to the door and gestured him outside.

The thugs eyed me warily – they were anxious for the order to tear me to pieces. I didn't much fancy my chances with them.

'Just follow your orders,' I told them. 'And we'll all be fine.'

They glared at me, and I wondered if I shouldn't try to make a run for it, after all. Then the door opened again and Alebayo shouted something at the thugs. They leapt up and ran out after him.

I looked in astonishment at the empty room. After about thirty seconds, I stood up myself, picking up my bag from the floor. At the door, I met the man with the red face. A hand was thrust out from a striped cotton sleeve.

'I'm Geoffrey Manning,' he said. 'Welcome to Lagos.'

VI

As we stepped out of the airport, a mob of taxi drivers swarmed around us.

'Where you go, mister?'

'I offer you best price!'

Manning waved them away and steered us to a blue Peugeot on the other side of the road.

'Did you catch the rugby on Saturday?' he asked as he unlocked his door. 'The Welsh seemed on good form.'

I climbed into the passenger seat. 'I missed that,' I said. 'Do they show the matches out here, then?'

'If only, old chap, if only. I caught the report on the World Service. Who's your money on to win the whole thing?'

'I haven't really followed it, I'm afraid.'

He grunted and locked his door, gesturing for me to do the same. When I had, he said: 'You're Larry Dark's boy, aren't you?'

I nodded.

'Fine fellow, your father. Never met him myself, but saw

him break the land speed record in '38. Extraordinary day —
were you there?'

I shook my head dully.

'Damn fine fellow.' He placed his key in the ignition and
started her up. 'Anyway, glad you made it. Imagine you'll be
wanting to get that suit off in this heat.'

He gestured at the back seat, on which an outfit identical
to the one he was wearing lay folded.

'Pyjama party at the Yacht Club — any excuse for a booze-up.'

I told him I was fine as I was.

We turned onto the main road and he swore under his breath.
'Not our night. Bad go-slow.' He caught my look. 'Traffic jam
in the local argot. Marjorie will be furious — she was expecting
me hours ago.'

'Marjorie?'

'The wife. Super girl. Don't deserve her, really. Fine stock —
Scottish blue blood, you know. Stuck with me through thick
and thin.' He mimed swigging a glass and winked conspira-
torially at me.

Pritchard had said things were a little haphazard, but I hadn't
imagined they'd be this dire. I'd seen plenty of Manning's type
before. He was a spook of the old school: stockbroker parents,
minor public school, army, Colonial Service. Most of them
had been swept away in '66 when the Service had taken over
responsibility for the colonies from Five, but Manning had
evidently managed to hold on.

I wound down the window and looked out. There was indeed
a go-slow. The street was a mass of cars, trucks, motorcycles,

and bikes, the drivers of which were all either tooting their horns or yelling at the drivers around them. Many of the vehicles looked on the verge of collapse, either because they were overloaded with passengers and luggage or were missing vital parts: windows, wing mirrors, bumpers . . . The Opel Kapitän alongside us was short a door on the passenger side. Looming over the scene was an enormous billboard with a picture of a tyre: 'GO BY DUNLOP – THEY LAST LONGEST!' It seemed a little like trying to sell sticking plasters on a battlefield.

As Manning searched for an opening in the traffic, I considered once again his presence at the airport. I prided myself on my ability to think several steps ahead, but it had taken me totally unawares – I hadn't imagined my colleagues would be anxious enough to want me on a leash for just one night.

'When did London cable to say I was on my way?' I asked.

Manning glanced across at me. 'About half seven. I was just changing when the office called.'

Half seven. That was fast – it usually took them a month to agree to buy a light bulb.

'I told the driver to take the night off and drove straight out here,' Manning was saying. 'Your flight came in, but there was no sign of you. Then I spotted a soldier standing guard outside one of the doors leading to the dungeons. Thought I'd better take a look-see.'

I told him I was glad he had; he waved my gratitude away. 'That's my job. Can't have our people thrown in the stocks the moment they arrive in the country! Especially not Larry Dark's boy. Not on my watch. You were unlucky – Bernard's only in town for a couple of hours. Well, I say unlucky. Depends on how you look at it, of course. A few months back a chap from the *Telegraph* thought it was a good idea to disagree with him. Bernard had the fellow's head shaved, got him to do press-ups for an hour, and then forced him to write out the words "I am a crappy Englishman and have no say in Nigeria" a thousand times.'

He roared with laughter at this, yanking the car into an opening in the traffic as he did so. '"*I am a crappy Englishman and have no say in Nigeria!*"' he bellowed out of the window at a startled motorcyclist, who nearly swerved into the drain as a result. 'Bernard was always a damn fool,' he continued calmly once we were safely ensconced in a line just as slow-moving as the one we'd left. 'Even at Sandhurst. That's where I first met him, of course, many moons ago. I was an instructor there. Know quite a few of the commanders in this war from those days, as it happens.'

'What's he doing in Lagos? I thought his division was miles away.'

'Yes, he's over at Port Harcourt. I asked him the same question myself, and he said he was picking up troops and supplies. Apparently he can't trust the other divisions not to steal his stuff unless he comes up and supervises things personally. Typically African way to run a war.'

I remembered the soldiers I'd seen on the tarmac. 'What's he up to? Preparing for the final push?'

Manning snorted. 'There's been a final push every blasted month of this war. They're calling this latest one the *final* final push – but nobody believes it.'

The traffic was at a complete standstill now, and it looked like we might be in for a long wait: Manning said it could sometimes take hours to clear. I took out my Players and watched as a mangy dog with great gaps of fur and a missing leg wandered up between the lanes of cars. Despite its limp, it had a strangely proud demeanour – almost as though it knew it would reach the centre of Lagos before us.

'What else did London say?' I asked Manning.

'Not much,' he replied, somewhat blithely. 'That Chief's gone missing. Reading between the lines, there's a flap on that he may have something to do with the double agent this Russian johnnie has told us about, and you've flown the nest to prove them wrong. Am I right?'

'Close enough,' I said. 'Did London mention when Pritchard would be arriving?'

'No, just to expect him soon. Good chap, Henry. Came out here a few months ago. Thrashed me at golf. Beautiful swing.'

'What were your instructions?'

'What? Oh. To pick you up at the airport, then provide you with any assistance you required.'

'I need to arrange accommodation,' I said. If they were going to assign me a nanny, I might as well make use of him.

'Of course. I'd have done it already, only nobody was sure what cover you'd be using.'

'Robert Kane. *Times* hack covering the Wilson visit.'

'Yes – so I gathered from Bernard. Well, we can check you in somewhere now if you'd like. Any preferences?'

'What's the best-known hotel?' I asked, and Manning glanced

over at me. Most agents would have wanted somewhere discreet, but I wanted to make my presence felt in the city, fast.

'The Victoria Palace,' he said. 'It's the closest Lagos gets to the Ritz. Not that it's particularly close . . .'

I knew the name. Pritchard's dossier had mentioned it a couple of times, notably because an Ibo had tried to blow it up in advance of a peace conference a few years earlier. That it was enough of a landmark to be a target meant it was precisely the kind of place I was looking for.

'I'll drop you there,' said Manning. 'If this traffic ever gets going, that is. Oh, and before I forget . . .' He plunged a hand inside the pocket of his pyjama jacket and fished out a small package, which he passed over to me. 'You'll also need these.'

I opened the box and took out a dozen white tablets sandwiched between some cellophane.

'Paludrine. Anti-malaria. Take them once a day. It's all there in the instructions: "Best absorbed with evening G and T."' He had another chuckle, and I began to wonder if he might simply be drunk. He caught my look. 'Sorry. But see it from my view, if you can.' He gestured at the Lagos night. 'Stuck out here in the sticks miles from the bloody war and suddenly people start flying in looking for Chief – this is the most excitement we've had in yonks.'

I nodded, and packed the medicine in my hold-all.

'Seems we're in luck,' said Manning, pointing ahead. The cars were starting to move.

*

The hotel was a horrendous white modernist building that looked like a collection of giant window-boxes, but the car park was stuffed with diplomatic plates and flagpoles jutted importantly from the entrance marquee, so it was clearly the right spot. I told Manning to wait for me and walked through to the reception, where a sullen-looking young woman behind a marble counter sold me an air-conditioned double room for a hundred and eighty Nigerian shillings a night — the single rooms were all gone, she claimed. After filling in the registry and handing over my passport, I took the stairs to my room on the third floor.

It didn't quite live up to the picture I'd been given in reception, but it looked like it had the basics: the air conditioning worked, and there was a telephone and a radio. Was it secure, though? I threw my bag and jacket onto the mattress and checked the strength of the door from the outside. After a few minutes, I was satisfied that anyone wanting to break it down would have to make a hell of a noise to do so. The windows also shut firmly, and I rigged an elastic band across the two handles to make sure. They led out onto a fire escape, which would come in handy if anyone tried anything. I was directly above the swimming pool. Despite the lateness of the hour, there were still a few people lounging on deckchairs sipping from long-stemmed glasses: diplomats, or aid workers. Nice life. Not mine.

There was a tiny en suite bathroom with a sink that trickled lukewarm water, and a cracked mirror above it. After splashing my face and drying it on my shirt — towels didn't appear to be part of the service — I called reception and asked them to put me through to the Soviet Embassy. Amazingly, this took only a couple of minutes.

'*Da?*' The voice was cold. Night shift.

'Hello,' I said in Russian, but playing up my English accent. 'Could you put me through to Third Secretary Irina Grigorieva, please?'

'Everyone's gone home,' she said. 'Do you want to leave a message?'

'Yes,' I said. 'Tell her it's an old friend calling: name of Paul Dark. I'm at the Palace Hotel on Victoria Island, room 376. Did you get all that?'

She said she had, and I replaced the receiver. Slavin was my first priority, because he was planning to defect and might have more information that could point to me. But Anna could also expose me — she wasn't volunteering to do so, but she could — so I had to get hold of her, too. She would be unlikely to return to the embassy until the morning, and they wouldn't have given me her address, so I'd taken the next best option, which was to leave a message to try to bring her to me.

I locked up, and headed downstairs.

★

'Everything okay?' asked Manning.

'First class,' I said, fastening my seat-belt.

'What are you doing?'

'Tell me what you know about Slavin,' I said.

'Slavin?'

'Yes. Russian johnnie. Was there anything you didn't mention in the dossier you sent?'

He looked at me blankly. 'Like what?'

'How about the woman he mentioned – Irina Grigorieva? What's their relationship?'

'I have no idea,' he replied, irritated. 'I sent all the information we have.'

I smiled. 'Just double-checking. I'd like to talk to Slavin – see if I can make him open up some more.'

'You can do that tomorrow morning. He's due at the High Commission at nine . . .'

'I'd like to talk to him tonight.'

He tensed up. 'Sorry, old chap, I don't follow.'

'Tomorrow may be too late,' I said. 'Did he have any surveillance on him when he arrived at the High Commission?' He stiffened, but gave no reply. 'And when he left?' No reply. 'So you see, we have no idea how secure his position is, let alone how he's handling the pressure of being about to defect. He could already be under suspicion, or he could be getting horribly drunk and about to spill everything to one of his colleagues while we sit here discussing it. Have you put his home under surveillance?'

He shook his head defensively. 'Too risky. He was quite clear we should make no further contact until tomorrow.'

'But you know where his house is?' A nod. 'Well?'

'It's in Ikoyi, near the Russian Embassy.'

'Near, but not in?'

'That's right. Most of the Russians have their own villas, same as us. But I don't—'

'Right, then. We'll go and knock on his door, see if he's still alive, alive-oh, and then you can head off to your party and I back to my little rat-hole.'

He frowned. 'If he's under surveillance, we could blow him.'

'If he's under surveillance,' I said, 'he's probably already been blown. London told you to hold my hand, and that's precisely what you're going to do.'

After a while, he shook his head and let out a deep sigh. 'You'll have to think of something to tell Marjorie,' he said. 'She'll be livid.'

*

Like many others in the neighbourhood, the villa sat behind an imposing set of iron gates. 'Villa' was Manning's word, and was perhaps a little generous. It was a large but plain-looking bungalow, with mosquito nets on the windows and a jacaranda tree in the drive helping to mask the peeling paint.

Slavin's house.

We were at the easternmost edge of the city: Ikoyi was the last island. On the way over, Manning had told me that many of the city's expatriates, himself included, lived here. I could see why. Its houses, even the run-down ones, were spacious, its gardens neatly trimmed and, in comparison to the cacophony of traffic elsewhere in the city, it was eerily quiet: the only sounds I could hear were the mosquitoes buzzing around my ears, the ticking of my watch, and the creaking of leather as Manning shifted his bum in his seat.

A Peugeot 404 was parked in the drive, so it looked as if

Slavin was in. However, I had no way of knowing whether he was in there *alone*. I'd made Manning drive around the neighbouring streets to check for surveillance. I hadn't found any, but that wasn't conclusive: they could be watching us from inside the house itself. And so could Slavin. I'd told Manning that surveillance would mean he was already blown, but that wasn't strictly true. This man was a KGB officer and, if his work was important enough, he could be guarded around the clock as a matter of course.

Manning was also right to worry that this kind of approach might tip off Slavin's colleagues that he was intending to defect. If they were to get the slightest sniff of that, he would immediately be deported, and probably shot on arrival in the motherland. But that wasn't my plan: for the time being anyway, I wanted Comrade Slavin to stay alive. I had to find out what he knew, and how he'd discovered it. He had claimed that Anna had loved me, but had she been the source for that, or someone else? I had to get to him, but I had to find a way to do it without the Russians being alerted.

It wasn't looking promising. We'd been here for twenty minutes and there hadn't been a flicker of activity from inside the house.

'It *is* the cocktail hour,' Manning said, finally.

I looked at him. 'You think Slavin might also have a pyjama party on tonight?'

He shrugged. 'He might even be at the same one.'

'You socialize with the Russians?'

'Sometimes. Plenty of diplomats, from all over, are members

of the Yacht Club. The Russian ambassador joined last year —
chap called Romanov. Charming fellow, actually, and quite a
good sailor—'

'Is Slavin a member?'

'Not that I know of. But anyone who is could sign him in.
And it's quite a big bash tonight, so perhaps he'd want to go.'

I found it hard to believe Moscow would allow anyone
important out on the cocktail circuit: it was almost an invita-
tion to defect. Still, Slavin *was* planning to defect, so perhaps
they had as tight a rein out here as the Service appeared to,
employing buffoons like Manning. Perhaps Lagos was just one
big pyjama party.

Or perhaps I was just tired. Manning was worried about the
rocket he was going to get from his wife and was probably
using the slightest possibility that Slavin would be at the same
party as a pretext to stop my goose chase around Lagos. But
it *was* a possibility, however slight, and now he'd put the thought
in my head it was hard to dismiss. It would be too painful to
bear if we were staking out his house while he was lording it
up over the road in his nightgown and slippers.

'How far away is this party of yours?'

Manning jollied up. 'A fifteen-minute drive — less at this
time of night. It's over on Lagos Island.' He pointed in the
direction we'd come. As he did, I noticed the field lying in
darkness by the side of the road.

'What's that? A golf course?'

'Yes. Part of the Ikoyi Club. I'm a member there, too. Not a
bad little course, as it happens. Henry—'

I didn't want to hear about Pritchard's birdie on the ninth, so I opened the door and climbed out.

'Wait here,' I said.

*

As I approached the gate, I saw that behind it and to the right, partly shielded by bushes, was a small hut, wooden and painted blue. I pressed a buzzer, and after a few seconds a bulb went on and a man emerged from it. He was wearing grey flannel trousers and a sweater with epaulettes.

'Who goes there?' he called. His handsome face was half-lit by the bulb, highlighting deep symmetrical scars down his cheeks. I could see the silhouette of his rifle: from the way he gripped it, he looked to be an amateur. Surely a KGB colonel would have more protection than this?

'Who goes there?'

'Is Mister Slavin in?' I asked.

He peered out at me. 'He expecting you, sir?'

That was good. 'Sir' was good.

'Yes,' I said. 'I'm here for the party.'

He didn't register either way, but he raised his rifle a little. I'd guessed wrongly: there might still be people in there, but he wasn't convinced it classed as a party.

'Listen,' I said quickly. 'What's your name?' I needed to change direction.

'Isaac,' he said warily.

'Isaac, could you do me a favour?' I patted my pockets absent-mindedly. 'Do you have a piece of paper I can write on?'

He went into his hut and came back a few seconds later with a newspaper. It was the *Daily Times*, Alebayo's read of choice. As he approached the gate, I saw that his rifle was now pointing towards the ground. His neck shone under the corona of the lamp. It would have been the easiest thing in the world to overpower him at that moment. But what then? What if I broke in and Slavin had company? At best, he'd be blown. At worst, I'd be dead.

Fifteen minutes, Manning had said. I looked at my watch: it was already half ten. I handed Isaac the note. 'Please give Mister Slavin this, and let him know I visited.'

*

'Any luck?' Manning asked, back in the car.

'Not much.'

'So what now?'

What now, indeed? It was getting on, and I was no further ahead. Come tomorrow morning, I was going to be in trouble. Even more trouble than I was already in. But I couldn't see a way past it – the odds were too high.

Manning was looking at me expectantly.

'All right,' I said. 'Just for half an hour.'

He turned the key in the ignition.

*

'The bar only opened last year, you know,' said Manning as he handed me my drink. 'Very controversial – the debate raged for years. A lot of us were worried the place would fill up with non-sailing types. There was even one chap – German, wasn't he, Sandy?'

'Dutch, I think,' said Sandy, who was a small elegant man in a long white nightshirt.

'Oh, yes,' said Manning, popping a peanut into his mouth. 'That's right. Dutch. Well, he came along one week and asked if he could join just to *socialize*. Brazenly admitted he had no intention of sailing at all! Put him right, didn't we?' He snorted, and Sandy nodded his head sagely.

'Oh, Geoffrey! I'm sure Robert isn't interested in the intricate workings of the Yacht Club.'

Marjorie Manning had been flirting with me outrageously since we'd arrived. She might have been a beauty twenty-odd years ago, but too much drink, sun, and Geoffrey had shaken most of it from her.

'What would you rather discuss, dear?' Manning asked her sweetly. 'The shops in London?'

'Why not?' she said. 'What's in fashion this season, Robert? Tell us, please. We have to rely on the local supermarkets to provide us with our clothes, and it's hardly Yves Saint Laurent.'

'I don't think fashion's quite Robert's patch,' said Manning, winking at me.

I'd been a bloody fool to listen to him, of course: there was no sign of any Russians, let alone Slavin. The party reminded me of dozens I'd been to in Istanbul and elsewhere: several dozen expats, mostly Brits, getting sloshed on brandy and sodas and munching stale crisps. We were seated at a table outside, making the most of the faint breeze coming in off the water. Stewards in white uniforms and guests in nightclothes milled about the lawn, giving the place a somewhat ghostly air. A group of men directly behind me discussed the merits of fibreglass hulls and wondered how long it would be until the rainy season. The consensus seemed to be that it would arrive any day now.

I glanced at my watch: twenty-five past ten. My note had asked Slavin to meet me at eleven. Despite the needless detour, this was still marginally preferable to sitting in the car with Manning for half an hour, which was what I would have been doing otherwise: and staying on for that length of time might have been unwise if there had been any sort of surveillance of the street from inside Slavin's villa. I took a sip from my drink and wondered again if he was being guarded. Perhaps he was being questioned about my note right now: perhaps I'd blown his defection. And that would be disastrous, because I couldn't afford for him to be carted away before Pritchard arrived. But I was being too pessimistic, surely. The most obvious explanation was the most likely: he hadn't been at home. Perhaps he was working late at the embassy. Men about to defect often become conspicuously loyal to those they are about to betray. If he *was* at the embassy, it was stalemate – I couldn't get near him there.

'Mister Kane?'

I looked up. The man called Sandy was speaking to me. 'Sorry?'

'I said, "What is your patch, exactly?" I can't remember seeing your byline in *The Times*.'

I'd been wondering when he would pounce. Manning had introduced him as a property developer, but I recognized his name – he'd been a BBC correspondent in the war, and was now connected behind the scenes. Still did some work for *The Mirror*, I seemed to remember.

I mentioned a few of the stories that had appeared in *The Times* credited to Robert Kane in the past couple of years. Each had been written for short-term operational reasons, using the name as a convenient blanket – they hadn't been intended to build cover in the field. If Farraday hadn't suddenly fancied having a go playing at spies, Manning could simply have introduced me under my own name as a second secretary at the embassy. Instead, I was going to have to be on my back foot defending a half-formed legend.

'Out here for the PM's visit, I suppose?'

I nodded. 'My editor wants something about the feel of the place, how the Brits see the war, that kind of thing. Perhaps I can interview you at some point?'

'Certainly – just call my office. I was here for the Queen's trip in '56, so I'm quite used to the pomp and ceremony. Wilson's rather small potatoes, isn't he? Reminds me of a bank clerk in those silly raincoats he wears.'

'He'll have to ditch them in this heat,' said Manning.

We all laughed politely.

'Is Lagos as safe as everyone says it is?' I asked Sandy. 'It seems very quiet.'

'Oh,' he said, 'we haven't had any action here since one of the rebels' planes attacked the Motor Boat Club two years ago. Didn't do much harm, though everyone got frightfully excited, of course.'

'"Rebels"? You don't think secession was justified, then?'

'Not really. Ojukwu's a thug, and Gowon's doing his best to control a very difficult situation.'

'What about the accusations of genocide? I've heard there were seven thousand Biafran deaths a day due to starvation over the summer.'

He grimaced. 'A lot of do-gooders with no idea of how this part of the world works are swallowing the genocide line whole. Propaganda, of course – people throw around these enormous figures, but nobody really has the slightest idea. I think the Federals have actually dealt with the situation very well, considering the paltry support they've received from our government – and I'll be telling the PM that when I meet him at State House on Thursday. At the moment, we seem to be simply watching from the sidelines, as usual. Nigeria will carry on with or without us.'

'Wawa,' said Manning, nodding his chin.

'Sorry?'

'West Africa wins again. Another drink, old boy?'

'It's all right,' I said, 'I'll get it.'

I pushed my chair back and headed for the bar.

*

A steward in a gleaming white uniform and scarlet cummerbund stood behind a makeshift table crammed with bottles and paper cups. With all the poise of a Sotheby's auctioneer, he surveyed the small crowd gathered round him, eventually nodding to a man in khaki shorts and deck shoes.

'Star,' said the man, in the manner of someone who had been wandering through the desert for forty days and nights.

The steward leaned down, scooped a bottle of beer from an icebox, opened it deftly, and handed it to the man.

And that was when I saw her.

She was sitting by herself on a stack of breeze blocks just beyond the bar, in a black bathing suit, a cigarette dangling from one hand. Her face was turned away in contemplation of the water, but the line of her jaw was unmistakable. I made my way through the crowd, stepped over the steward's icebox and tapped her on the shoulder.

'Anna.'

She turned and peered at me in puzzlement. And for a fraction of a moment, it was her — but her twenty years ago. And then the illusion faded, and I was apologizing for my error. What a fool I was! What a bloody fool to mistake the first dark-haired stranger for her. I was losing grip, and fast.

'You do not wear pyjamas,' said the girl. Her accent was French, as was her tone. I looked at her again. She had one of those androgynous cat-like faces that were so much in fashion, the effect highlighted by her lack of make-up and slicked-back hair. She was more conventionally beautiful than Anna had ever been, but there was something rather hard about her. She looked like she should be marching through Parisian boulevards holding a placard.

'No,' I said in answer to her comment. 'But neither do you.'

'I was swimming.'

I glanced down at the water — it looked filthy.

'It is not so bad once you have entered,' she said, white teeth flashing in the dark face.

I offered her my hand. 'Robert Kane.'

She shook it perfunctorily. 'Isabelle Dumont. Tell me, who did you think I was just now?'

'Someone I knew a long time ago,' I said.

She smiled softly. 'I see. So what do you do, Mister Kane? I haven't seen you here before.'

'I've only just arrived. I'm a reporter, for *The Times.*'

'That is a coincidence. I write for Agence France-Presse. Are you here for your prime minister's visit?'

I nodded, already bored of the pretext.

She grinned again, and lifted her chin. 'Look on the good side of it: you meet such very interesting people.'

I followed her gaze back to the table I'd left. Manning was stuffing his face full of peanuts, his wife was laughing like a hyena, and Sandy was trying to fish a dead fly from his drink with a spoon.

'Yes,' I said. 'Why is it one can never stand one's countrymen whenever one meets them abroad?'

'One has no idea,' she said, curling her lip a little.

'Still,' I said, ignoring the crack. 'I've met you. You're interesting. Have you been out here long?'

'I grew up here,' she said. 'My father was the French ambassador.'

'Have you seen much of the rest of the country?'

There was a noise from further down the jetty, and we both looked up. A woman in a cocktail dress was squealing as a man lifted her over his head and threatened to throw her in the water. People at other tables stopped their conversations to stare at the scene, but nobody did much, and a few seconds later there was a splash as her spine hit the water.

The woman swam to the shore and helped herself out, ignoring the man's insincere apologies. The steward ran over to offer her a towel, and she took it, wrapped it around herself, and marched through the crowd into the clubhouse.

A few moments later, the man walked past us, a wide innocent smile on his face.

'Kraut,' he said in an American accent. 'Can't take jokes.'

We watched him trudge up to the clubhouse, and then Isabelle took a puff of her cigarette and said in a very still voice: 'I was at the front in January. I must now get back. But it takes very long to obtain authorization to fly there.'

She was looking out at the sea instead of me, at the lights of the trawlers. Her brown skin, the sheen of her bathing suit, the lapping of the water behind her, the alcohol still warm in my throat . . . for a moment, I forgot about Slavin and Anna and Sasha and Pritchard, and felt like a human being. Then a ship hooted in the distance and I woke up. That life was an illusion, and I couldn't afford to slip back into it.

'I'm afraid I can't help you,' I said. 'I've only just got here.'

She turned, and shot me a withering look. 'I was not requesting your help,' she said. 'I make my own arrangements.'

I looked at my watch. It was quarter to eleven.

'It was nice meeting you,' I said, and her looks softened for a fraction of a moment.

*

Back at the table, I took Manning to one side and told him I needed to borrow his car.

'Whatever for?' he said. 'Not that Slavin business again?'

'Well, he's not here, is he?'

'But how am I supposed to—'

'Sandy can give you a lift home,' I said, lifting the keys from his jacket pocket.

*

I stood on the eighteenth brown and looked around. Nothing.

Nigerian golf courses didn't have greens, Manning had explained to me. It was too hard to maintain grass in such a climate, so instead they had 'browns': they were made of a mix of sand and oil, which the caddies would sweep for you before your putt.

He was already ten minutes late. Had I just blown him? I had counted on his being senior enough to read his own messages without being challenged, but now I was having doubts. What if he was under such close supervision that his correspondence was read as a matter of course? I had no choice but to wait and find out.

Behind me were the banks of villas and embassies. I could see Slavin's street, but there didn't seem to be any sign of life in it. And then something moved in my peripheral vision, and I turned to catch it. It was just a shape in the darkness, but it hadn't been there before.

'Who's that?' I called out.

The shape stopped, and now I saw it was a man. He ran up

the incline onto the far edge of the brown. He was tall with stooped shoulders and, I could just make out, a widow's peak.

Slavin.

*

I exhaled deeply. I had left London this morning with the aim of reaching this man before anyone else, and I'd succeeded.

'You are not Mister Manning,' he said, and I fancied he backed away a step.

I held up my hands. 'I work with Mister Manning at the High Commission,' I said in Russian. 'He told me to arrange a meeting with you.'

'Why? I thought it was clear that the interview was tomorrow.'

'It is,' I assured him. 'And I'm sorry we broke our promise not to contact you before then. But we had to. Some questions have come up in London.'

He took a couple of steps closer, and the moonlight struck his face. Anxiety was etched across it.

'Questions?' he asked. 'What questions?'

'Irina Grigorieva,' I said. 'We need to know more about her.'

He took another few steps, and now we were standing face to face, within touching distance.

'Irina?' he said, confused. 'But she has nothing to—'

He stopped, and I wondered if he had changed his mind about whatever it was he'd been about to tell me. But then I saw the dark red patch on his throat and my mind caught up with the sound, half-drowned in the wind.

Shot.

VII

Slavin fell into my arms. I dropped him and ran in the direction of the noise. As I clambered down the bank, I saw a figure on the fairway: a white man, running. I followed him.

Was he heading for Slavin's house? Had he been one of his guards? He looked to be heading for the road, certainly. On the drive here, I hadn't seen anybody on the streets – curfew descended at midnight, and expats were unlikely to wander around anyway. They had gins to drink, boats to sail, women to throw in the sea.

He still had the pistol in his right hand, and he turned to fire at me. It missed, and I wondered if it had been deliberate – he'd had no trouble with Slavin.

He was heading through a band of bushes to cut across to another hole, which sloped down to the gardens on Slavin's street. When he reached the crest of the hill, he stopped, staggering a little, standing back and bellowing at me. I couldn't understand it – the echo was too confusing. But it was a jeer. He raised his hand to fire again, and I dropped to the ground. He disappeared over the brow of the hill.

And now it started raining. It began gently, bringing the smell of the earth to the fore and refreshing my face, but within seconds it was a sheet. It attacked like hot needles, and the noise of it on the nearby roofs was deafening.

The rain wasn't good for the shooter, either, as he was stuck in weeds in the rough, bogging him down. I was on the fairway and started gaining ground. I saw that another mound was coming up, and from its position I guessed what lay behind it.

As he reached the brow, I shouted out at him, and he turned back for an instant. With a surge, I carried myself over and onto his back, tumbling us both into the bunker. He grunted and waved his arms around as though he were drowning, and I realized that I'd have to be quick; he was a younger, stronger man, trained, with a gun. I wanted him alive, but it might not be possible. I swung wildly at his head, trying to get at his eyes or nose. I felt the cracking of bone and heard him scream, so I immediately brought the other hand round in an axe-chop to follow through, but he rolled to avoid it and then he was climbing on me. A fist slammed into the small of my back, sending a wave of agony up my spine, and I tried to get the momentum to push back into him, hoisting my elbows towards his face, but I merely scraped his chin and he was grabbing me around the neck and pulling me towards him. His breathing was fast and I could smell him, could smell his sweat and his desire to kill me. As I started to lose control of my throat muscles, I freed one hand and grabbed at his groin. His grip loosened for a moment and I managed to turn enough to bring my other hand into play, gouging at one of his eyes. My fingers came away wet, but I lost my footing and fell face first into the mud. It took me a while to get back up, but I couldn't see anything and the nerves in my spine were stabbing at me. Where the hell was he? Everything was black, and the rain was hammering down. Suddenly I saw a glint of light. The moon? No, it was moving! I rolled away from it and heard a slashing sound behind me as I did. I leapt at the shape in the dark, lashing out with my feet and catching him hard in the stomach. He fell against the side of the bunker and I pinned him, locking my arms around his neck and squeezing. It was a thick neck: the neck of a KGB thug. Rage surged through me. Sasha had broken his promise.

'Who are you?' I screamed into his face in Russian, but he was incapable of answering, so I loosened my hold and concentrated on his left arm instead.

'Who? Tell me!'

He didn't answer, and after I'd asked him a few more times, I broke the arm in one movement. But there was no scream from the Russian, and I wondered what was wrong. His face suddenly looked pale; I realized what he was doing and frantically tried to prise open his jaw to get to the pill.

Too late.

I searched him. There were no identifying papers, of course, but there were some Nigerian shillings and a box of matches. The matchbox had something scribbled on it in pencil. I held it up to the moonlight. It was one very familiar Cyrillic word: "АЭРОФЛОТ".

I shunted it to one side of my brain, to deal with later, picked up the rake and started shovelling the mud over his body, as the rain kept coming down around us. Then I trudged back up to the eighteenth to look for Slavin and do the same thing.

VIII

In the front seat of Manning's car, away from the rain hammering into my back and drowning out my thoughts, I considered the implications of what had just happened. They were, all told, pretty bleak. The death of a KGB officer on the eve of his defection would trigger the order for an immediate investigation from London. I could have handled that if it had been run by Manning, but Pritchard would be in the city in a matter of days, possibly even hours, and he would be much harder to fob off. Especially as I had disobeyed orders to come out here, had then insisted on meeting Slavin ahead of the scheduled time – and had been the only witness to his murder.

There was nothing I could do about any of that now. If I went underground – moved hotels, cut all contact with Manning – I might as well paint a cross on my back. Pritchard would have a pack of hounds sent over on Concorde. No, my only option was to carry on the pretence I was searching for the traitor, even if that meant Pritchard breathing down my neck and giving me even less room for manoeuvre. It was precisely the situation I'd wanted to avoid – and precisely what I'd warned Sasha would happen if he got Moscow to send a hitman into Lagos.

Now I *had* to find Anna. The Service knew she had recruited Radnya, so would almost certainly investigate her next. I knew she was somewhere in this city – probably even somewhere in this neighbourhood. Perhaps that house, there, with the jacaranda trees swaying in the wind. Perhaps she was in that villa, wrapped up in pleasant dreams, while I sat here with my shirt dripping and my fingers caked in blood as the minutes wound down until Pritchard's plane landed.

I took the torch from the glove compartment and ran it over the assassin's effects. I wasn't expecting to find anything that would identify him: he'd been a professional. But there were clues. There were always clues.

The most obvious one was the word scrawled on the matchbox: 'AEROFLOT'. My first thought was that it was a reminder to book his ticket back to Moscow: after all, even hitmen need to organize their travel arrangements. But why would he write that down? It wasn't as if he would forget the name of the national airline.

Next thought: perhaps he had a contact at Aeroflot's office here. That made more sense – it was a common KGB cover. But again, why make a note of it? Bad form and, again, it wouldn't be too hard to remember.

I was missing something. I hadn't been in the field in over five years, and it was taking me time to get back into the old ways of thinking. Too much time.

I picked up the Russian's gun. It was a Tokarev TT. I had always thought it a brutish-looking weapon: unpainted and almost devoid of markings, it looked more like a cast of a pistol than the real thing. This one had been worn smooth with years of use, so that only one of the Cs in 'CCCP' arranged around the grip was still legible.

I emptied the chamber, because it had no manual safety and I didn't want to blow my knees off, and asked myself why a KGB assassin would be carrying this gun. The TT hadn't been produced in years — most KGB now used the Makarov. The army had continued to use it for a while, but I'd read a report just a few months ago saying that they had also abandoned it. Perhaps he had been in the army many years ago, and had kept the gun? I tried to remember his face, before its features had been contorted by pain. Late twenties — no older than that. So too young to have been issued with a TT even if he had been in the army. Perhaps someone he knew had been in the army, and had given it to him. Or he had it for other reasons — like I had my Luger.

I wasn't getting anywhere. My thoughts turned to Slavin — were there any clues there? He had started to say something about Anna before the shots had interrupted him. 'But she has nothing to . . .' What? Nothing to do with this? Nothing to gain? Nothing to lose?

The shots. There was a clue. The first had gone through Slavin's windpipe; the second had nearly taken off my ear. But why had he wasted valuable seconds shooting at me? Simply because I was a witness to murder — or because I was his second *target*?

A chill went through me. Had Sasha ordered me 'dispatched', too?

I would have to make a move soon. I lit a cigarette with one of the dead man's matches. As I made to put the box in my pocket, I noticed that his scribbled 'eh' looked more like a stylized 'ehf'. That didn't help me much: so I knew he hadn't been an especially literate assassin. But then I saw that two other letters also looked wrong.

I flicked the torch across the surface again.

He hadn't written them down incorrectly – I'd misread them. The word wasn't 'АЭРОФЛОТ', but 'АФРОСПОТ'. I was so used to seeing the name of the airline in Section reports that my mind had automatically taken in a similar-looking word and jumped to the wrong conclusion.

So what the hell was 'Afrospot'?

*

At the Yacht Club, the party had moved into the bar. Manning was deep in discussion with his wife and Sandy: West Africa, no doubt, was winning again. When he caught sight of me, he nearly tripped over himself running over.

'Bloody hell!' he said. 'What happened? Did you get caught in the rain?'

'No,' I said. 'I decided to take a shower and forgot to undress.'

He coughed into his hand. 'Did Slavin show?'

I took him by the arm and led him down a corridor and into the men's changing rooms. I gave the place the once over, glancing into the WCs and the shower stalls to make sure nobody else was there. Once I was satisfied we were alone, I turned to Manning.

'Slavin made contact about half an hour ago,' I said.

'Did he have any information about the woman?'

'I don't know. Someone put a bullet through the back of his neck before I could find out.'

It took an instant for the words to penetrate, and then his face crumpled and his eyes lost their spark.

'Christ,' he said. 'That's rather a blow.'

'Yes,' I said. 'It is, rather.' I wondered if he was so comfortable out here that he'd forgotten what our game was about, or if he was just worried about Pritchard's reaction, and was seeing his pension float away. I walked over to a basin and washed some of the mud off my hands and face.

'Did you see the shooter?' Manning asked.

I took a towel off a nearby peg and dried myself. 'Not clearly. He got away very fast.'

'Ah. Pity.' He picked up a piece of tarpaulin peeking out from beneath one of the benches and stood it up against the wall. 'Terrible mess some people make,' he said. 'I'll have to raise it at the next meeting.' Then he looked up at me, as if he had suddenly remembered that his role in the Yacht Club was of secondary importance to a dead Russian. 'The office called,' he said. 'London cabled to say that Henry's flight lands at oh-eight-hundred tomorrow.'

On the drive over from Ikoyi, I'd held, somewhere at the back of my mind, the hope that Pritchard might not be able to make it out here for a few more days. Now it was settled: I had just over nine hours until he arrived and started asking questions – and all I had to go on was a word scribbled on a matchbox.

Manning was shuffling his feet, anxious to get back to his drink.

'I'll meet you at the airport at half-seven,' I told him. 'But tell me something – does the phrase "Afrospot" mean anything to you?'

He considered it for a moment, then shook his head. 'Perhaps a local brand of pimple cream?' He chuckled, pleased with himself.

'Did you notice the woman I was talking to earlier on?'

He grimaced. 'Yes, I saw her,' he said. 'But don't you think you should leave the love life for later, old chap? Go back to your hotel, have a good night's sleep, and we'll sort all this out come morning.'

I counted out ten beats, timing them to a dripping tap some-where behind me, letting Manning understand that I was not interested in talking sex, or rugby, or my father, and that this would be the last time I wasted valuable seconds on him. He coughed after the seventh beat, and I relieved him of the tension.

'Did you notice if she left?'

'I saw her setting out for the hard about ten minutes ago. Might still be there.'

'The hard?'

'Um – near the jetty – take a right and you'll see the path leading down to it.'

'Thank you,' I said, and headed for the door.

'What about my car?' Manning called after me. 'Sandy's already giving another couple a lift, and I'm not sure Marjorie and I will squeeze in.'

'I'll let you know in a couple of minutes,' I shouted back.

*

I checked the bar just in case, but she wasn't there, so I hooked my jacket over my head and headed outside. The chairs had been stacked up in columns and a steward was doing the rounds of the tables with a tray, picking up bottles and glasses and bowls while the rain blew against him.

I found Isabelle in a lifejacket, tethering her boat to a pole.

'Didn't fancy another swim, then?' I said.

She looked up, startled, and then smiled a little wearily as she put the voice to the face.

'You didn't say you had your own boat,' I said.

'I didn't have the chance. You left. Anyway, you have to be a regular sailor to be a member of the club. They don't . . .'

'Allow social members. I remember.'

'Are you angry with me?'

'Angry? What gives you that idea?'

'You left very quickly. As though I had said something wrong.' She finished tying the knot and looked up, her gaze challenging me.

'You didn't say anything wrong,' I said. 'I had a meeting to go to. An interview.'

'At this time?'

'I'm back now.'

'Do you expect me to bow down at your feet?'

So she was going to play it that way. 'Look,' I said. 'I'm sorry.'

She didn't answer.

'Have you ever heard of something called Afrospot?'

She stared at me for a few moments, and then gave a sudden, astonished laugh. 'You want to take me there?'

'No,' I said, 'I just want to know what it is.'

She jumped into the boat, and I thought for a moment that she was going to unmoor it and sail off. But instead she removed the lifejacket, then lifted one of the seats and took out a black hand-towel and a pair of boots.

'It is a nightclub,' she said, raising her arms and wriggling into the centre of the towel, which it transpired was a dress. 'In Ebute Metta.'

'Is that in Lagos?'

She nodded. 'About half an hour away by car. Do you have a car?'

I glanced up at the bar, and saw Manning standing at the window, looking worried. 'Yes. What road do I need to take?'

She smiled, and pointedly looked me up and down. 'They'll never let you in, *mon vieux*. Not without me.' And she jumped out of the boat.

IX

I steered us onto the main road and Isabelle indicated I should take a right. Manning wouldn't be too pleased when he realized I'd left, but he'd soon get over it: I was Larry Dark's boy, after all.

'It is not a new club,' she was saying. 'But it has a new owner recently, and more people visit. It is fun – you will see. Now it is your turn to speak: tell me why you are so interested in this place.'

'Oh,' I said. 'Just that I heard it mentioned and wondered if there might be a story in it.'

She laughed softly. 'I am not a fool, Robert! You didn't even know it was a nightclub. This means there already is a story. Something big, *non?*'

I had no idea. It was just a word on a matchbox. But the Russian had only written the name of the club – no date or time. That suggested he was confident he would meet his contact whenever he turned up there, which in turn pointed to that contact being either a regular at the club or, more likely, someone who worked there.

Isabelle was looking at me expectantly. 'There might be a story,' I told her. 'I'm not sure yet.'

She eyed me keenly and told me to take the next left.

*

We arrived at the club just before midnight. A ramshackle two-storey house, it looked like it was hosting a private party that had got out of control. An overpowering smell of marijuana wafted from the doors, along with the muffled sound of frenetic music. There were a few dozen people by the entrance, talking and dancing in the fug while they waited to be let in. A hand-painted sign announced that tonight's performance would be by 'the magnificent Black Chargers'.

As we approached the door, the Nigerians in the queue looked us up and down. A young man wearing a wide leather belt and an open-necked dress shirt shouted something to his friends, who all laughed uproariously.

I glanced at Isabelle.

'You don't want to know,' she said.

I asked her if she could try to find a way through the queue. If this was a dead-end, I didn't want to spend the rest of the night on it. She walked over to one of the doormen and started talking in very fast pidgin English with him. The man listened to her solemnly, then gave a nod and let us past, much to the chagrin of some of the crowd.

'I told him we are press,' she whispered to me. 'He said the intermission is coming soon and we can interview the owner. Is that okay?'

As there was a chance that the owner himself might be the Russian's contact, I told her it was fine. A group of heavies frisked us, Isabelle paid the entrance fee and I followed her onto a tiny but packed dance floor.

'Let's dance!' she shouted into my ear and, before I could answer, she had whisked me into the centre of the floor, where we were absorbed into the crowd of young Nigerians flailing their limbs around. The music was now deafening. On stage, at least a dozen musicians were playing trumpets, guitars and several sets of drums, all at a feverish pace. Every once in a while, a blast of notes emanated from a trombone attached to a small, wiry man in an iridescent suit, who seemed to be the chief Black Charger. It was like listening to a big band accompanying a voodoo ceremony.

Isabelle was swaying back and forth, her eyes fixed on me. I tried to play along with her, but my mind was too occupied to do anything other than shuffle my feet aimlessly and try to avoid colliding into others. The song was very repetitive, almost like a stuck record. With the heat and humidity, the frantic jostling crowd, the headiness of the marijuana and the nearness of Isabelle's body, I struggled to keep a clear head. After a few minutes, the song built to a dramatic climax, and my ears were left ringing in the relative quiet that came after.

Isabelle was smiling ecstatically, sweat dripping off her. 'C'est magnifique, non?' she shouted in my ear, and I nodded. The band began making their way offstage, and were disappearing through an entrance covered by a beaded curtain. Isabelle found the doorman who had let us through. Money changed hands, and we were passed to one of his colleagues. Another swift transaction and we were shown through the curtain and led down a long corridor until we reached a door marked 'Artists' Green Room'.

*

'Welcome to the Afrospot, my friends!' said the trombonist, after he had been told by the doorman that we were press. 'My name is J. J. Thompson-Bola. Have you been enjoying the show?'

We nodded our heads like obedient schoolchildren. The room was almost as packed as the dance floor, with musicians and hangers-on chatting and smoking and laughing. Standing in one corner was a rather stern-looking middle-aged woman in a traditional dress and headgear made from the same material. She was looking at me with an expression I couldn't place — it was almost as though she knew me, or thought she did.

J. J. was now bare-chested, and a couple of young women were wiping his torso down with a sponge: he looked like a boxer limbering up for another round. As he rotated his shoulders and rolled his head around, his eyes fixed on Isabelle. 'You are reporter?' he asked her. 'For which newspaper?'

'Agence France-Presse,' she said. 'It's a news agency . . .'

'I know what it is,' he snapped, bringing his head back to its natural position. He paused, perhaps realizing there was little point in antagonizing the press unduly. 'I think I have met you before. Is that so?'

'Yes,' she said. 'I wrote an article on the cultural festival last year——'

'Ah, yes, I remember.' A woman handed him a bottle of Fanta orange squash and he gulped down a few swigs. 'So why have you returned? Could you not resist my charms?' He grinned impishly, and the middle-aged woman smacked her lips in mock disapproval. Could she be his mother, come to cheer on her son's performance?

Isabelle smiled at the flirtation. 'I told my editor about how your brand of high life is becoming more popular, and he was interested in another story, but this time to be centred around only you.'

J. J. beamed. 'Is that so? Well, tell your editor that he is a fine person with wonderful taste.' He laughed suddenly, and looked around the room for approval – some of the hangers-on joined in the laughter. He held up a hand and the laughter stopped. He turned to me. 'And who are you?' he asked.

'Robert Kane,' I said, stepping forward. '*The Times* of London. I'm also writing a piece on Lagos nightlife.'

'*The Times*!' he exclaimed. 'I know it well.'

'Oh, yes?'

'Certainly – I used to take it when I lived in London. Last year you ran an excellent article about my cousin. He has been imprisoned by the government on bogus and trumped-up charges for the last eighteen months, and he is rotting in a cell in Kaduna at this very moment.'

'I'm sorry to hear that,' I said.

'But how is London these days? I often think fondly of the

nightclubs I used to visit there. I am trying to recreate a certain aspect of them here in Lagos. The Flamingo, the Marquee, Ronnie Scott's . . .'

'Ronnie Scott's? I was there last night! I saw a very good American group.' I struggled to remember the name, but my mind had gone blank.

'Dexter Gordon? Ben Webster? What instruments? I saw all the big names when I lived there. But now these Americans, they try to take over our country with this new soul sound. It is not real music. Our audience here' — he gestured dismissively in the direction of the dance floor — 'wants us to play James Brown, James Brown, all night. That does not interest me — to be James Brown in my own place. I studied for three years at the London College of Music. It was an excellent grounding in the kind of thing I am trying to achieve here.'

'I've heard they have a very good course,' I said.

'Ah, so you know it?'

'I know of its reputation,' I said, which seemed to satisfy him. I wasn't sure how far I could push things. The Russian probably had an introductory phrase to feed his contact — without it, I was lost. I didn't even know if this man was the contact. But it was moot: before I could think of anything else to say, he abruptly announced that it was time to go back on stage, and everyone began shuffling out of the room.

'Did you get your story?' Isabelle asked me as we moved back through the crowd.

'Not really. I might try to talk to him again after the show. Do you mind staying on?'

'No,' she said. 'I haven't danced in a long time.'

As J. J. and his band settled into another of their numbers, and Isabelle started twisting and turning round the floor, I considered the encounter. I wasn't sure what I had been expecting, but it hadn't materialized: I was no nearer to discovering who the Russian had wanted to meet here. J. J.? One of his musicians? One of the bouncers? It could be almost anyone. Or perhaps he hadn't been due to meet anyone. Perhaps it was just somewhere he had heard about and intended to visit, or had visited, as recreation. Because it was a terrible choice for a meet. Any cover that might be offered by the crowd was completely offset by the fact that, apart from Isabelle and me, everyone in the place was black. Not ideal if you were a Russian looking for a secret rendezvous. If I were the contact, I'd certainly not have agreed to it.

Unless, of course, the contact wasn't actually supposed to make contact. What if the Russian had instructions to come here to find some*thing* rather than some*one*? That would explain why he hadn't needed a date or time — whatever he was after would simply stay here until he came to collect it.

I was suddenly wishing I had paid more attention in the green room.

I looked over at the entrance we'd come through from backstage. Two of the heavies were meant to be guarding it, but they had both advanced into the hall too far, and were now out of visual contact with each other. I shuffled round the back of them, waiting for my chance. It came a few minutes later, when J. J. had the crowd moving their arms up and down with the horns — the heavies got swept up in it, and I quickly slipped through the curtain and into the corridor.

*

There was no answer when I knocked on the green room door, so I stepped inside. Empty. I got to work at once, pulling out drawers, looking in bags and boxes, scanning every inch of the room as I moved around it. I found a collection of J. J.'s garish stage outfits, a sizeable stash of marijuana, and a few bottles of whisky and rum. The papers on the table were either posters for upcoming concerts or set lists. I didn't even know what I was looking for, and God knew what I would do if one of the heavies were to walk in now. In desperation, I turned to some larger cases for instruments that had been propped up against the wall, shoved in a small space behind a rickety bookcase. I squeezed past the bookcase and ran my finger down the line clicking open their latches one by one. Empty. Empty. Empty . . .

A piece of sacking fell towards me. I caught it with both hands and sat it upright immediately. It wasn't sacking, in fact, but a soft canvas bag with leather straps. A gun bag. I undid the straps and saw the curved magazine. An AK-47? I leaned forward. No — it was a sniper rifle. As I took this in, I heard something move behind me. I snatched the rifle out of the bag and swivelled round, pointing it at the figure in the doorway.

'You should leave this room now,' said Isabelle. 'The police have arrived.'

X

The music in the club had stopped and I could hear the clatter of boots coming down the corridor towards us.

'What the hell are they doing here?' I asked.

'I don't know. Perhaps looking for drugs. Raids are frequent in this city.'

Or they'd found the bodies on the golf course and I was the focus of a manhunt. But how had they known who to look for — and where to find me?

The questions could wait.

'We need to get out of here,' I said. 'Try the window.'

She ran over and started trying to prise it open. It was jammed. There was no time to fiddle with straps, so I just put the rifle back in its bag and threw that into the trombone case, then joined her. The footsteps in the corridor were now accompanied by shouted commands, and sirens had started wailing outside. I smashed the case against the glass. Now the sound of the steps shifted in our direction. I swept away the shards with the back of my arm, then helped Isabelle crawl over the frame. Once she had jumped to the ground, I passed the case to her and followed her over. The door of the room crashed open as I was landing and a voice called out: 'Federal police! No one leave the building!'.

I took the case back from Isabelle and we started running. Several policemen jumped down from the window and started pursuit. As Isabelle and I reached the front of the building, I glanced to the right and saw people streaming from the club in a panic. They were being greeted by a large contingent of police, all of whom were armed with machine guns. I could see J. J. and his entourage engaged in furious debate with them, and the man in the dress shirt who had laughed at us earlier was being pushed into the back of one of the unmarked cars that were parked behind the police line.

Those cars stood between us and the Peugeot.

I shouted to Isabelle to follow me, and headed towards the garden of the neighbouring house. The fence was already half-trampled and bent in on itself, so it was easy enough to leap over. I could hear Isabelle right behind me and, just behind her, shouting and gunfire.

We ran through the garden, passing a couple of frightened club-goers crouching behind an empty bathtub, and navigated the next fence, and the one after that. I carried the trombone case above my head – it made running easier, and protected my eyes from the hammering of the rain. At the fourth or perhaps fifth garden, I gestured to Isabelle that we should move back towards the street. Manning's car was directly opposite, and we headed for it. A few seconds after we emerged onto the road, the men following us reached it, too. They alerted their colleagues down by the club's entrance, and we won a few seconds as they shouted about us to each other. Then some of the men by the entrance headed towards their cars.

Isabelle reached Manning's car just before me.

'Let me drive!' she called out. 'I know the city.'

I threw her the keys. She jumped in and started it up, and I ran round to the passenger side and leapt in just as she was moving off. She reversed a few yards, making the men behind us stop in their tracks, and then headed straight for the police cars now hurtling down the street towards us.

There was a succession of shots from both directions. Nothing hit us, but it wasn't for a lack of trying. Struggling in the enclosed space, it took me a few seconds to get the rifle out of the case and find the ammunition. Then I wound down the window and leaned out to fire at the cars coming our way. I didn't hit anything, either: it was a self-loading semi-automatic, and although it could manage twenty to thirty rounds a minute, it was designed for accurate shooting at close quarters – not against moving targets while moving oneself. Isabelle pushed the accelerator down as far as it would go, and several of the cars veered out of the way. We caught two of them as we passed, and for a few yards we skidded on the wet tarmac and I thought we were going to end up in one of the storm drains that lined each side of the road, but she brought it round and pulled us back into the centre at the last moment.

Some of the group who had chased us through the gardens

had reached their cars and were now coming up fast behind us. The man in the car closest was leaning out of the passenger window and firing his Kalashnikov, and he aimed well because there was a dull crack and thousands of tiny tributaries suddenly filled the rear window, before the whole surface gave way and fell into the back seat like a sheet of crushed ice.

As Isabelle took a sharp left turn, I carried on firing, but my knuckles were under assault from the relentless needles of rain and there were no streetlights, making my view through the sight next to useless.

There were now five cars on our tail: three dark, two lighter-coloured, all Peugeots of various models. Bullets were now peppering our bodywork every few seconds, and I realized we had to do something fast, before they hit a tyre, or the engine, or us. There were hardly any other cars on the street – it was well after curfew – which meant we couldn't easily create a diversion or block them. But the lack of lighting might help: if we got far enough ahead in a residential area, we could lose them in the darkness.

As if reading my thoughts, Isabelle took a late left turn, dimmed the lights for two streets and then swerved into a sudden right. Now we had just three cars in pursuit, the other two not having been tight enough on the turnings and skidding past, the Doppler effect of their sirens echoing after them.

I had run out of ammunition, but our pursuers didn't seem to be holding off on the shooting. It seemed unlikely they would have brought this much firepower with them had they just been out on a routine raid of the club. But I still couldn't figure it out: if they were chasing me for the Russians on the golf course, how had they known where to look? They clearly hadn't followed us out here. Did they think we were someone else? Alarm bells were ringing in my head – and most of them involved the person sitting at the wheel next to me.

I threw the rifle onto the rear seat, then grabbed the Tokarev from the glove compartment and leaned back out of the window. We passed, finally, a lighted building – another club? – which gave me a clear view of the driver of the nearest car for one vital second, and I managed to shatter his windscreen. There was a scream and the car swerved wildly – another of our pursuers was lost to the drains. But the remaining two cars suddenly loomed out from the darkness. As a series of shots thudded into the dashboard, bringing up a storm of sparks, Isabelle momentarily lost control, and then there was a horrific scraping sound as both cars came alongside us, squeezing us between them, and I was looking right into the face of one of the policemen as he raised a pistol and fired.

Isabelle slowed the car at the same moment, trying to gain control, and the shot went wide, but as a result both cars drew ahead of us and they immediately started turning to block off the road. I leaned over Isabelle and, shoving her away, grabbed hold of the wheel and spun it towards with me with as much force as I could manage, one hand over the other. The next few seconds were a havoc of screeched tyres and broken headlights and gunfire as we bumped across open ground, until finally, by some miracle, we hit tarmac again, and Isabelle put her foot down and I fell back into my seat. Through the rear-view mirror

I could see that the police were busy trying to disentangle themselves from their roadblock, so I shouted at her to take a quick turn, then another, then another, until eventually I couldn't see any headlights behind us and my breathing slowed and I put away the gun and told her to keep driving.

They couldn't have been after me: they wouldn't have cared enough about a couple of dead Russians to shoot to kill. They must have been looking for something else.

'Do you know the Victoria Palace Hotel?' I asked Isabelle.

She nodded, and we headed for it.

*

The street was dark but for a shimmering yellow pool where the moonlight struck the rain-soaked macadam. I stepped back from the curtain and looked at Isabelle. She was sitting in the easy chair by the bed, her chin resting on one hand.

'Strip,' I said.

She looked at me from out of the darkness, but didn't move.

'Are all Englishmen this romantic?' she said, tilting her head.

'It's not a come-on,' I said. 'Strip now, or I'll do it for you.'

'Do you enjoy the rough stuff, is that it?'

'No,' I said. 'That's not it. It's that I don't like being taken for a fool.' I took the pistol from my holster and pointed it at her.

Her eyes widened. Then she stood up, shrugged, and started to unlace her boots.

'How did you know I was in the green room?' I asked. 'At the club.'

She looked surprised. 'I saw you slip away. I guessed you had seen something backstage and wished to return for another look.'

'And the police?'

'Yes?'

'I don't believe, even in wild and woolly Lagos, that the police fire on people just for fleeing a raid. There were five cars chasing us, and they were shooting to kill.'

'So were you, *non?*' Her boots off, she started unbuttoning her tunic.

'How long have you been with French intelligence?' I said.

She stretched out her arms so the dress fell to the floor, leaving her in her bathing suit. 'How long have you been with British intelligence?'

She hadn't even denied it. I walked over and slapped her across the face. 'Where is it? Where's the transmitter?'

She grabbed my forearm – she had a strong grip – and wiped her face. '*T'es fou, ou quoi?* Why would I let the police know we were at the club? I came to warn you they were there, remember?'

That was true. But her story stank nevertheless. Nobody else had known where I was going, and I didn't believe that the police were acting on their own initiative. We were white: if they hadn't known who we were, they should at least have been worried about causing a diplomatic incident. They hadn't looked in the least bit worried.

I turned my attention back to Isabelle. 'What are your instructions regarding me?' I asked her.

'None,' she said. 'I haven't been in touch with my people yet. And as you can see,' she added sarcastically, 'I don't have any transmitters hidden on me.'

'So why are you here?'

'When we met at the Yacht Club, I thought you were British intelligence—'

'Why?'

She shrugged. 'Instinct. Then, when you asked to go the Afro-spot, I decided to come with you and see. I always enjoy an adventure.'

Despite the slap of a few moments ago, she was smiling. I recognized the sort: she was still under the misapprehension that espionage was a glamorous business. She'd learn the hard way; everyone did, eventually.

'We were good, weren't we?' she said, bringing my hand back up to her face, where I'd hit her. 'Me driving, you shooting . . .'

'Is that your idea of kicks?' I asked, but she was good, better than she could possibly know, because my mind was moving without me being able to control it, moving back many years, to another room.

She started moving my hand across her cheek, making me caress her, and I didn't resist, just stood there as she did it. One of my fingers brushed against her mouth, and she grabbed it with her lip, and then her hands were in my hair and she was leading me over to the bed, where she kissed me. I could taste the sweat on her, from the club, from the car. She moved her hands across my sodden shirt and lifted it, touching my stomach, and there was a fluttering there that I hadn't felt in years, and I let myself be transported back, let myself drift away in her skilful arms. As she unhooked her bra and I bit into her flesh, we fell into the cool grey sheets and she cried out to me – 'Robert! Oh, Robert!' – but I wasn't there. I was in another place, many years ago, and so I couldn't speak, couldn't *do* anything but lie there as she rubbed her body against mine, two animals in the dirt and the heat, and my mind cried back, shouting out in its little cell, again and again, despite everything: 'Anna! Anna! Anna!'

XI

Tuesday, 25 March 1969, Lagos

I woke with a start and reached for the gun. The room was pitch black and my chest was soaked in sweat. There was a sound, and it took me a moment to locate and identify it. It was coming from the woman lying next to me: her body was rising and falling in a gentle rhythm, and a low whistling was emanating from her nostrils.

The previous night's events flooded back. I flicked the bedside light switch, but nothing happened. Taking care not to wake Isabelle, I climbed out of bed and walked over to the door. The main light wasn't working either. That explained why I was drenched − there'd been a power cut, so there was no air conditioning.

I looked at the luminous dial of my watch. Twenty past five. Pritchard's plane would be here in just over two hours. I had to get dressed and get outside. But to where, and to do what, exactly? It was too early for Anna to be starting work at the embassy, and I would be too conspicuous hanging round there at this time of night. There was nothing more to do until dawn.

The wind was shooting volleys of rain against the window, making an eerie fluttering noise every few seconds. I went over, parted the curtains by a finger's breadth and peered through the mosquito net. I couldn't detect any movement, either in the street or in the cars parked by the entrance. The rain was beating furiously against the surface of the swimming pool – no diplomats sipping cocktails now. Across the dark water, the lights of the trawlers pulsed softly.

I took a seat in the corner of the room and considered the naked woman sprawled carelessly across the bed. I'd deliberately brought her back here, blowing my base, because if she was working against me that was the quickest way to force her hand. It had been my strategy from the start, and in some ways it seemed to be working. Since my arrival in Lagos less than twelve hours previously, Slavin had been killed, his assassin had taken his own life, and I'd been shot at by the local police. Someone was working against me, and pretty effectively. Was it Isabelle, though? I was starting to have second thoughts. She hadn't been out of my sight since leaving the Yacht Club, except for those two minutes in the Afrospot when I'd left her to return to the green room. But even if she had found a telephone in that time, the police couldn't have reached the club so fast. There had been close to a dozen cars. Perhaps she had given a signal earlier – to one of the bouncers, or even someone at the Yacht Club.

But none of this seemed to fit the woman sleeping so easily a few feet away from me. After we had made love, I'd feigned sleep with one hand gripping the Tokarev, waiting for any sudden movement. But she had drifted off faster than most husbands. If she had wanted me dead, would she have slept naked and unarmed in the same room as me, knowing I had a pistol and rifle within easy reach?

It wasn't just Isabelle that didn't add up. In the turmoil of the previous evening's events, I'd made several assumptions on the hoof — as light began to seep into the room, I went through them again.

I started with the killer on the golf course. My first reaction had been fury at Sasha: I had presumed that, despite my threats, he'd sent someone out to kill Slavin. But that couldn't be right. The rifle had been left at the club for the Russian, but it had not been involved in the killing of Slavin — that had been accomplished easily enough with a pistol. A cold thought swept through me: Slavin's killer had to have already been out here.

But why?

I thought back to the Afrospot: had I missed anything? Quite possibly — I'd had very little time to investigate. I tried to picture the green room again, but nothing new came to mind. What else had been there — and why had that woman stared at me like that when she'd first seen me? Perhaps she was the contact, and had thought I was the Russian. When I hadn't quoted poetry at her, she'd realized her mistake and retreated.

My immediate instinct was to return there at once and

forget meeting Pritchard, but I rejected the idea just as quickly. Slavin's death implicated me as the traitor, and unless I gave a plausible explanation for it, Pritchard would come hunting my hide with the full might of the Service. I'd have to give him the impression we were working together, while at the same time not allowing him to draw too close. It would be a delicate balancing act, especially if my thoughts about the rifle were correct, in which case he'd stick to me like glue. I could, of course, neglect to tell him about the rifle. But Pritchard had clout, and I might be able to use some of it to get some more answers.

I picked my shirt from the carpet and reached for the cigarettes in the pocket. There were twelve left in the pack. I wondered if I would find Anna before they had all been smoked. I changed the focus of the thought: I would find Anna before they had all been smoked. The phrase from Slavin's interview that I had been trying to avoid thinking about once again slipped into my mind: 'the one true love of her life'.

A muscle in my stomach tensed. It was partly hunger — except for a handful of peanuts at the Yacht Club, I hadn't eaten anything since getting off the plane. It was partly fatigue — I'd been under huge strain and had only managed a few hours' sleep. But I knew that it was also partly a sudden, over-powering longing for Anna. Something had awoken when Isabelle had touched me, but I had to put it to sleep. It didn't matter if Anna had loved me, or I her — that was over twenty years ago, and a lot of blood had passed under the bridge since. She was a highly dangerous professional who had gone to extraordinary lengths to betray me, and who had almost certainly had a hand in murdering Father. This was not a woman to long for. This was a woman I had to find.

I finished my smoke, then felt for the case beneath the chair and lifted out the rifle. The night hadn't been a complete waste, after all: I had found this. Perhaps, if I looked hard enough, it might offer up some clues as to what was going on.

It was in perfect condition. Even in the dim light, the laminated hardwood had a noticeable sheen. That meant it hadn't been used yet – gum would have been applied to lessen its visibility in the field otherwise. I wasn't sure if that meant anything, but I stored the thought anyway.

Then I started to feel my way around the weapon, figuring out how it fitted together. It was a very different beast from the Enfields I'd used in the war. The sight, as I had already discovered, was mounted over the receiver instead of the butt-stock, which was itself unusually long and sleek. Hard to transport something this size. How had it been brought into the country? Diplomatic bag?

I spent several minutes sorting through all the thoughts that came to me. When my eyes had fully adjusted to the dark and I thought I could see how the rifle worked, I began a field-strip.

I detached the magazine, then lowered the safety and emptied the cartridge chamber. Then the sight. The eyepiece was still a little wet, so I took hold of a corner of curtain and dried it as best I could. Finally, I detached the cheek plate, followed by the receiver cover and retracting mechanism . . .

'What you are doing?'

I looked up to see Isabelle staring at me from the bed.

'Good morning,' I said. 'I'm cleaning the rifle. There's been a power cut.'

She sat up and rubbed her eyes. 'It is what time?'

I told her. She picked her damp dress from the floor and slipped it over her head with a shudder. It was a shame to watch her body vanish beneath the fabric – I had an urge to get up and help her take it back off.

I placed the rifle back in its case and walked over to the bed.

'I'm sorry about last night,' I said, seating myself beside her.

She pushed her hair behind her ears and smiled, her teeth gleaming in the soft bluey-greyness of the room. 'You have nothing to be sorry about.'

'Not that,' I said. 'Earlier, when I made all those accusations. Mistaking you for a spy.'

She tilted her head up sharply. 'Why do you say that?'

It was my turn to smile. 'Last time I checked, French intelligence still insists its agents have basic driving skills.'

She punched me in the shoulder. '*Connard!*' But it was said with affection. 'Did you also search my clothes for transmitters after I fell asleep?' I didn't react, and she punched me again.

'What story did they give you?' I asked. 'They didn't say it was your chance to help *la patrie*, I hope?'

She shook her head. 'That wouldn't have worked.' She paused, wondering whether or not she could trust me. Then, perhaps realizing she now had little to lose, she shrugged her shoulders and continued. 'Before I was due to travel to the front last year, an old colleague of my father approached me. He said they were doing everything they could to end the war here, but if I could provide any information on what I saw it might help end it sooner.' She narrowed her eyes and looked at me straight on. 'It might save lives, you know?'

I nodded. 'The usual lie.'

It was too quick for her and she bristled. 'I forgot – you are British. Of course you say this. Your government arms the Nigerians so they can isolate Biafra and starve innocent women and children. How could you think any differently?'

I smiled tolerantly. 'I never discuss politics before breakfast.'

She looked at me with all the scorn she could muster. 'Do you treat all questions you cannot answer this way?'

'No,' I said. 'I treat all questions asked by people who have already made up their mind this way.' She stared blankly at me. 'All right,' I said. 'We're supplying the Nigerians with arms. So are the Russians, and others. Guns, tanks, planes . . .'

'That is your justification? That you are not alone?'

'Your government only started selling arms to the Biafrans last year,' I went on. 'Its contribution is still tiny compared to what the Nigerians receive from us and Moscow. And no heavy weapons. At its current level, France's support isn't enough to give Biafra even the slimmest chance of victory. That's because the idea isn't to help Colonel Ojukwu win the war – it's to help General de Gaulle win votes. Your government doesn't give any more of a shit about starving Biafrans than mine, and any information you've given your father's friend has, like the arms he has supplied, merely prolonged the bloodshed. You haven't saved lives – you've helped take more of them.'

I saw the slap coming, and steeled myself for it. Now we were even.

She started crying soon after, so I took the rifle case into the bathroom and sat on the edge of the tub. I reached for the collapsible rod tip: the bore looked filthy.

She didn't know anything about Anna, or Slavin, or any of it. She was just an amateur, a hopeless idealist caught in the crossfire.

'I have to leave soon,' I called out. 'Can you get ready?'

I went over to the basin. A dead rat lay face up in it, its eyes staring glassily at me from the darkness. I opened the window and threw it into the street below. Perhaps that's what I am, I thought: a dead rat flying towards a gutter, where larger creatures wait to devour me.

Melodramatic fool. I was as bad as she was. Nobody was going to devour me. I'd devour them first.

The water from the tap was tepid, but I splashed it all over my face and body anyway.

'I leave now.' She was standing in the doorway.

I dried myself, and she waited for the words of kindness that were not going to come from my lips. I suppose she was used to men begging her to stay.

'If you have to pay any traffic fines, the AFP office has my details.'

There was no need to humiliate her, so I smiled. 'You're heading back to the front, then?'

She nodded. 'This afternoon.'

The phone started ringing in the main room, and I went through to answer it. Could this be it? Could it be her?

'Paul,' said the man's voice on the other end. 'It's Geoffrey. Have you seen this morning's *Daily Times*?'

I looked up to see Isabelle walking past the bed. 'Best of luck,' I said to her. She nodded, but didn't make eye contact. The door made barely a click as she closed it behind her.

'Who are you talking to?' Manning was saying. 'Hello, is anyone there?'

'Hello, Geoffrey,' I said. 'No, I haven't read the papers yet – it's barely dawn. Why?'

'The entire front page is about bodies being dug up from bunkers on Ikoyi golf course, that's why!'

Alebayo had been right – it wasn't a bad paper. They'd put the story together in under seven hours. I told Manning we could discuss it at the airport.

'I'm not sure you should come,' he said. 'I don't think we should be seen together. It might—'

'What?' I asked. 'Blow my cover? You've just used my real name on a line that may well be tapped, so I think it's a bit late to be worrying about that, don't you? I'll be at the airport at half seven, as agreed. I'm leaving your car here – the police will be looking for it. Send one of your secretaries to come and pick it up.'

'Looking for it? Are you pulling my leg?'

'Unfortunately not.' I didn't tell him the back window had also been shot off, but he'd find out soon enough. Instead, I told him that the Afrospot had turned out to be a club, and that the owner was a certain J. J. Thompson-Bola. I spelled it out for him, and when he'd got it I told him to see if there was anything in the files.

Then I hung up and called the Soviet Embassy again. It was a different clerk, but much the same message: Third Secretary Grigorieva had not come into the building yet and no, he had no idea when she was due. I left my details again, this time leaving my name, then dressed, reassembled the rifle, and called reception to order a taxi. Part of me wanted to direct it to the embassy, so I could sit and wait for her to turn up, but I knew I couldn't. There was something else I couldn't put off: it was time to face Pritchard.

*

The rain had finally stopped, and the sun was rapidly climbing the sky. It looked as round and yellow and artificial as a child's drawing up there, but its effect on me as the taxi sped along the main road was real enough: my cheek facing the window felt like a branding iron had been placed on it. The city outside seemed flat and colourless in the glare and the haze, and I felt a little dizzy and nauseous – perhaps the previous night's activities had taken more of a toll than I'd realized. Luckily, there were few cars on the road, so we arrived at the airport in good time. The driver charged me two Nigerian pounds, despite a sign saying it was a fixed fare of one and ten bob the other way. There were more important arguments to be had, so I paid him.

'Robert!' Manning shouted at me as I entered the arrivals

terminal. He was keen to rectify his earlier mistake, even if it meant making a few more in the process. He marched towards me, waving away a small collection of flies buzzing around him. He'd traded the nightwear for a khaki linen suit and deck shoes – it made him look only slightly more trustworthy.

I asked him if Pritchard had landed yet, and he shook his head. 'Some sort of a hitch in Madrid, apparently.' He dropped his voice to a whisper. 'Look, Paul, I really think this situation—'

'Did they say how long the delay was?' Perhaps there was time to go to the embassy and come back – it wasn't so far away. Perhaps Pritchard's flight would have to turn tail to London, and he wouldn't come out at all.

Manning dashed the thought: 'An hour at the most.' He suddenly noticed the case. 'I do hope that's not what I think it is.'

It admittedly wasn't ideal, carrying the thing around in the airport, but it wasn't safe leaving it at the hotel either. I wasn't in the mood for a lecture on tradecraft from Manning.

'Perhaps I wasn't clear enough on the phone,' I said, keeping my voice even. 'Everything that happened last night was necessary. Everything except for the police shooting at me, that is. That might have been because the nightclub you'd never heard of was a KGB drop.'

He quietened down then. 'Sorry about that,' he said. 'Jungle dancing's not really my thing, you know.' He tried to get a smile out of me, but when he realized it wasn't going to happen he swivelled his head around the hall theatrically, then leaned over and handed me the newspaper, from one end of which peeked a plain brown dossier. By the time he'd finished the manoeuvre, even the woman cleaning the floor was watching.

'Turns out we have a dossier on the family,' he said.

'Anywhere in here sell food?' I said, trying to move the conversation to a safer subject. There didn't seem to be any police around, but I didn't want to attract more attention if it could be helped — one trip to the dungeons had been enough.

'There's a stall in the car park,' said Manning. 'Nowhere else is open yet.'

I fished some coins out of my pocket and handed them to him. 'Fruit if they have it,' I said. 'Bananas or citrus. Failing that, anything with sugar in it.'

He didn't disguise his anger at being ordered around, but I was London — I might be in trouble with Pritchard, but he knew that a few choice words about his cock-up over the Afrospot could force him into early retirement. So he chewed his lip and waggled his eyebrows, and walked over to the exit.

I found a seat and examined the front page of the *Daily Times*. 'CORPSES ON THE GOLF COURSE!' was the headline, and the story contained full descriptions of both men and some lurid speculation from unnamed sources about their manners of death — but no clue as to the perpetrator. I read it twice and decided I was fairly safe: it would be very difficult for the police to prise anything out of the Russians, and judging by the number of other crimes reported in the city on the inside pages, they already had a fair amount on their plate.

I turned to the dossier. It was a dull affair, by and large, filled with lengthy accounts of impossibly trivial matters relating to seemingly every member of the extensive Thompson-Bola clan. After struggling through it, I came out with two files of interest. One involved a Daniel Talabi, the cousin Thompson-Bola had mentioned at the club: he was a writer who had been imprisoned by the government for aiding the 'rebels'.

But by far the most substantial dossier was on Thompson-Bola's mother, Abigail. The harmless-looking woman in glasses and headdress was apparently something of a firebrand. She had a decades-long history of anti-colonial protest – and was, according to the file, a hardened Communist. She had been one of the first African women allowed behind the Iron Curtain, where she had met Mao. If there had been any doubts in my mind about the family's knowledge of the drop, this put paid to them, and she was now my prime suspect for the contact.

Manning returned with my breakfast: an unripe banana and a bottle of Fanta.

'I checked on the flight's progress,' he said. 'No news.'

The hour had passed – the delay was now edging up to two. I decided enough was enough, and told Manning to set up a meeting with Pritchard for the afternoon – I had a few errands to run.

'Are any of your safe houses near the Afrospot?' I asked. But he wasn't even listening to me – he was focusing on something over my right shoulder. I asked him if he had heard, and his eyes flicked over to meet mine. He pointed across to the customs official taking down the barrier in front of passport control.

'They've landed,' he said.

*

Pritchard came through ten minutes later, striding confidently past his fellow passengers. In his dark suit and tie, white shirt and dark glasses, he looked like an upmarket funeral director. He caught sight of us and walked over.

'Hello, Henry,' said Manning, beaming. 'Welcome to Lagos.' It was evidently his line for airports.

'Hello, Geoffrey,' said Pritchard. 'How's Marjorie?' They shook hands and exchanged a few more pleasantries. Then Pritchard turned to me, and gave me the kind of look I saved for dead rats.

'Paul,' he said, dipping his head.

'Henry,' I nodded back.

Manning lifted Pritchard's bag and we walked back outside and hailed a taxi.

*

The return journey was conducted in silence, save for Manning's barked instructions at the driver. Pritchard sat next to me, staring sullenly at the landscape. It made sense that he didn't want to talk shop with others present, but what was he thinking in the meantime? I ate my banana and tried to clear my mind.

About forty-five minutes later we reached a large square, in the centre of which a street market was setting up. Manning paid the driver and led us through the aisles, past traders laying out their wares. One stall was apparently a grocer's, but although the fruit and vegetables were abundant, they were rotten and already covered in flies. A handful of Westerners were wandering around, waving their money and cameras, and I realized that this was probably where the photograph of Slavin had been taken.

Manning made a show of haggling over an intricately carved knife for a couple of minutes, before leaving off and pointing us to a grand colonial house on the corner of the square. He led us through a side entrance and down a narrow dirt path until we came out at a small garden in the rear of the property. He pushed open a rickety door and we followed him through several rooms. Chandeliers, chaises longues, candelabra: it was like walking onto the set of *The Forsyte Saga* after hours. Some of the furniture was in covers, and fat balls of dust sat contentedly in the corners. Manning explained that the local building industry had long been dominated by the Ibos, but that most of them had returned to the East when it had seceded, leaving dozens of unfinished and unsupervised buildings dotted around the city.

It was an unconventional choice for a safe house, but I had to admit he wasn't quite as daft as he looked. The market was popular with tourists, meaning that white faces were less likely to stick out, and the building was so conspicuous that nobody would think twice about anyone who entered it.

We climbed a flight of stairs to the second floor, which was home to a large ballroom that Manning had cleaned up a bit. I sat in an easy chair by a large electric orchestrion, and Pritchard walked over to the window and looked out at the rooftops.

'Depressing-looking country, isn't it?' he said. He swivelled on his heels and inspected his Patek Philippe. 'So. What time did you tell Slavin to get here for?'

Manning looked over at me anxiously.

Pritchard registered it. 'Problem?'

I broke the news. He didn't react for a long time, just stared at a spot on the floor in front of his shoes. Then he looked back up at Manning.

'Thank you, Geoffrey,' he said. 'You've done very well. We can take things from here.'

'Oh,' said Manning. 'Right-oh, then. I'll be at the office if you need me.' He gestured to a phone on a mahogany dresser, then scuttled away, leaving me alone in the room with Pritchard.

XII

'So,' he said, removing his sunglasses and placing them carefully inside his jacket. 'You came to meet me. You've got balls,
Dark, I'll give you that.'

'You're still angry I left London ahead of you, then,' I said.

'Angry?' He tilted his head and considered the idea. Then
he walked over to me, the heels of his brogues clicking loudly
across the floor. He came right up, until his face was just a
couple of inches from mine. 'Put it this way,' he hissed. 'If you
ever do something like that again, I will *destroy* you.' He rocked
back on his heels, pinching his nose as though trying to stop
the rage from bursting out. 'Do you understand?'

I said I did, and let silence consume the room for several
seconds.

'But you decided to run me anyway.'

He stepped away and laughed a joyless laugh. 'Believe me,
this wasn't my idea. I pushed for them to recall you, but Farraday
told me to make the best of the situation and come out as
your control.'

'Farraday is a fucking fool,' I said.

He sighed. 'He's also our fucking Chief at present, and unless you're tendering your resignation we are going to do precisely what he fucking says.'

'What if I refuse?'

'Apart from getting the sack, you mean?' He smiled. 'I'll blow your cover to the Nigerians and you'll be locked up and being buggered by the natives before you know it.'

He took off his jacket and placed it over the back of a nearby chair. Then he rolled up his shirtsleeves, revealing pale but muscular forearms. It was a clear signal: beneath the funeral director's garb was a man it would be wise not to mess with. But I already knew that.

'Now before you give me a thorough explanation for the complete *shambles* you seem to have created since arriving here,' he said, 'I'd like you to tell me what really happened in Germany in '45. You can start with Larry.'

He'd thrown it out fast, but I'd been expecting it. 'I wish I knew,' I said, and ignored his open look of disbelief. 'He disappeared looking for Meier,' I went on. 'Remember him?' Pritchard nodded slowly. I took out my pack of Players, lit one, and sucked in the rich welcoming glow. 'We'd found all the others, but Meier had been much harder. We just hadn't seemed to be able to pick up his trail. Then, in September, Father announced he had traced him to somewhere near Hamburg. He left in the jeep that afternoon – and never came back. Obviously, something happened with this nurse, and I mean to find out exactly what.'

He pondered this for a moment, then sprung: 'Why did he leave alone? Why didn't you go with him?'

'You remember what happened with Shashkevich,' I said, and did my best to look ashamed.

'I see. But why didn't you mention at the Round Table that you were in Germany at the end of the war?'

I took another drag of my cigarette, and said I could well ask him the same question.

He ran a finger along the mantelpiece, then inspected the dust that had gathered on it. 'So you were just waiting for me, is that it?'

'You heard William: there were hundreds of people working in intelligence in Germany at that time.' I let a note of right-eousness creep into my tone. 'Anyway, we were discussing a traitor in our midst. Your theory was that he might even have been in the room, so it hardly seemed like the best moment to reveal it.'

'You could have told Farraday after the meeting, surely? Unless you think *he* might be the traitor?'

'Why, after all these years, would I tell Farraday about Sacrosanct and risk—'

'Incriminating yourself?' he inserted. Then he relaxed a little and smiled. It looked painted on. 'I can see your point. I felt the same myself. But perhaps Farraday should be let into the secret now. It might look worse if he learns about it later and neither of us had mentioned it.'

I couldn't read his tone, but I didn't like the sound of that one bit.

'How could he learn about it?' I asked. 'Seeing as you and I are the only two who know? Anyway, I'm not sure he would understand even if we did tell him.'

'Oh, don't underestimate Farraday,' he said. 'He's sharper than he looks.'

Sharper indeed, I thought, remembering the way he had steamrollered Osborne at the meeting.

'Tell him, then,' I said. 'I suppose it's too late for all the repercussions you and Father were worried about, anyway.' I ground out my cigarette on the floor and opened the bottle of Fanta by tilting the top against one of the arms of the chair. It tasted warm, flat and oddly metallic. 'Perhaps you could also give him a thorough account of your operations in Gaggenau at the same time.'

His eyes were tiny marbles devoid of recognizable emotion. 'I think,' he said finally, 'that you could now debrief me on the current situation.'

We left it at stalemate, and I did as he had asked. It didn't take me long: one pyjama party, two dead Russians and a car chase.

'What about the bodies?' he said when I'd finished. 'What did you do with them?'

I handed him the newspaper. He read through it quickly and then put it to one side.

'Well, that's sure to enrage the Russians — let's see what they do. Have you looked into Grigorieva yet? Slavin claimed she recruited the double, so she would appear to be key to the whole thing.'

'I haven't had time to stake out the embassy yet, but I imagine they've trebled their guard now. What do you have in mind? Approaching her as a possible defector herself?'

He nodded. 'Yes. Although if she was recruiting double agents twenty years ago, I imagine she'd be a fairly hard nut to crack. And I'd like to have at least some idea beforehand of why her death was staged.'

'What about Chief — has he not turned up yet?'

He walked back to his position by the fireplace and shook his head.

'That's a pity,' I said. 'I'm starting to wonder if Farraday might have been right. This hit on Slavin makes me think he might be involved in this, after all.'

Pritchard turned and faced me. 'Oh, no,' he said. 'We know Chief's not the double. He was murdered.'

*

I took out another cigarette. I was down to ten, but it didn't matter. I needed something to calm me down — and something to keep my hands from shaking.

I'd allowed Chief's death to drift to the back of my mind in the last few hours. I should have known it wouldn't go away for very long. I took a deep draught of the cigarette and asked Pritchard why murder was now suspected.

'Five have found traces of blood and matter in his living room,' he said. 'And a bullethole in one of the walls. The killer had tried to conceal it by moving the piano. They're looking into what kind of gun might have been used. At any rate, he was shot. Most probably by the real traitor. By the way, are your fingerprints on file?'

Despite the sunlight streaming into the room, I suddenly felt very cold. I shook my head. 'Why?'

'Oh,' he said. 'Five are planning to take prints of anyone in the office old enough to have been turned in '45. It's more so they can rule people out than anything. Lift any clouds of suspicion. You can have yours taken when you get back.'

'Of course.' I made the extra effort to keep my voice steady. 'Why would the traitor want to kill Chief, though?'

Pritchard shrugged. 'Perhaps he knew something that would give him away. Perhaps . . .' He stopped. 'I must say, you don't appear too surprised.'

'That Chief was murdered? Of course I'm surprised. I'm just trying to think it through.' I thought I had sounded flabbergasted, but Pritchard was evidently now viewing my every utterance with suspicion. 'Has Vanessa been told?'

'Not yet. But they'll have to do it soon, because she's already going spare. Osborne's speaking to her tonight.' He gestured at the case lying by my feet. 'Is that the item you found in the nightclub?'

I nodded, relieved to be moving onto safer ground. I took out the rifle and positioned it on the floor so he could have a good look.

He walked around it, twice. 'Looks like an AK-47,' he said. 'But it's not, is it? It's a sniper rifle.' There was no visible reaction on his face, no sudden dawning realization.

'Yes,' I said. 'It's a 7.62 mm Dragunov SVD. First produced in competition with Kalashnikov, in fact. It was adopted by the Red Army six years ago.' I picked it up and placed Pritchard in the crosshairs. He didn't flinch. Once again, it crossed my mind that I should kill him while I had the chance. But I was on a knife-edge already – another corpse would leave no doubt in London's mind. I didn't fancy running for the rest of my life or rotting away in Moscow, so I leaned down and placed the rifle back on the floor.

'Why didn't your man on the golf course use this to kill Slavin?' Pritchard was saying.

'I've been wondering the same thing myself,' I said. 'I reckon killing Slavin must have been a last-minute idea. The killer was out here on another job when he was told he had to take care of a defector as well, and fast. He didn't have time to go to the club to pick up the rifle, so he used an unmarked pistol instead.'

'"Another job"?'

'He had an L-pill on him and he *used* it. He had to be protecting something pretty major to take his own life.'

'Perhaps he was simply a well-trained servant of the Motherland.'

'I don't think even the Russians are that brainwashed,' I said.

'All right. If he didn't need a rifle to kill Slavin, what would he need it for?'

I nodded. 'I thought of that, too. What if Slavin was killed, not because someone was afraid he was going to reveal the identity of Radnya, but because he might reveal the identity of *another target*? The man on the golf course was no ordinary thug – he knew hand-to-hand combat, and he was a crack shot. Ever heard of SMERSH?'

He nodded. SMERSH had been the Russians' method of dealing with those they felt might escape justice after the war. They hadn't bothered burying their bodies.

'Officially, they were wound up in '48,' I said, 'but we have some evidence that the new KGB chief, Andropov, has reformed them. Remember those chaps who took over Prague airport last year? Very similar m.o.'

'I don't remember seeing any reports on this,' said Pritchard.

'We've not had solid proof of it. I've mentioned it to Chief a few times, but he keeps − kept − putting me off.'

'Assassination units in peacetime? Isn't that stretching it a little?'

'Have you forgotten, Henry?' I said. 'You helped my father set one up.'

He didn't say anything to that.

'Slavin was shot with a pistol,' I went on. I pointed at the rifle. 'So why was *that* waiting for him in the Afrospot?'

'Could be a number of reasons,' he said. 'The country is at war, after all . . .'

'Fine,' I said. 'Leave it, then. Let your petty hatred of me get in the way of you doing your job, and watch the PM have his guts smeared all over the street. Hell, you don't agree with his politics anyway, so perhaps you're ecstatic about it.'

He frowned. 'My personal feelings don't come into it. My problem is simply that what you're suggesting doesn't sound plausible. What would the Russians have to gain by killing the PM?'

'Nigeria, of course. If he were assassinated in Lagos, it would be seen as a direct result of his policy to provide arms to the

Federals. Whoever succeeded him as prime minister would be under enormous pressure to end Britain's involvement here. That would leave the Russians free to step up their arms sales, end the war and move their men into the presidential palace shortly after. And with one of the largest countries in Africa in their grip, they'd soon start exerting influence elsewhere.'

'You didn't like the domino theory yesterday,' he said.

'I've learned a few things since then.'

He walked around the SVD, considering the implications of what I was saying. I needed him to conclude I was right, because the authority he had with Farraday might be useful to me — and could be very dangerous if turned against me.

'You're assuming too much,' he said after a minute or so, and I let my breath out slowly, trying to contain my disappointment. 'It's all rather circumstantial. Quite a lot of what you say is circumstantial, I find.'

I was getting sick of him. 'Look, Henry,' I said. 'I know you don't like me much. That's fine — I can't stand you, either. But if you would just listen—'

He put a palm up.

'You may be onto something. I was simply noting that you have no proof of it.'

He walked over to the dresser and rang Manning, asking him to get hold of a copy of the schedule for the Prime Minister's visit as a matter of urgency.

When he'd put the receiver down, I asked him what he thought he was doing.

'What do you mean?'

'I mean you just said I'm onto something. So when are you going to signal London and tell them to cancel the visit?'

He gave a sharp shake of his head. 'Can't do that. The PM has made quite a fuss about this visit. He'd have to have a very good reason to back out now.'

'A better reason than an attempt on his life?'

He ran his tongue along his teeth. 'If he pulls out now, it would be an enormous loss of face for the Nigerians, and it might lose us all the influence we've earned in the last couple of years. And it was hard earned, believe me. But more importantly, it would deprive us of the opportunity of finding out what the hell the Russians are up to – and perhaps finding this traitor. That's why we're both here, after all.'

'Doesn't the traitor become a slightly lower priority now that the PM's life is at risk?'

He tilted his head and let the way I had phrased it settle. 'If there was a plot to kill the PM,' he said, eventually, 'it would seem to have been extinguished.' He pointed at the rifle. 'We even have the weapon they were going to use.'

'They're not going to call it off because of that!' I said. 'Golf Course Man had written down the name of the place he was to pick up the gun. No professional would do such a thing unless they had to. He must have been the back-up.'

He considered this for a moment. 'Where's the original sniper gone, then? And what weapon will he use?'

'I've obviously no idea where they are, but weapons are easily replaceable.'

'Yes. So are prime ministers.' He misinterpreted my look. 'Oh, don't wet yourself. If I thought for a second we were endangering the life of the PM, I wouldn't joke about it. I agree that there seems to be a wider plot, but it can't be a coincidence: it's surely linked to Slavin's decision to defect. As Slavin is dead,' – he pursed his lips at me – 'he can't tell us how, but we need to find out because it may help identify the traitor. And that is paramount: as long as he is operating, we have no idea how much damage he has done, or even in what areas. If we tell Cabinet Office about this, they'll either whip the PM out of the country before we can blink, or wrap him so tight in cotton wool the Russians will immediately smell a rat. Either way, they will roll up whatever it is they've got going, and you'll be no closer to finding out what Slavin knew or how it connects to the double.'

It was a beautiful speech. The twist in it was lobbed in so elegantly that it took me a second to catch up to it.

'Me?' I said.

He nodded. 'The note you left in your office said you wanted to find the real traitor – so far all you've done is got our only lead killed. I'm not yet sure if that was cock-up or conspiracy, but here's your chance to prove your innocence. We now know Chief is not Radnya – I think it's time you earn your spurs and find out who is. If not,' he paused, 'well, I might be able to help the police in their investigation into the deaths of two Russian diplomats.'

XIII

In the harsh light of day, and without the wail of saxophones and trumpets emanating from it, the Afrospot was revealed as just another nondescript Lagos townhouse on just another nondescript Lagos street. The patch of lawn in front of the entrance was strewn with empty beer bottles and tin cans, and a gang of stray dogs barked at the young boys who were half-heartedly kicking around a punctured football.

'You're in Marjorie's bad books,' Manning was saying, as we surveyed the scene from a car across the street. When I didn't respond he turned to Pritchard, who was in the passenger seat next to him. 'He's in Marjorie's bad books.'

'Why's that?' said Pritchard, not moving his eyes from the entrance to the club.

'Because I've had to hide the car. This is one of the firm's spares. So you can imagine – she's not best pleased.'

It was a white Peugeot estate, and, if anything, it was in better condition than Manning's had been. But I didn't argue – there were other things to think about. I'd seriously miscalculated the way Pritchard would react to the idea that the PM might be the target of an assassination attempt. I had tried to convince him of it, partly because I didn't like the idea of sitting on information that someone might be about to get his head blown off, whoever he was, but also because it suited my own aims. I'd thought Pritchard would immediately arrange for the trip to be cancelled, which would tie him up in red tape and give me the space and time to get to Anna. I hadn't imagined he would be mad enough to use Wilson as *bait*. Still, I couldn't deny his logic – it was essentially the same strategy I'd used with myself: move close enough to the flame to be able to blow it out.

According to the schedule Manning had brought with him, the PM was due to arrive in just under fifty-one hours' time. I glanced again at the sheet of paper.

<u>Visit of the Prime Minister to Nigeria</u>

<u>27-31 March 1969</u>

Programme

Thursday 27 March

16.00 Prime Minister and British Delegation
      arrive.

20.00 Working dinner on board HMS Fearless.

Friday 28 March

09.00 Formal talks with General Gowon.

```
13.15   Depart Lagos by air.
14.30   Arrive   Enugu.   Visits   to   the   ICRC
        Rehabilitation Camp at Udi and to the
        British Child Medical Care Unit at Enugu
        Hospital.
19.00   Arrive Lagos by air.
20.30   Informal  dinner  with  General  Gowon  at
        Dodan Barracks.
```

And so it continued, until he flew off to Addis Ababa on Monday morning. In four days, he would visit dozens of buildings and meet hundreds of people. Without anything more to go on, narrowing down the time and location of an attempt on his life would be impossible. But Pritchard was right: there must be a connection with Slavin's move to defect, and as he had opened his negotiations by providing information about me, I wanted to know what it was.

'Why is he bringing the *Fearless*?' I asked Manning.

'Show of strength,' Pritchard answered, and Manning nodded vigorously.

'Precisely. The Russians have been building up a presence in the harbour over the last few months, so this will put them in their place.'

I ruled it out as a possible target — it would be far too heavily guarded. From Pritchard's dossier, I knew that Enugu and Udi were both former Biafran strongholds now in Federal hands. They also seemed unlikely; for propaganda purposes, Lagos seemed likely to be the Russians' first choice. My instinct, for the moment, was that they would be keen to strike as soon after he arrived as possible – perhaps even at the airport.

'Do either of you fancy telling me what this is all about?' asked Manning.

'Just stay here, Geoffrey,' I said. 'Look after the case, and if the police – or anyone else – arrive, come in and get us.'

*

'Remind me,' said Pritchard as we crossed the street. 'What are you hoping to find?'

'I'm not sure,' I said. 'I'm just worried I might have missed something.' It was partly the truth – it had been niggling at me since I'd read the files Manning had brought me on the family – but it was partly because Pritchard was now going to follow me wherever I went, so I couldn't go to the Soviet Embassy to wait for Anna. I wanted that meeting to occur alone. He hadn't been that easy to persuade, but I had insisted that the security situation there would make us too conspicuous.

The boys stopped their game as we approached. The tallest of the group ambled over and stood between us and the front door, legs akimbo and arms folded.

'We closed,' he scowled.

'Good morning,' I said. 'We're looking for Mister Thompson-Bola. Is he in?'

He looked us up and down, and slowly shook his head.

'It's important,' I said. 'We want to talk to him about Daniel Talabi.'

He wasn't convinced: perhaps the name didn't mean anything to him. But someone had been following the conversation, because there was a sudden scratching at one of the windows. The boy took a couple of steps back, listened for a few moments, and then gave a small nod of his head and stood to one side.

Pritchard and I walked into the Afrospot.

*

The room was a degree or two cooler than outside, but every bit as lifeless: there were beer stains on the floor, and smears on the windows. In the doorway stood J. J. Thompson-Bola. He looked tired, but otherwise the same as when I'd last seen him: he was still in his silver trousers, and between two fingers he held a marijuana cigarette so large it looked about to collapse in on itself.

'I remember you,' he said. 'The journalist. Where's your girlfriend?'

I could sense Pritchard stiffen beside me. 'She wasn't my girlfriend,' I said. 'But I have to apologize – I'm not really a journalist. I work for the British High Commission, as does my colleague here.' Pritchard showed his diplomatic passport: he was a second secretary, impressive cover to have set up in less than a day.

J. J. took a long drag of his joint. He didn't seem too surprised. 'What do you know about Daniel?'

'Is there anywhere we can sit down and talk?'

He nodded, and gestured for us to follow him. We walked down the corridor, past several doors, until we reached one, which he pushed open.

189

It was the green room. It didn't appear to have been touched since I'd been here – I supposed the police had occupied them for most of the rest of the night. It evidently also served as a dormitory of sorts, as there were a few mattresses on the floor, and as a dining room: several people sat eating at the central table, among them Abigail. She was wearing the same kind of traditional outfit as previously, but the headdress had gone. She looked up as we walked in, and immediately recognized me. She rattled something off to J. J. in their own language; they were Yoruba, I remembered from the file. J. J. replied in kind – I caught only 'Daniel'. She looked at him in surprise and, with a few words, immediately dismissed him and everyone else from the room.

When they had all gone, she addressed me: 'You want to talk about Daniel?'

I walked over and sat down at the table opposite her. Pritchard stayed put by the door.

'We believe we may be able to arrange his release,' I said. 'Would that be important to you?'

'How?' she said. The eyes behind the thick lenses were unflinching, proud, and unafraid. 'How would you be able to accomplish that? I saw you run from here yesterday night. Run from the police. So I ask again: how will *you* arrange for the long-awaited release of my nephew from unlawful imprisonment?'

I could see how she could be trouble. Her voice was that of a natural orator – and she was no fool.

'Last night was a misunderstanding,' I said. 'I work for the

British government, and we have called in some favours with the people who are dealing with Daniel's case. They are more than willing to cooperate. Provided,' I added, 'that you can help us with another investigation we are conducting.'

I scanned the instrument cases leaning against the wall. They looked untouched. The table was the same mess of glasses and bottles and musical paraphernalia, only now with a few half-finished plates of what looked like curry.

What was it I was looking for?

'You are not here to help Daniel,' she said.

Her tone was calm, but there was defiance in her face — a lifetime of defiance, against men who looked like me. I wished I could reach across to her and tell her that I was no enemy, that I shared her cause. But I couldn't — because I didn't think I did, any longer.

'We're not here to help Daniel,' I admitted. 'But if you don't help us, things may become worse for him.'

She looked at me with disgust. 'You think you can black-mail me?' she said. 'I have nothing you can take. Nothing! Not even Daniel. I will not be forced against my will to do your bidding.'

I took out the Tokarev and leaned across the table.

'I think you will.'

She didn't avert her gaze. 'Why must men always revert to violence?' she said.

'I believe you've met Mao. The answer's in his book. "Power grows out of the barrel of a gun."'

'That is incorrect. It is *political* power . . .'

'This is political.'

'Shoot me, then,' she said, in the same calm voice. 'Shoot me with your gun. I don't think your masters would look kindly on it.' She glanced at Pritchard. 'Do you approve of this behaviour?'

Without moving the pistol, I glanced over my shoulder at Pritchard. He adjusted his sunglasses and gave the slightest of nods, either in answer to her question or to tell me to carry on.

I carried on.

'Tell me about the man who was meant to collect the rifle,' I said, placing a touch more pressure on the pistol.

And then she reacted. It was just for a fraction of a moment, but her eyes flickered to a spot a few degrees above my head. And in that instant I thought I saw something she'd not wanted me to see: not exactly panic and not quite fear. Confusion? And then she was staring straight at me again, expressionless, as though it had never happened.

I turned to follow the line her eyes had taken. Pritchard. But why would she look at him? And then I noticed that something was hanging on the back of the door, directly behind him. A white sheet, it looked like.

I placed the gun back in its holster and walked over. Pritchard gave me a puzzled look, but stepped out of the way. I unhooked the sheet, and found it wasn't a sheet at all. It was an apron. Embroidered on one sleeve was a small red cross. It also had a pocket across the front, out of which poked a small piece of white cloth, which I took out. A cap.

The roof of my mouth felt dry, and I could hear a drumming in my head.

They hadn't been expecting a man to collect the rifle.

They'd been expecting a woman.

*

I didn't find out how much more Abigail Thompson-Bola knew – perhaps it was just that there was a nurse's apron hanging in the green room of her son's nightclub. But even if she had known more, she wasn't going to give it to me without a long struggle, and I didn't have the time for that.

I had until Friday afternoon. Manning's programme didn't make clear the precise time the PM was due to arrive at the Red Cross camp in Udi, but the earliest it could be was half past two, so that was my deadline.

Anna had been due to pick up the rifle. She had been a Red Cross nurse in Germany; the assassin was to use the same cover. It couldn't be coincidence, and explained several other things. Abigail's odd glance at me when I had entered the green room of the Afrospot: she'd either been expecting a woman or wondered if I was her last-minute replacement, Golf Course Man. And why nobody had searched my room at the hotel, despite my doing everything to try to draw Anna out of the embassy. Because she wasn't in the embassy, but three hundred and fifty miles away.

But there was a lot it didn't explain. What had prevented Anna from picking up the rifle and the nurse's uniform? Why the sudden change of plan? Perhaps she had found out Slavin was about to defect. Panicking that he knew about the plot to kill the PM, she had left for Udi early, leaving one of her team behind to dispose of Slavin and pick up the weapon and apron.

These were all grim thoughts, though, because her involvement in something of this magnitude suggested that she had not only known about the plan to kill my father, but was more likely to have been the one to have pulled the trigger. I realized that a part of me had been harbouring the hope that she might have been almost as much of a pawn in the Germany operation as I had been. But this didn't look like someone who could have been used in that way. This looked like a ruthless professional assassin.

Pritchard had realized the ramifications of the apron within seconds, of course — I'd bloody given him the file in which it stated her cover in '45 had been as a nurse. That meant it was now more important than ever that I found her. Because if he got to her before I did, he had ample reason to put her in a room and squeeze her for everything she knew. And that meant I was dead.

As soon as we had left the club, Pritchard had headed for the High Commission with Manning to work on getting transportation to Udi, and had told me to check out of my hotel and get down to the Government Press Office in the centre of town to apply for a permit to fly to the front. We were due to meet back at the safe house for a progress report at 15.00 sharp.

It was now half past two. I had checked out of the hotel, but I hadn't been to the press office and I wasn't intending to go. Presuming that Anna had not changed her plans, there were now seventy-two hours on the clock, rather than forty-eight, but Pritchard had an awkward problem to solve: if he told London that the Prime Minister's life was in danger, they'd cancel the trip and he'd lose his chance to find out how the plot related to Slavin's defection. But any request for airborne transport would have to be cleared by the Federal side, and I already knew from Isabelle that the authority for that could take weeks. At any rate, they wouldn't let me on board, not after a British newspaper had just accused the Nigerian air force of deliberately targeting Biafran civilians. There were tank convoys, of course, but Udi was a hell of a long way away. Even in peacetime, getting across a country like this could take a while. In the middle of a war, three days would be pushing it.

I'd thought of a better idea. I had disposed of the rifle, dismantling it and leaving it in the wardrobe of my hotel room. Then I had taken a taxi to the Agence France-Presse offices, which were housed in a concrete office block opposite one of the Arab embassies in Ikoyi. I told the driver to wait and rang the bell. A tanned Frenchman in shirtsleeves answered the door, and I told him I was looking for Isabelle Dumont.

'I am sorry,' he said. 'She has already left.'

'Where from? What time was her departure?'

He smiled tolerantly – Isabelle and her lovers – and looked at his watch.

'Three o'clock,' he said. 'From the main airport.'

I shook his hand and ran back over to the taxi.

*

Through one of the windows, I could see that the Nigeria Airways DC-4 that had been on the tarmac when I'd arrived on Sunday was still there – or perhaps it was another DC-4. But just one soldier stood beside it now, and as I watched he threw his cigarette stub to the ground and began to climb the steps of the ladder.

'That's my plane,' I told the customs official. 'If it leaves, prepare to receive a very stern note from Government Office headquarters.'

He was a small man with an oversize cap and a neat row of pens in his shirt pocket. 'I am sorry, sir,' he said. 'But I need to see your authorization before I can let you through.'

'And I've already told you that I don't bloody have it! It's on the plane with my colleague, Isabelle Dumont. There was a mix-up at the office, and she left without me. Call the control tower, stop the plane, and ask her if she works with Robert Kane – or you can say goodbye to any chance of promotion!'

Something in that lot – perhaps the idea he'd be stuck talking to the likes of me forever – penetrated, and he hurried off to a back office. I lit another cigarette – forget my silly game, my body needed the nicotine – and watched the plane.

It was starting to move. Damn it, he had to hurry. I wondered if I should go in there and make the call myself. The plane was taxiing towards the runway, and with it my chances of getting to Udi. I had no other plan. I'd have to sit it out and wait for Pritchard to arrange something, but the chances were that they would allow only him to go, and that would be it . . .

The plane stopped. The official beckoned me.

XIV

The inside of the plane looked just like the one I'd flown in from London, only the seats were filled with sombre-looking soldiers instead of diplomats and aid workers. But it still bore many of the markings of civilian travel, right down to the emergency information card and sick bag in the seat pockets.

'Which division are we with?' I asked Isabelle a few minutes after we had taken off.

She gave me a puzzled glance. 'The first,' she said. 'Why?'

'No reason,' I said. I stood up and placed my bag in the overhead locker. 'Thanks again for your help, by the way — you needn't have.'

'It was nothing.' She rummaged around in her bag until she had found a camera. 'Take this,' she said, handing it to me. 'If you're coming as my photographer, you may as well take some pictures. That's a Nikon F — the best. Just point it at anything you think is interesting and press here.'

I strapped the camera around my neck and peered over at

her window: the city was receding rapidly below us, the sun reflecting off the water as we swung inland.

'So what brings you back to me?' asked Isabelle. 'What is your mission in Enugu?'

'I'm not telling you that!' I said. 'I don't want it all over the French papers tomorrow.'

She gave a short, indignant laugh. 'So I risk my neck for you and you are not even gentleman enough to share with me the reason . . .'

There was a flirtatious upturn to her mouth, but anger lay just below the surface. She didn't realize that my not telling her was protection, for both of us.

'Perhaps later,' I said, picking the tourist map from the seat pocket in front of me. 'How long do you think it will take to reach Enugu?' I asked. It was very close to Udi.

'Get ready,' she said.

I glanced over at her: she was looking down the aisle. I raised my head a little and saw that one of the soldiers was walking towards us. He was a tall, lanky fellow, and from the way the others stepped out of the way as he passed, I guessed he was in charge.

'You are journalists?' he asked when he reached us. He wore a thick sweat-stained camouflage jacket with a grenade dangling from each pocket, and the word 'GUNNER' was written across his helmet in white paint.

'Yes,' said Isabelle. 'I am a reporter.'

'And I'm her photographer,' I said, holding up the camera.

Gunner gave me a sharp look.

'You are English?'

I nodded.

'BBC?'

'No,' I said. 'We're with a French agency—'

'You want interview me?'

I looked at him — he seemed serious.

'I'm sorry?' I said.

'Interview. I give you exclusive,' he said.

I tried to explain that I was just Isabelle's cameraman. 'I don't do interviews,' I said.

He didn't seem to hear, and gestured that I follow him. I glanced at Isabelle, who gave me a nod and passed me up a notebook and pen. I squeezed past her and followed Gunner down the aisle.

He was heading for the rear of the aircraft, which was partitioned off with a grubby green curtain. Behind it, the seats had been stripped out and the space had been filled with crates of AK-47s and ammunition, lashed to the floor with ropes. Gunner seated himself on the floor between a couple of the crates and waited for me to ask him a question.

I crouched down beside him. The only thing I really wanted to know was how long it would take for us to get to Enugu, and how I could get to Udi from there. But that obviously wouldn't do. After a few seconds of silence, he gave me a look that indicated he wasn't impressed with English journalism so far.

'How long do you think the war will last?' I said — the first thing that had come into my mind.

He thought about this for a moment, and then replied solemnly: 'Hopefully, it will end soon. But first we must finish it.'

I dutifully noted down this pearl of wisdom, and tried to think of another question that might satisfy him.

'Do you think it is a just war?'

He looked up sharply.

'Just?' he snorted. 'Of course. Ojukwu tried to break this country into pieces. But to keep Nigeria one is a job that must be done.'

He was parroting Federal slogans at me — I'd seen the last sentence on a poster on a street in Lagos just a couple of hours previously.

'So you don't think the Biafrans have a case for secession?'

'What case?' He leaned forward and made sure I met his gaze. 'I am from the East. But I no agree with this so-called "secession". It no serve the interests of our region, and it no serve the interests of Nigeria. It only serve Ojukwu and his rebel clique.'

'You're an Ibo?' I said, surprised.

He held up one finger imperiously. 'Please, Mister BBC Journalist, do me the courtesy of allowing me to finish. I am Ibibio. I no like this Biafra idea from start, so I go leave the East and join the army to help crush the rebel movement.'

'That's an excellent quote,' I said, and he straightened his shoulders a little and jutted out his lower lip. 'Thank you very much for taking the time to talk to me.' He looked disappointed, so I asked him his name and rank to round the thing off for him.

'Captain Henry Alele,' he said, proudly, and I noted it down. He looked at me expectantly.

'And can I just ask, for our readers, how you got your nick-name? Were you on anti-aircraft duty?'

He looked at me blankly, and I pointed to his helmet.

'Ah,' he said. 'Arsenal.'

I looked down at the crates. 'You make sure the weapons get to the front?'

'No, no,' he said, looking at me like I was a fool. 'I support Arsenal Football Club!'

I started laughing. It must have been a physical need welling up in me, because it wasn't the funniest joke I'd ever heard and yet tears were soon running down my cheeks. After a few moments, Gunner joined in, nervously at first, and then full-bloodedly. It changed the shape of his face, lighting it up, and I realized just how young he was. He couldn't have been more than eighteen or nineteen.

Then, abruptly, he stopped.

'Why you laugh at me?'

'I'm not,' I said, between heaves. But how to explain to him that I found his devotion to an English football team surreal without insulting him? And then something occurred to me. 'You lost the cup to Swindon . . .' But that thought just set me off again, and Gunner's eyes, which were starting to bulge with anger, only made it worse.

'Do not mention this word!' he shouted. 'I do not want to hear about these Swindon thieves!'

I waved a hand at him to stop, and he actually went quiet until

I'd regained some control. Then he looked at me very seriously, and I wondered if he was going to ask to see my press pass.

'Tell me, honestly, Mister — what is your name?'

'Robert Kane.'

'Tell me, Mister Robert, have you ever heard of such a bunch of crooked sportsmen in your life as Swindon Town?'

'No,' I said, trying to match his tone. 'I haven't.'

My exclusive interview with Captain Alele came to an abrupt close just then, as the curtain was drawn and an anxious face peered out at us.

'Captain — we have some trouble with the plane. The pilot wants to know how to proceed.'

*

The trouble, Isabelle told me when I had returned to my seat, was that a message had come through from Enugu saying it was not safe to land there. Gunner and the pilot were now locked in heated debate about what to do. Isabelle's theory was that the Biafrans had coordinated one of their rare air strikes.

'What other airports do the Federals have?' I asked her.

'Not many,' she said. 'We already passed Benin City, so perhaps they will have to try Port Harcourt.'

I looked at the map. Suddenly the world wasn't so funny. Port Harcourt was a good hundred miles south of Udi. It looked like my strategy had completely backfired — we were now heading away from my target.

Things soon got worse. Over the next couple of hours, it began to rain again, after which we found ourselves flying through lightning. We were buffeted about in our seats, our stomachs churning, our fingers gripping the arm-rests. Just minutes before we reached Port Harcourt, the pilot decided to land in the bush.

And so, as night fell, we came down with an almighty bump in a muddy field somewhere in the forests of eastern Nigeria; I noticed a few of the soldiers crossing themselves when we finally came to a standstill.

Gunner moved swiftly into action. He might not have been the world's greatest interviewee, but he knew how to deal with his men. He picked out five of them to accompany him on a reconnaissance mission, and gave a short speech to the rest of us explaining the situation.

'We go see if we can find some transport for us to leave here.' He gestured at the two soldiers sitting in the aisle seats in the front row, and for a moment I thought he might point out the emergency exits, like in the safety demonstrations. 'In the meantime, Njoku and Otigbe, keep watch on your windows. If you see anything suspicious at all at all, raise the alarm. Everyone, stay close to your weapons. When we return, we knock four times on the door. Do not let anyone in who no knock four times. Understand?'

Everyone shouted that they understood, sir, and Gunner and his group started gathering up their weapons and back-packs.

'We're sitting ducks,' I said to Isabelle. 'A fully lit plane sitting in the middle of a field. What's to stop the Biafrans from attacking us?'

'Fighting is finished for today,' she said.

'You sound very sure of that.'

She nodded. 'There is a routine, followed by both sides. Usually, they fight in the morning, then have lunch and a siesta and then they fight for a few more hours in the afternoon. They do less during the rainy season – there is too much mud. In any case, it is very rare that there is fighting after dark, so we should be completely safe.'

Siestas? It seemed I had stumbled into a joke-shop war. Still, if what she said were true, then perhaps there was some hope. We had only been a few minutes from landing in Port Harcourt, which was a Federal stronghold. That meant there should be plenty of transport around. If we weren't under threat, I might be able to find some. I got out of my seat.

'What are you doing?' said Isabelle. 'Wait for me.'

I found Gunner and told him that we wanted to come along on the expedition. 'This could be a big story,' I said. '"Captain Leads Unit To Safety After Aircraft Downed By Storm".'

He considered the idea. 'You do as I say at all times,' he said eventually. 'Otherwise I tell my men to shoot you on the spot.'

*

The eight of us piled down the small staircase into the field. The rain whipped against us; I'd forgotten how strong it could be. Within seconds, my clothes were stuck to my skin.

The lights of the plane cast an eerie glow, but it made visibility easier. The field was surprisingly lush, although there didn't seem to be any crops in it – looted by soldiers, perhaps.

Palm trees swayed menacingly around us, and the air was thick with the buzzing of mosquitoes.

'Be careful,' said Gunner, as we stalked through the field. 'There may be rebels close by. But there may also be our own soldier – so look before you shoot!'

After about a mile, we reached a small dirt track, which Gunner decided we should take. It was the right move, as it led us straight into the centre of the nearest town.

If you could still call it a town. It seemed completely abandoned, and the unmistakable stench of decaying human flesh hung in the air – we all took care to breathe through our mouths. We walked through streets littered with spent ammunition, broken bottles and the occasional corpse, grey and inflated. The buildings were almost all ruined. One still bore a sign reading 'Bank of Biafra', while another had been a cinema: I glimpsed a poster advertising a showing of James Stewart in *It's a Wonderful Life* flapping from an empty window frame.

There were plenty of vehicles around, but they were either charred to a cinder or missing wheels. The lights of the buildings were all out – it didn't look as though there was any electricity here at all. My hopes of jumping in a jeep and driving off to Udi were looking pretty slim. The main road had been cut anyway, with trees laid across it at regular intervals, so even if I had found a working set of wheels, I'd have had difficulties getting anywhere.

Suddenly the wind intensified, bringing the rain up off the ground. As I struggled to keep my footing, I saw Gunner raising his arms and gesturing at a nearby building, which looked like nothing but a small hut with an open entrance. I reached it just after him, with Isabelle following close behind me.

The hut seemed much bigger inside, a dark cavern that receded into nothingness. As I came further in, I was conscious of light, and with a start realized it was eyes: the whites of dozens of eyes staring at me from the silent gloom. The men were stick-thin. Their uniforms, if you could call them that, consisted of torn T-shirts and sweaters dyed green, and trousers that could barely hold themselves together. The women wore ragged cotton sheets and little else, their breasts bare and their ribs exposed so much it almost hurt to look. But it was the children that sent a shiver through me. Naked and pot-bellied, they stood there silently as the rain roared outside, calmly looking at the strangers entering.

'Nobody shoot,' said Gunner. But his men were frozen.

'The camera,' Isabelle whispered to me urgently. Perhaps Gunner's words had made her think of it. 'Give it to me now.'

And while we all just stood there, I handed it over and she crouched down on one knee and began photographing the scene, the sound of the shutter almost obscenely loud.

'Who is your leader?' said Gunner.

After a few moments, a stoop-shouldered old man shuffled forward.

'We just want food,' he said. 'We are all hungry.'

Isabelle stopped her clicking.

'We must take them back to the plane,' she said. 'We must help them.'

Gunner didn't say anything for a long time. Then he nodded, and we started taking them out.

*

'Order, order!' shouted Gunner from his position at the head of the aircraft. 'Now listen, men. I am glad to report that our reconnaissance mission has been a tremendous success.'

I saw a couple of the group glance at each other. There were now eighteen more bodies in the plane, and they were the enemy to boot.

'We are very close to a town that has recently fallen to our side,' Gunner continued. 'This is good news.' He looked out at us, and seemed to lose his train of thought for a moment. 'This is good news,' he stressed. 'This means our soldiers must be close by. Divisional HQ must not be far away. When morning comes, we go locate the HQ and proceed to Port Harcourt. We move at first light. In the meantime, please look after our . . .' He looked around at the Biafrans hopelessly, searching for the right word. 'Our guests. Keep them warm. Pass around blankets and cushions. Share your rations with them, please – there will be plenty of food tomorrow.'

He didn't say what would happen to the Biafrans tomorrow, and nobody asked. After water and bread had been passed around and some of the most severely affected and youngest children given as much treatment as the plane's first-aid kits could provide, some semblance of normality began to take hold. Guided by Gunner's skilful diplomacy, the Biafrans started to talk. One of the Nigerians recognized one of them from his schooldays, and soon they were comparing the fates of friends and family members. As the atmosphere warmed up, I told them how something similar had happened in the First World War – or 'the Kaiser War', as they knew it – when British and German troops had played football together in No Man's Land one Christmas Eve. It wasn't the same, of course – the men of the group were deserters, and had stayed in the bush when the town, which they told us was called Aba, had fallen months earlier. They had been trying to live off the land since. The field we were in had contained cassava, but it had long gone. But, despite the differences, my historical comparison went down well, and made everyone feel better for a moment.

It didn't last. A few minutes later, as everyone began preparing to bed down for the night, there was a loud banging on the rear door of the plane.

Everyone went quiet and listened to the sound. A few of the men quietly reached for their machine guns.

The banging came again, a dull but insistent thudding.

Gunner walked over to the door and stood a few inches away from it. 'Who goes there?' he shouted. Everyone tensed: fingers gripped around triggers, shoulders hunched and all eyes fixed on the door.

'This is Colonel Bernard Alebayo of the Third Marine Commando Division,' called out a familiar voice. 'Who goes *there*?'

XV

Alebayo stood at the front of the plane, his back and shoulders parade-ground straight. Although our encounter in the belly of Lagos Airport had been less than twenty-four hours earlier, it seemed much longer ago than that, and my image of him had changed in the interim. I was surprised at how small he seemed, and how young – with his short sleeves and slight frame, he looked more like a cadet than the most feared and celebrated commander of the war. But as he stood there, motionless, it was almost as though he were waiting for his presence to ripple around the cabin, and within moments I was remembering just how unpleasant he had been.

He was flanked by about half a dozen soldiers, all of them well-built and heavily armed. Rain dripped from their helmets, darkening the green and white Nigeria Airways logo that was repeated across the thin carpet. Alebayo's eyes slowly swept the cabin. As I followed the line of his gaze, the incriminating details seemed to leap out: the Nigerians in their smart uniforms;

the rising sun insignia on the sleeves of the ragged Biafrans; the half-eaten loaf of bread.

When his eyes finally reached mine, they paused for a fraction of a second, and I fancied they glowed with a touch of triumph. He looked like he was about to say something, but if so he thought better of it, for he continued his visual tour. When he came to Isabelle, there was another flicker, but this I couldn't decipher. Concern, perhaps? Or just surprise to see a woman, and a young white woman at that, in these surroundings?

He jerked away. 'Who is in charge here?' he said, and his voice reverberated through the plane.

Gunner stepped forward and saluted smartly. 'Captain Henry Alele at your command, Colonel. This no be as it appear, sir. I apologize most heartily—'

Alebayo raised his hand. 'There is no need, Captain.' He extended an arm and patted Gunner on the shoulder, and at the same time a strange smile broke through his stern features. 'I applaud you, for you have done the right thing. We must rejoice, today of all days – it is only proper. It came as a shock to me, that is all. I hadn't heard, you see. When did the news come through?'

Gunner frowned. 'The news, sir?'

'Yes,' said Alebayo, his smile still fixed in place. 'It cannot have been long ago – I listened to the radio just before leaving my headquarters, and there were no reports of a ceasefire then.'

Gunner lowered his head for a moment – perhaps to gather courage – and then looked up at Alebayo. 'I have not heard about a ceasefire, sir.'

'Oh?' said Alebayo, raising his eyebrows in a caricature of puzzlement. He slowly withdrew his hand from Gunner's shoulder and set his eyes travelling around the cabin again, in the manner of a lawyer making sure everyone in the jury appreciated that he had just caught out a witness. Then, in a louder, more menacing voice, he said: 'So why are you fraternizing with the enemy, Captain?'

Isabelle shuddered beside me. I knew how she felt – it had been a nasty little trick.

'I know it begin look that way, sir,' said Gunner. 'The truth—'

'Save it for afterward,' said Alebayo. He lifted his hand again, and as though he were signalling the start of a race, or were a Roman emperor ruling on the death of a gladiator, he suddenly brought it down, slapping it against the side of his trouser-leg. 'Arrest them,' he said quietly. And as his men moved forward to carry out the command, he looked across at Isabelle and me with something that looked very much like disgust. 'Arrest all of them.'

*

The rain beat against the tarpaulin above us, and I watched it bounce off the receding mud track, so thick it was almost impossible to see past. I was getting my ride, but it wasn't in a jeep and it wasn't to Udi. Instead, I was shackled to my seat in the back of a dilapidated lorry, headed in the direction, presumably, of Alebayo's headquarters in Port Harcourt.

Alebayo was in one of the vehicles ahead of us, along with

Gunner, his men and the Biafrans. Before setting off, he had assigned three men to guard me and Isabelle. Our bags and the camera had been confiscated, and we'd been chained together and pushed into the truck with about a dozen soldiers.

So we sat, thighs touching – it was hard to tell where my sweat ended and hers began, even through layers of fabric. The smell of sweat was so heady in the confined space, in fact, that I was finding it a struggle to focus on our guards. They were seated on the opposite bench; all three had sub-machine guns aimed at our legs, and were keeping their eyes glued to us.

There was no reasonable hope of escape – I'd realized that at once. I was in poor shape to attempt it, anyway, as the last couple of days were choosing their moment to catch up with me: my eyes were stinging, perhaps because I'd only slept a few hours since leaving London, and I had a nagging ache in my back and down my left thigh, both of which were probably gifts from a nasty little Russian with a sand rake. None of this compared to my thirst, though; my tongue was working frantically in a desperate attempt to create more saliva. I hadn't had any of the water that had been handed round in the plane – I'd spent enough time in tropical climates to know not to drink from an open bottle – but now I was sorely regretting the decision. Thinking about it would only make it worse, I knew, but I couldn't help myself. My eyes only saw moisture: the rain outside; the sweat on the faces of my companions; even the polished metal poles that ran around the roof of the truck holding the tarpaulin up seemed to have a liquid quality to them.

I tried to empty my mind of such thoughts and concentrate

on the problem at hand. The lorry's suspension was almost
non-existent, and as we seemed to be taking dirt tracks through
the forest, it felt like we were sitting on a drunk camel. The
first time we had hit a sizeable bump, a couple of miles back,
Isabelle had let out a yelp, and all three of our guards had
tensed, as had a few of the other soldiers. But the guard on
the left, the one with the scars on his cheeks, had let out his
own cry, almost simultaneous with Isabelle's, and raised his
gun, enough to make me think he was serious about using it.

I had no idea if Isabelle was aware just how precarious the
situation was: a bigger bump, a bigger yelp, and one or both
of us could get a round through the legs, or worse. I'd seen
Alebayo give instructions to the men before they had taken
us in hand, and I guessed he had told them that the two
Westerners should not, under any circumstances, be killed —
hence their aiming at our legs. And I was confident that they
would try to carry out the order, because Alebayo had a reputation for rough justice: the report I'd read back in London
had recounted how he'd had one of his soldiers executed by
firing squad for shooting an unarmed Biafran. But would he
take into account the bumps in the road, and Isabelle's nerves?
If I were accidentally killed, the man responsible might also
face a firing squad — but that wouldn't help my corpse.

'Do any of you speak English?' I said to the guards, in the
clearest, calmest voice I could muster.

All three coiled in response, and I could feel Isabelle doing
the same beside me. Coiled, but there was no harm done, yet.
Fingers gripping triggers, but no shots fired, yet.

'Do not speak,' said the man with the scars. 'The colonel told us if you speak, we shoot you.'

'That's just it,' I said quickly, before he could think about it. 'I'm worried you might shoot us by accident. My colleague here is very nervous, and if we hit a big bump, I'm worried someone might . . .'

'Do not speak,' said the man. 'If I were you.' But he gave a tiny nod and kept his eyes locked on mine, as if to say he understood the problem. A few minutes later, he leaned over and whispered in the ear of the guard next to him, who in turn whispered something to the third man. And a few minutes after that, Scarface quietly put his gun onto safety, and the other two followed suit.

It was an opening. There was nothing now between me and the road — well, nothing but chains and a dozen armed soldiers. But supposing I could bound forward with enough force to break the chains? My hands were attached to the underside of the bench, meaning that if pressure were exerted at the right angle, I could use it as leverage. The bench was quite wide — I could press my feet back at least fifteen inches. It was perhaps even a little too much, but if I sat bolt upright, the distance shortened until it felt almost like a natural starting block.

And the soldiers? Most of them were not on their guard. This was just another journey back to headquarters. They would be looking forward to putting some food in their bellies, perhaps a beer or two, and sleep. They knew there were a couple of prisoners in their midst, of course, but they also knew that three of their colleagues had their weapons trained on us. We were not their responsibility. And unless they had been paying close attention, they wouldn't have known that those weapons were now on safety. I would have the benefit of surprise.

But, of course, the danger would not be over once I had left the jeep. It would take the fastest of the men only a few seconds to recover, if that, and I would be picked out even through the rain and the mud and the darkness in only a few seconds more. And nobody would face a firing squad for shooting a prisoner who had tried to escape.

My other potential lever was sitting beside me: Isabelle. If I managed to bring her with me, the soldiers would have two targets, rather than one, and added to the rain and the mud and the darkness that might just be enough to save me . . .

I stopped the line of thought. It was an exercise, that was all, an exercise I had hoped might reveal a way of prising open the chink. But I knew even as I went through the options that none of them was viable. Even if I managed to pull Isabelle and myself into the road, the chances of survival were too small to take the risk. The fact that escape was possible was no comfort – it had to be likely. In short, it was the kind of plan that looked good on a blackboard in the Home Counties, but when it was your life on the line in the middle of the night in the African bush, it was only good for keeping your mind distracted.

And right now I had more important things to think about. Chiefly: Alebayo. The good news was that I hadn't done anything I wouldn't have done had I, in fact, been a photo-journalist. If he interviewed Gunner or any of the other men who had been on the plane, they wouldn't be able to report anything incriminating. And there was nothing in my bag that shouldn't have been there.

The bad news, of course, was that I had already crossed paths with him. He had been suspicious of my cover then, and it had changed since. Not substantially, but perhaps enough to be a problem. I'd told him I was working for *The Times*, assigned to follow the PM's trip in Lagos. If he remembered that (and I had a feeling he might), he would naturally want to know what I was doing several hundred miles away, and under the aegis of Agence France-Presse.

I decided the best thing was to bluff it out, and insist that I was still working for *The Times*, but simply teaming up with Isabelle. As long as she didn't crack and I stuck to my guns, there would be no easy way for him to prove otherwise. My trump card was that I was British. That meant he couldn't do too much without provoking an international incident – if I made enough of a noise, perhaps nothing at all. Hopefully I'd be away from here within a couple of hours, leaving me plenty of time to find my way to Udi.

More light was entering the jeep now, and the road had suddenly become much smoother. Peering through the rain, I saw rows of small houses, a few of them with lit windows, and then what looked like a grass tennis court. That must have been a mistake, though, because I couldn't imagine many towns in the area had a tennis club.

The truck started to slow, and our guards took their guns off safety with an audible click. It was our stop. Without a word, the soldier with the scars on his face released our chains, and we were pushed out onto a smooth asphalt surface. The truck sped away.

Where the hell were we? It didn't look like it could be a Nigerian town, or even an officers' mess — it looked like one of the new towns outside London. Neat white Snowcem bungalows lined both sides of the road, and each had a small garden in the front fenced off by low hedges. There were even a few sun loungers, and I wondered for a moment if we had fetched up in some sort of luxury holiday resort; perhaps I had fallen asleep and we'd driven into some tropical paradise. But that wasn't right — it was quarter to ten, so we couldn't have been more than fifty miles from Aba, and probably less as the roads would have slowed us down. The smell of the swamp was still here, too, and every bit as fetid.

Before I could contemplate my surroundings any more, I was prodded in the back again, and Isabelle and I were marched towards one of the bungalows. We reached a small wooden gate and one of the men struggled with the latch for a few seconds before getting it open. We walked up the narrow path to the door.

A small plate was fixed next to the doorbell: '561. Sebastian Tilby-Wells and Family'. A former British army base, then? But why would the British have a camp out here? And looking down the street, it looked very grand for the military — even Fort Gosport didn't have this level of build. I tried to imagine Sebastian Tilby-Wells, and saw a very tall man with a neat ginger moustache and a burnt pate, bossing around his fat little wife and their fat little children.

Scarface fiddled in his shirt pocket and brought out a key with '561' stamped on it. He unlocked the door and we were pushed into darkness.

'Stay here,' he said. 'Do not try to leave, or you will be shot.' He cocked his trigger to make sure we'd got the message, then closed the door and locked it.

XVI

I ran my hand along the wall until I found the light switch. We were in a large living room: two armchairs, a divan, a coffee table, a couple of dead house plants. At the far end, an integrated kitchen, long metal windows – and an air conditioner. I walked over and switched it on, but nothing happened.

Isabelle slumped into one of the armchairs and asked me if I had any cigarettes left. I tossed her the pack and lighter, and walked over to take a look at the windows. They were unlocked.

That was interesting. I rolled them back to find a veranda, complete with deckchairs and flowers sticking out of what looked like old petrol drums.

'They had it good, didn't they?' said Isabelle.

I turned. 'Who? Where are we?'

She laughed, her face momentarily obscured by a cloud of smoke. 'You are very serious. "Who? Where are we?"'

'Fill me in,' I said, 'and I'll tell you all my knock-knock jokes.'

She sat up and ground out my sixth-to-last cigarette in an

ashtray on the coffee table. 'We're in the Shell—BP camp at Port Harcourt. I thought you knew — Alebayo is using it as his headquarters.'

Of course. While I'd been feverishly fantasizing about throwing myself into the road, we must have been waved through some gates. The windows were unlocked because it didn't matter if we left the house: we wouldn't be able to get past the perimeter. I turned back to the window: the moon was dim in the rain, but I could make out a few more bungalows and, beyond them, the outline of a high concrete wall. I couldn't see any machine guns in turrets, but it amounted to the same thing.

I had another look at the room. The Tilby-Wellses appeared to have left the place rather quickly. Magazines and paperbacks were still scattered across the coffee table: a two-year-old issue of *Life* featuring the lost notebooks of Leonardo da Vinci shared space with *The Collected Short Stories of Somerset Maugham*, *My Family and Other Animals* and a booklet about West African birds. Apart from the standard pieces of furniture, the only unusual items were a drinks cabinet and an antique radio set. The kitchen was home to a disconnected fridge and a rusty stove. The cupboards were empty, except for a couple of cockroaches and several tins of Bartlett pears. No tin-openers, though.

It was like a safe house, I decided. The thought comforted me somewhat, and I made my way back to the drinks cabinet, where I found the dregs of a bottle of Drambuie, a sliver of Tio Pepe, and about a quarter of a litre of lime cordial. A not-too-dirty shot glass was resting on the board, and I poured the lot into it and downed the result. It tasted vile: my teeth felt as though they were rotting away as they came into contact with the liquid. But for one exquisite moment it relieved the dryness in my throat. I also hoped it might contain enough sugar to send some much-needed aid to the pain surging through my lower back and thigh muscles.

Behind me, Isabelle announced she was going to find the bathroom to powder her nose. I investigated the radio set. It was in working order, so I tuned it to the BBC's African Service. They were reaching the end of a bulletin – I wanted the headlines, to see if Pritchard had cancelled the PM's trip. I turned the volume up as loud as it would go, and the weather report blared across the room. Cairo was hot. Oslo was cold.

'What are you doing?' Isabelle called from offstage.

I walked towards her voice. 'The room may be bugged,' I said, taking a left at the kitchen. 'You might want to watch what you say.'

'You should check the plants. Isn't that where they usually hide them?'

If there were microphones, they could be anywhere – in the ceiling, the walls, the furniture. It would take at least an hour to turn over the place, and I didn't know how long we had.

'The radio is fine,' I said. 'Where are you?'

'Here!' she said, leaping out from behind the wall. 'So what do you think?' Instead of her usual Zazou black, she was now in a turquoise ankle-length dress.

'What the hell do you think you're doing?'

'You don't like?' she said angelically. 'I could no longer wear those wet clothes.' She scrunched up her nose in disgust, then raised a finger. 'I find something for you also.' She vanished behind the wall again for a few seconds, then reappeared clutching a pair of silk turquoise trousers and a white tennis shirt. '*Voilà!* You will match me perfectly.'

I took her by the wrist and exerted some pressure. 'We're not going to a bloody fashion show,' I said.

She pulled away. 'What happened to those jokes you promised me?' she said. She walked back into the living room, seated herself in one of the armchairs and pouted.

I didn't have time to waste on games — somewhere in this compound, Gunner and his men were being interrogated. And any minute now, it could be our turn.

'Listen,' I said. 'Do you have your press accreditation from Lagos?'

She looked up. 'No — it was in my bag. Why?'

That was what I'd been afraid of. 'Here's what we're going to do,' I said. 'I'm working with *The Times*, but at the last moment I got ordered to the front, and we decided to work together. All right?'

She took it in, then nodded. 'All right,' she said. 'But I think you should relax. We're not in danger now. It's a story for your friends back in London, I think. A story for myself also — my office will be very pleased to hear it. Some of the photographs I took in the hut may change the course of the war. This level of suffering — it will shock people into action.'

She looked so smug, I could have smacked her. I pointed

out that Alebayo might not be too keen to let her call her office, or hand back her camera. She didn't hear me, so I moved closer and said it again.

She laughed, smoothing the pleats of her new dress with one hand. 'I think he will give it back. He can be tough when he's ordering his men to kill innocent Biafrans — I would like to see how tough he is in front of a member of the world's press.'

'These ones aren't all innocent, though,' I said. 'The men are deserters.'

She looked at me, aghast.

'Did you see the condition they were in?'

The silly bitch seemed to have forgotten we were in the middle of a war. It was bad news — if she tried to take Alebayo on, she'd really put the cat among the pigeons.

'Alebayo hates the world's press,' I told her. 'In fact, he hates anything that smacks of interference by the West. If you want to help the Biafrans, and yourself, you would do well to remember that.'

We listened to the football results in sullen silence for a few minutes. Finally, the familiar notes of 'Lilliburlero' whistled merrily into the room, and I turned it down slightly so we could listen to the bulletin more comfortably. Pakistan had a new president, there was fierce fighting in southern Vietnam, and John Lennon and his new wife were staging a protest in bed in Amsterdam. No mention of Nigeria or the British prime minister. I wondered where Pritchard was — probably a deal closer to Anna than I was.

'That was about your operation, wasn't it?' said Isabelle when the report had finished and I'd turned the volume back up. 'There was a coded message in one of the items!'

I shook my head. 'We don't do that any more.'

'What, then?' she said. 'You might as well tell me now.'

'The less you know, the better.'

It was a shame to have to treat her like a child, but she had a glint in her eye and it was worrying me. She was notching it all up for her exclusive report from the Biafran front, where she had been imprisoned in a bugged room with a British secret agent on a mysterious mission. It would make thrilling reading at breakfast tables across France – if we got out of here in one piece.

We listened to the radio for a while longer, and she cadged another of my cigarettes. I went over the story with her one more time, and then the door opened and Scarface marched in.

'Move,' he said, gesturing with his sub-machine gun.

*

The streets of the compound were quiet and deserted, but I caught a few glimpses of the site's new purpose: a couple of camouflaged armoured cars and a Land Rover parked outside one of the bungalows, and a small obstacle course that had been set up on the other side of what had once been tennis courts. It was still raining, and Isabelle was having trouble with her new outfit, which was sticking to her in all the wrong places. God knows what Scarface made of her get-up; he didn't say a word, just gestured which turnings we were to take and kept a close eye on our movements in case we decided to make a run for it. There was little chance of that, unfortunately — the only thing to do now was to talk Alebayo into letting us go as soon as possible. At one point, we passed a street that led to the entrance into the compound. It was a massive iron gate, and I managed to count eight guards before we had to make a turn.

After about a ten-minute walk, we arrived at our destination: a grand villa standing on the crest of a small hill. We walked up a path through the large and well-kept garden, passing jacarandas and palm trees. As we got nearer to the house, the sound of music spilled out onto the lawn, an American soul number with swishing drums and a plangent male voice singing about the end of the world. The doors to the place were open, and a handful of soldiers were pulling crates off a jeep in the forecourt. It looked a little like preparations were being made for a party — I half-expected to see a marquee being erected.

Scarface took us into the house, which still had the appearance of a private home — presumably this was where the managing director had lived. The paintings and mirrors still hung on the walls and there were vases filled with flowers. We walked down a short corridor, passing several soldiers on the way, their boots pinging off the tiled floor as they went about their business. Nobody gave us a second glance.

The music became louder with every step, and the instruments and voice started to mesh together. Scarface pushed open some double doors and we entered a large hangar-like room. It was dark, but I could make out desks, chairs, filing cabinets, telephones, several standard radio sets and a few SSBs. I could make out a faint glow from the rear of the room, and Scarface indicated we should head for it. As we got nearer, I saw that the light was emanating from a small area sunk a couple of feet into the floor. There was a campbed, a wardrobe and a mahogany table. On top of the latter was an antique gramophone player, from which the closing notes of the song blared, and a lamp, which cast a small pool of light on the tatty leather armchair in the centre of the 'room'. Seated in this was Colonel Alebayo, his head tilted back, apparently asleep. He was wearing a black and gold kimono-type number and matching slippers. His uniform lay folded neatly on the bed, his cap resting on top of it.

We stood at the edge of the pit for a few seconds, watching him. Then Scarface coughed. Alebayo's eyes snapped open, his head jerked upright and he jumped to his feet. Without looking at us, he strode the two feet to the table, stopped the needle and replaced the record in its sleeve.

'The prisoners are here, sir,' said Scarface unnecessarily, and gestured for us to walk down the three steps that led into the den.

Alebayo turned. 'Thank you,' he said, with a hint of a smile. 'I can see that.' Scarface thought about replying, but Alebayo waved him down. 'At ease, at ease.'

Isabelle and I took up position side by side in front of the armchair, like two schoolchildren summoned before the headmaster. As he and his men had done earlier in the aircraft, we silently dripped rain onto the floor.

Alebayo seated himself again and looked us over. It was very quiet in here, more noticeably so after the din of the music. Alebayo's face was as smooth and placid as a marble bust – it reminded me of the masks I'd seen in the market in Lagos.

'Mademoiselle Dumont . . .' he said, finally, and his voice was lilting, almost tender. 'I'm sorry – are you married?'

She shook her head. Alebayo stretched an arm out from the depths of a satin sleeve and plucked a piece of paper from the table. His voice rose: 'Mademoiselle, this is your authorization to be at the front. Is that correct?'

She glanced at it. 'Yes.'

'You have been a reporter for a long time?'

'Four years,' she said.

Alebayo nodded, and turned to me. 'And how about you, Mister Kane? Where is your authorization?'

'He's my photographer,' put in Isabelle.

Alebayo pursed his lips. 'Really?' He looked back down at her papers. 'But it says here that you work for Agence France-Presse. Mister Kane told me in Lagos just the other day that he worked for *The Times*, and that he was covering the visit of the British prime minister there.'

'That was true then,' I put in. 'But I got a cable from my editor this morning telling me to get out to the front and find a more interesting story. I proposed teaming up with Miss Dumont here. She agreed to it, as did my editor.'

Alebayo lightly waved Isabelle's authorization, as though fanning himself. 'They may well have, Mister Kane. But the Press Office of the Ministry of Information in Lagos did not. If they had, your name would also be on this piece of paper, or you would have your own.'

'Here's the thing,' I said. 'I did have my own, but we had a very bumpy landing and I couldn't find it afterwards. I must have dropped it.'

'How terribly careless of you,' said Alebayo, amused at the flimsiness of the excuse. He folded Isabelle's paper and placed it back on the table, then gave me a searching look. 'Do you know David Ashton of *The Daily Telegraph*?'

This game again. He'd tried it with Churchill back in Lagos.

'By reputation,' I said. 'I've never had the pleasure of meeting him.'

Alebayo pressed his fist against his chin as if thinking. 'How about Bill Turner of *The Express*?'

'Don't think so,' I said.

'Jack Stern? He's at *The Observer*.'

I shook my head apologetically. 'I'm afraid I'm not very sociable – I tend to stick to my work.'

He nodded. 'I quite understand. I am much the same.' He leaned forward in his chair. 'But here's the *thing*, Mister Kane. Those three gentlemen are all staying at a hotel very near here. So are several other British journalists. I took the liberty of calling earlier and asking if any of them had ever heard of or met a Robert Kane of *The Times*. And do you know – not a single one of them ever had?' He eased back into his chair. 'You must be *very* unsociable.'

There had always been the danger of my cover being blown. I hadn't designed it for use in the field, and I'd only had time to take the most limited of precautions, namely securing the initial accreditation for Lagos. So it was no real surprise it was coming under strain. I didn't say anything. It was his inter-rogation − he'd have to do the work.

'No,' said Alebayo after a few moments. 'I don't feel your story has a shred of credibility. But I admire your quick wits. The British Secret Service trains its agents well.'

'I was wondering when you'd get to that,' I said. 'I told you before I'm not a spy.'

'No?' he said. 'Do not play games with me, Kane.' I didn't like that − I'd been getting used to the 'Mister' bit. 'I am not buying the act.' His voice was now tinged with that familiar sharp edge. 'You are not an innocent journalist. You are a British spy, and you are in Nigeria to disrupt Russian involvement in this war.'

'That's absurd,' I said. It was, really.

'Is it?' He let the words hang in the air for a moment, and we locked eyes: his were openly triumphant. 'Do you deny that you have been monitoring our arms supplies?'

'What arms supplies?'

'The crates in the aeroplane you flew here on, Mister Kane. They contained weapons provided to us by the Soviets − as you well know.'

'How the hell would I know that?'

'They were all clearly marked with Russian identification. And Captain Alele has confirmed to me that you and he had a conversation in the rear of the craft . . .'

'At his request!' I said. 'He wanted me to interview him!'

'Come, come. Do you expect me to believe that if a trained

British operative wants to investigate the hold of a plane, he cannot present himself to a junior officer in a certain way so as to ensure he gains the access he seeks?'

'Look,' I said. 'It's clear we've got off to a bad start. You didn't like me when you met me in Lagos and it's a shame we've run into each other again, because you seem determined to see my actions in the worst possible—'

Alebayo had one hand in front of his mouth, and it took me a moment to realize that he was quietly chuckling to himself.

'"Run into each other"?' he said. 'Is that what you think we have done? Do you think I just happened to be passing by Aba? Let me enlighten you, my friend – I was *looking* for you. Two Russian diplomats were murdered in Lagos last night, and this afternoon the police put out an alert at all airports for a British journalist by the name of Kane, whom they urgently wish to question. When you turned up again at Lagos Airport, a very efficient customs officer, Mister Igbaweno, a distant cousin of mine, as it happens, radioed through to me to ask what he should do. I advised him to let you on the plane and promptly contacted divisional headquarters in Enugu. They were very understanding, thankfully. We have had a few minor disagreements, our two divisions' – he offered a preview of a smile, then shut it off abruptly – 'but when I explained that there was a British spy and murderer flying in their direction, and that I had already come across him and would like the opportunity of dealing with him myself, they were only too happy to let the plane be diverted. When the winds came up and your plane failed to land as your pilot had announced to our control tower, I sent some of my men out to see what they could find. It didn't take them long to track you down. On arriving at the spot, I found that you had persuaded some of our troops to fraternize with the enemy. So you see,' he concluded, folding his hands in his lap, 'there is really no question of my misinterpreting your actions. They speak for themselves.'

Blown.

The police had known to look for Kane.

Blown by *Pritchard*.

What a fool I had been. I'd completely misread the man – desk work had killed my instincts. I was a fucking amateur, of no more use than Manning or, indeed, Isabelle. Because I should have – how could I not have? – realized what the bastard had been up to. When I had suggested delaying the PM's trip, he had raised a few polite objections and then backed down, nodding that cadaverous skull of his at me. It was so obvious now that it felt like I'd been kicked in the stomach. He hadn't simply strongly suspected me: he hadn't bought my story for a moment. He'd realized I was Radnya the moment I'd fled London. Farraday hadn't told him to come out and run me; he'd told him to come out and find proof.

How terribly clever I'd thought I was being – but Pritchard had seen through my game from the start. He had *expected* me to run again, which was why he'd given me the deadline to meet him in town. Perhaps he'd had me tailed – in my rush to find Isabelle, I'd neglected to take the usual precautions – or he could simply have made a call to the Palace and discovered I'd checked out. That would have been confirmation enough, because there had been no guarantee he would find transport by nightfall, so it could only have meant a run.

He'd come out to Lagos certain I was the double, and I had confirmed it for him. So he had delivered on his threat, and blown me to the Nigerians. One anonymous call to the local police station would have done the trick. Result: I was in the middle of the jungle, surrounded by soldiers armed to the eye teeth, in the hands of a man with a taste for sentimental songs and a hatred of journalists, spies, the West, and especially, it appeared, me.

All of this shot through my brain as I listened to Alebayo's crowing little speech. There were a few cracks in his logic, though, and I leapt on them ravenously.

'With all due respect,' I said, 'your accusations don't make much sense to me, Colonel. If my mission had been to assassinate a couple of Russians, why would I flee to the front? I can think of safer places to hide from the police. And why would I also be checking your cache of arms and encouraging fraternization? My knowledge of espionage is extremely limited, but would any agent really be given so many objectives to complete?' I was surprised to find myself drifting into the same kind of cod-legalistic language he favoured, but decided it was a decent strategy: he might be more likely to free me if he felt we saw the situation in similar terms.

But he wasn't impressed. 'The precise nature of your

operation does not concern me,' he said sharply. 'There is enough evidence of nefarious activity to condemn you several times over. As well as persuading Captain Alele to show you the weapons on board the craft, you also took photographs. Perhaps the Russians got in your way – or perhaps you decided to kill two birds with one stone.' He waved the argument away. 'In any case, you leave me no choice but to hold you here.'

I sensed Isabelle flinch beside me. Had she thought it would be so easy?

'What purpose would that serve?' I said, trying not to sound as though I were pleading. 'My editor will soon wonder where I've got to, and then he'll be in touch with the High Commission, and then you'll have to release me – and I'll have a very good story to publish.'

'You think you can negotiate because you are British? I told you in Lagos that I care not a jot for international incidents nor my reputation, which has been besmirched time and time again until we have all become tired of it. It would be more convenient if you were not from one of our so-called allies, and our one-time colonial masters at that. Of course, I admit that freely. It is a nuisance. However, we cannot deal in hypotheticals, but in the realities with which we are faced. The reality of this evening is that you are revealed as a spy, and as such I cannot allow you to leave here until the end of this conflict.'

'Until the end—'

'Allow me to finish, Mister Kane. It will do you good to listen. I am confident this war will not continue for very much longer, so you need not fear your incarceration will be a lengthy one. The rebels are on their last legs, as the sorry specimens you encountered today testify.'

'Will you also jail them?' asked Isabelle. 'After all, they may also be spies.'

Cat, meet pigeons.

Alebayo didn't take long to answer. 'I already have,' he said simply. 'They are enemy combatants. The women and children will be cared for by our medical staff, of course. What would you suggest I do in the circumstances?'

Isabelle nodded, but I could feel the anger surging within her. 'And me? Will you imprison me, too, Colonel?'

Alebayo inspected his slippers for a moment, then looked up at her. 'Yes,' he said. 'I am afraid I must. It is unfortunate, but I have no means of knowing if you are involved in Mister Kane's dirty work.'

Isabelle took a step forward, but Scarface was there at once, holding her back.

'*C'est un scandale!*' she shouted. 'My government—'

'Will be very angry.' Alebayo nodded at Scarface to let her go, and he did, reluctantly. 'Yes, Mademoiselle, I am well aware of it. My superiors will be equally concerned. There will be pressure on me from all sides to release you both. But I tell you now: I shall resist that pressure for as long as I am able. Because this is a war I am engaged in.'

'And my camera?' said Isabelle. 'Does freedom of expression mean nothing to you? Will you hide what is happening in this country from the world?'

Alebayo snorted. 'I will certainly hide military secrets from foreign powers,' he said. He tilted his head, and softened his tone again. 'Mademoiselle, if you are indeed innocent of any involvement with this man, please accept my apologies. But would you not agree it is a sound principle of war that if one finds a spy moving freely among one's troops, one jails him and anyone associated with him?'

She was shaking her head furiously, like a child who doesn't want to hear why she can't have any more boiled sweets. 'My father was ambassador to this country for fifteen years, and he knows people who will think nothing of ordering your dismissal from this disgrace of an army.'

'Mademoiselle—'

'*Non!*' she cried. 'You are a madman, and a bully, and a butcher!' And she leaned forward and spat in his face, a full globule that slowly ran down his cheek and onto his neck and disappeared into the lapel of his kimono.

Alebayo didn't react for several seconds. Scarface was trying to restrain her again, and eventually he shook his head and Scarface let go. Alebayo then stood up and walked across to the wardrobe. He took a handkerchief from one of the drawers and carefully wiped his face, before turning back to Isabelle.

'I can assure you, Mademoiselle Dumont, that I am no madman. I am in full possession of my faculties. As for being a bully and a butcher, that is for others to judge. But during these difficult days, I often think of my time in the Congo with the United Nations, and something one of my colleagues there shared with me. "When two elephants fight, it is the grass that suffers." I believe it is a Swahili saying. At the moment, there are several elephants fighting on the grass of Nigeria. But two of the largest beasts are Great Britain — and France.' He pointed a finger at Isabelle. 'Your government is providing arms to the rebels. It is you that is making a mess of the grass. My job is to minimize that mess.' He nodded at Scarface, who stepped forward and placed the butt of his gun into her back.

'Put them with the others,' said Alebayo. 'I do not wish to see them again.'

*

The rain had finally stopped, though it wasn't much comfort. Scarface prodded us through the Toytown streets. Whereas earlier I'd sensed a tiny measure of warmth in his manner, something I might have been able to work on, now there was no mistaking his open hostility. We were no longer Europeans summoned to see his commanding officer; we were foreign spies, and his prisoners to boot.

I inwardly cursed Isabelle and her little performance — it was a wonder Alebayo hadn't had us shot there and then. The worry was that she wasn't finished. Just as I could sense Scarface's hostility behind us, I could sense her seething as she trudged along beside me.

I tried to keep my mind on tracing our bearings in relation to where I'd seen the entrance earlier, and concluded that we were heading north-east from it. It was a pointless exercise — if I was going to make a dash for it, now was the time, because there would probably be more soldiers wherever we were being taken. But I wasn't going to run, because Scarface had a sub-machine gun and he might be inclined to use it. And even if he didn't, or missed me, I had already seen that the entrance was well guarded. All my options had closed down. So I marched on, turning when told to, hoping that Isabelle had got it out of her system.

After about a quarter of an hour of walking in silence, we arrived at a series of interconnected bungalows. Scarface jabbed us towards one of the doors and we stepped through and walked down a long corridor with doors on both sides. Each had a name-plate and a title – it looked as though we were in a former office block.

We were pushed through a door marked 'Walker, Godwin – Chief Accounts Officer, B-3', into a sea of familiar faces. Everyone from the plane was here, seated in chairs or lying on mattresses on the floor. They all looked up at the limping secret agent and his elegantly attired accomplice. Gunner had removed his shirt, and there was bruising on his chest – it looked like he'd had a rough time of it. The Biafrans were mainly sprawled on the mattresses, eyes closed, limbs sticking out of their thin 'uniforms'. I noticed with relief that the women and children were not here, and hoped that Alebayo had been sincere when he had said they would receive proper treatment.

I quickly surveyed the rest of the room. It was the arche-type of an office: a massive square desk that looked like it had come in from a *Punch* cartoon, grey filing cabinets, dead pot plant. Perhaps the place was bugged. There were no other exits, no windows – and no guards. It was odd, but then why waste men? The prisoners would also have seen the gates and known the futility of trying to make a run for it, and they probably assumed someone was stationed outside the door anyway. They were also, of course, hardly in a fit state to escape. But still. It could be an opening . . .

'Do you think this is humane?'

It was Isabelle. She had turned to Scarface. Her hands were resting by her hips, but her glare was fierce.

'Do you?'

He stared back at her for a moment, his face expressionless, his arm clutched firmly around his gun.

'This is a war, Mademoiselle,' he said. 'You are enemy combatants.'

Isabelle was trying to hold back tears. 'That is what your superior said. What do *you* think? Do you think these people' – she gestured at the Biafrans on the floor – 'are a threat? They are starving to death!'

And then it happened. Scarface, perhaps about to launch into a more elaborate answer and wishing to make himself more comfortable, *lowered his gun arm*. And I saw the look in Isabelle's eye. It was sheer madness – you never attack a man holding a gun unless you really know what you are doing – but I saw what she had in mind. Too late, though, because she let out a terrifying scream and leapt at him and, Christ, it very nearly worked, because he stumbled backwards and she began scratching at his eyes and it looked, for the briefest of moments, as though she had managed to overpower him. But then the gun came up. My legs had barely started moving before the shot went off, and the two bodies crumpled to the floor, and there was stillness.

All told, it must have taken about five seconds.

I looked down at the floor. Scarface was clutching his eyes with one hand and using the other to try to prise Isabelle's body off him, but he was still holding the gun, so it was awkward. His first push managed to shift her a little, though, and as she turned I saw in one horrid moment the massive wound to her chest, the widening pool of blood, and the frozen eyes.

I placed my boot on Scarface's arm and took the gun from him. I knocked him unconscious with one blow of the butt, then looked around at the dazed faces and the walls spinning around me.

There was no time to waste – even in a rabbit warren like this, the sound of the shot would travel, and more men would be on their way. I had to find a way out of here, now.

XVII

I rubbed the butt of the gun against my trousers. When I looked again, the blood had gone. It was a Stechkin APS machine pistol – Alebayo's arrangement with Moscow clearly wasn't new.

Gunner was standing by the far wall. Like everyone else in the room, he was rooted to the spot. When I had 'interviewed' him on the plane, he had revealed that he was an Easterner who had specifically joined the Federal side because he didn't believe in secession. But he was clearly susceptible to their plight, because he had agreed to take the Biafrans from Aba and had fed them. However, I had no way of knowing what he might have done if Alebayo hadn't turned up – it seemed unlikely he would have let them go.

'Where are your ropes?' I asked him, and he looked up at me. His eyes were glazed, and he was having trouble focusing.

'What did you say?'

'The ropes they tied you with – where are they?' I said it a touch too harshly, a touch too loudly, because I was desperate to get through to him before more men came and the chance was gone, and that could be in five minutes or it could be in thirty seconds. As a result, some of the others started to stir, pulling their gazes away from Isabelle and Scarface as they realized that something new was happening in the room. I looked into Gunner's eyes and willed him to answer me. As every moment passed, my words sounded more and more like a mistake.

After what seemed an age, but which was probably less than ten seconds, he shook his head and pointed to the ground, where the ropes lay coiled against the inside of a table leg. I picked them up and looped them round one arm, then offered him the Stechkin.

He looked me over quietly. 'You are not a journalist.'

'No,' I said, forcing bonhomie and efficiency into my voice, trying to use the exchange of words as touch-paper. 'But we're going to pretend I am for just a little longer. I'm your prisoner. You're taking me to a hotel in Port Harcourt. Colonel Alebayo's orders.'

'Why?' he asked. 'You want me to desert my men?'

'What good can you do them if you stay?' I said. 'What good can you do anyone? If you want to help bring this war to an end, you have to get out of here. Now might be your only chance.'

He nodded slowly, weighing up the idea. Come on, man, come on! Somewhere in the room, a Biafran groaned, and the sound of it echoed against the walls. Taking his time, Gunner reached out and took the gun, and I became conscious of my breathing as he placed it in his waistband.

'I can only take two others,' I said, willing him to move faster. 'Your two most trusted men.'

That stopped him, and in the silence that followed I wondered if it meant the end of my trail and the rest of the war writing my memoirs on toilet paper. 'They will be here soon,' I said.

'I won't shoot my fellow soldiers,' he said.

'All right,' I agreed, thankful that that was all he needed to persuade himself. 'If we do this right, that won't happen.'

He spoke quickly to two of his men, and when they had saluted and gathered themselves together, we opened the window and climbed out.

*

As I landed on the grass with a thump, a wave of pain shuddered up my left thigh. A monkey that had been sitting a couple of feet away let out a series of ear-shattering shrieks before scampering back into the bush, his fading cackle taunting me. I stayed crouched for a moment, willing the pain to subside, then peered around the edge of the building.

There was no wind. It had stopped raining and the air was thick with mosquitoes – they whined past my ears, and I could sense them homing in on the spots of flesh exposed by the rips in my clothing. Above, a sickle of moon cut through a starless sky, and I wondered for a brief moment if Anna was looking at it, somewhere not so very far away.

Focus, Dark.

Directly ahead of me lay a patch of grass as smooth as a billiard table. Beyond that was the road, pools of which were illuminated by streetlamps.

There were no men. Yet.

On the other side of the road was the tennis court, and beyond that, if my calculations were correct, the street where I'd earlier seen the Land Rover parked.

The three Nigerians quickly took up position behind me. I whispered to Gunner to move to my left, towards the Nissen hut I'd spotted earlier. He nodded and scuttled off, disappearing into the darkness and re-emerging a few seconds later, a dim shape against the wall of the hut.

I looked at the other two men. One I recognized from Aba: he had a boxer's broken nose and split lip. The other was lean and tall, with skin so black and polished he looked almost blue, like a Senegalese. I suddenly felt very conscious of my whiteness, and wanted to scoop up a handful of mud and smear it across my cheeks. But there was no time, so I told Senegal to join Gunner, and took Boxer with me, towards the road. In darkness, it was best to spread out.

The surface of the grass was slick with rain, and I took care to keep my centre of gravity low and lift my heels after each step. In my peripheral vision, I could see Gunner and Senegal moving alongside us. There was still nobody else in view, but I didn't give it long: soldiers' ears are attuned to gunfire, and the camp was silent. They'd be putting on their boots and starting their engines. They'd be here, any moment now.

When we reached the verge of the road, I held out my hand and the three of them stopped. I told them to file behind me – we were approaching light, so we wanted to present a smaller target. When they had done this, I climbed up onto the road, and made for the space between two streetlamps.

This was no man's land, but there would be no football matches in it tonight. We were half-lit by the orbit of two lamps either side of us. If they came now, we would be seen at once and they would just pick us off. After a few steps, my heart was pounding through my shirt, which was sticking to my skin after several soakings of rain, and the blood was drumming in my ears. But I could still hear the trickle of rainwater through the drains and the splashing of our legs through the shallow puddles. All my senses were alert: for sound, movement, smell, or any change in the environment that meant it was time to raise my arm a little and squeeze the trigger.

None came, and we made it to the verge of the tennis court, which was surrounded by a wire fence. We scrambled down the bank to the gate, and ran, still in single file, around the outside of the court. I saw some fuzzy grey spots on the ground and my muscles tightened on the trigger until my brain registered what they were: lost tennis balls.

We clambered back up the slope and flattened ourselves against it — it was something of a relief, so I tried not to relax the leg too much. It was still tense from my rocky landing earlier.

I peered over and scanned the horizon. And there, parked quietly by one of the bungalows, was the sight I'd been hoping for: the Land Rover.

I waved my hand to the others and we went over the top. The pain was now working its way up my body, but I used it as a spur, pushing myself against it to see how much it would hurt, knowing that every moment counted. We weren't out of here yet. At the halfway point, the others overtook me — it had been a long time since I was their age, running round the glens of Arisaig with only a compass and a dagger to guide me.

There were no lights on in the bungalow and no keys in the Land Rover. I told Gunner to get behind the wheel and Boxer and Senegal to jump in the back, then climbed into the passenger seat myself and looped the ropes around my arms so it looked as if I was bound. The fuel tank was two-thirds full, so that was all right. I reached under the dashboard for the solenoid and the hot wire.

'Is anyone coming?' I whispered to Gunner, and he had another look around and shook his head.

I bridged the two wires.

Ignition.

*

'Slow down a touch,' I said. A speeding vehicle might blow the whistle. We had cover now.

Gunner obliged. I remembered the way he'd walked down the aisle towards me on the aeroplane from Lagos – cocky, swaggering. He was a different man now – the sweat was streaming down his face. He had gone from fraternizing with the enemy to deserting with a suspected enemy agent – he knew he would face a firing squad if we didn't pull this off.

'Keep calm,' I said. 'We're nearly there. Just act as though you've been given urgent orders by Alebayo. They won't argue.'

He nodded, but his jaw continued to shake after he had done so. I placed the Stechkin under my feet and tore away a piece of my shirtsleeve.

'Here,' I said. 'Mop your brow. You need to stay calm.'

Without looking, he took it from me and held the rag to his forehead, as though it were a steak on a bruise.

I turned to Boxer and Senegal, crouched down in the back. 'If there's any trouble,' I said, 'just follow my lead.' I couldn't trust any of these men, of course, but they might now believe I could, or think it enough to delay their reactions for a fraction of a second if things got out of control.

'Next right,' I told Gunner, and he veered sharply, nearly taking us off a couple of the wheels. Waves of pain again, but now I could feel them stretching out their tentacles for my chest. I slumped back as far as I could in the bucket seat and tried not to breathe in too many mosquitoes.

We made the turning, and the gate came into view at the end of the road. The light at the end of the tunnel. I desperately wanted to tell Gunner to slow down, but I bit my tongue. I was in too much pain to waste words, and he needed these seconds to gather his confidence and remember he was in charge. I was just his prisoner now.

He slowed down a few yards from the gate, triggering a light in the hut. One of the guards came out a few seconds later, rifle at the ready and arm raised. There had been eight when I had counted – how many would be on duty now?

'Where are you going?' said the man, the barrel of his Kalashnikov lined up with my head. 'It is past curfew.'

'Let us through,' said Gunner with an admirable tone of authority in his voice. 'The Colonel just ordered me to take this man to Port Harcourt.' He gestured at me.

The soldier took a step closer.

'Who is he?'

'That is none of your business,' Gunner snapped. The guard's jaw tightened and Gunner pretended to soften. 'A British journalist. The Colonel wants him out the way — tonight.'

Too much. He'd said too much. The guard swivelled on his heel and leaned in to look at his face.

'Who are you? I don't recognize you.'

'Captain Samuel Johnson,' he said. 'I arrived from Lagos this afternoon on the Colonel's orders.'

The guard weighed this up, then looked at his watch. I could almost read his thought: 'Is it too late to call through to the main house and check?'

'Call the Colonel now if you like,' said Gunner, who was evidently on the same wavelength. 'But he will not be pleased by interruptions now — he gave me the express order to chop-chop.'

The guard nodded and saluted Gunner.

'Go on with one Nigeria,' he said.

'Go on with one Nigeria,' said Gunner soberly.

The guard turned his back and pressed the mechanism to open the gate, which slowly started to swing back on its hinges.

I felt the air move before I heard the shots. I looked in the rear-view mirror — they were coming over the far lip of the hill, bearing down the road. Dozens of men and a Ferret armoured car, its two lights blazing and its black snout rapidly growing larger as it came towards us.

As I reached for the Stechkin, I shouted at Gunner to put his foot down, but he already had — we were heading straight into the gates. The guard turned, took in the approaching men and car, and began shouting to alert his colleagues inside the hut.

I aimed for the ground just in front of him as I opened the car door and bundled out onto the tarmac. I saw him throw himself flat, and I rolled over and fired off several rounds into the lever controlling the gate until I saw sparks, and then the first flickers of flames. I could hear the others behind me as I got to my feet, then squeezed through the gates and pounded my feet down the tarmac, until I realized what I was doing and veered off to the left, down a steep bank towards the bush. I had no idea what direction I needed to go in, but that wasn't important now. They had a Ferret, and it was bearing down on us at a rate of knots. I could feel the heat of its lights on my back, and the shots were thundering in my brain.

I leapt through the grass, feeling plants and insects stinging my skin and prying my shoes away from the mud with each step. Two of the others – Gunner and Senegal, I thought – overtook me, clattering down the hill with their arms outstretched, and I followed them without thinking, blocking the rest of the world from my head and concentrating on my feet and the ground directly in front of me. Soon, I couldn't hear the Ferret – perhaps the lever had jammed and they were still trying to prise the gate open. I was running so fast that it took several strides before it hit home. I couldn't hear the Ferret, but I couldn't hear anything else either: no shots, no footsteps, not even my own breathing, which had been so strong just moments before.

I had gone deaf.

XVIII

I began to slow down. The pain in my upper left thigh was sharpening with every step, and I was shivering with cold. It felt like I was losing my balance, and my face was sticky with sweat. My brain also needed to absorb what had just happened. Which was that all the noises that had been registering in my head moments before – the squelching of my feet in the rain-sodden earth, the buzzing of the mosquitoes around me, the machine-gun fire from the men in armoured cars trying to kill me – had, without notice, been replaced by complete silence.

I had never experienced *true* silence before. It had a rather frightening beauty to it: every detail of the world around me was intact – the rank swamp smell, the curtain of sky framed by darkened palm trees, the shapes of the other two men skidding down the slope away from me – but with one element removed, it seemed unreal.

What the hell had caused this? Surely not the sound of the gunfire – I'd heard plenty of that in my time. Hunger and fatigue, then? I suddenly remembered all those horror stories people liked telling in the basement bar after hours of agents collapsing of exhaustion or going mad in the field. That poor sod Carslake who'd started having headaches in the middle of an operation just outside Bangkok. He'd gone blind before finding a hospital, and the opposition had simply picked him off on the street. His corpse hadn't been a pretty sight, by all accounts. Was that my fate, then? One second all my faculties intact; the next running through a soundless world towards oblivion?

Run anyway – and then keep running. Think later. The car would break through the gate soon. Perhaps it already had. I forced my feet back into action, fixing on the path ahead and trying to block out the pain as I scrambled down the bank. I outstretched one arm to protect me from insects and branches, and kept the other hovering low in case I slipped. As I pushed aside some large fronds, glossy and greeny-black in the moonlight, I sensed something in my peripheral vision, and turned to see a blurred ball of dark matter propelling straight towards my head. As I leapt away from it, I realized it was a mammoth insect – perhaps a dragonfly? – but that was as far as I got because I landed on something sharp, which cut into my right calf and shredded my trouser-leg so a flap of it now hung loose, leaving the wound exposed to the cool night air: a feast for the mosquitoes.

I tried to right myself and felt something solid pushing down on my head. I looked up to see a pair of gleaming bloodshot eyes: Gunner! What the hell was he doing coming back for me? His mouth was moving urgently, shouting something behind the screen between us. I gestured at my ears and shook my head, and he pushed my shoulders down roughly. I followed his lead and flattened myself against some muddy roots.

We looked up the hill. Flickers of red and yellow light flashed over the rim, and I guessed that the Ferret was heading down the road.

They hadn't seen us.

We lay there for a few minutes, or perhaps it was only seconds – time was getting harder to judge – and then I turned to see that he had gotten up and had started running back down the mountainside.

With a mighty effort I stood up and leapt after him, pounding my feet every step of the way. It was excruciating, but if I pounded hard enough, I could 'hear' the pulse reverberating through my body – not as a sound but as a physical sensation. Somehow it seemed comforting, so I concentrated on making it happen, again and again, all the while watching Gunner's silhouette ahead, weaving through the plants.

As the slope finally started to flatten out and we waded across a narrow rivulet of swamp water, I felt a closer shuddering. Had they changed their minds? Were they coming down the hill? I didn't dare look back, and at some point I realized that these new vibrations were coming from inside my own head – my teeth were chattering.

It was shortly after I realized this that the sound came back. Just as suddenly as it had been shut off, someone lifted the needle and placed it back on the record. My panting breaths, the rush of the wind and the sound of my trousers pushing through the brush burst into my brain at what seemed like double the normal volume, but after a few shaky seconds where I nearly lost my balance, I was almost insanely happy. The deafness had lasted just a few minutes, and now it had gone! The swish of my legs now spurred me on – create more swish, more noise, let the sounds continue for as long as you can enjoy them – and I leapt over rocks and eddies and kept running, full pelt, towards Gunner, until I slowly started to bear down on him, my heart thumping in my ribcage.

*

'I need to get to Udi. Do you have any idea which direction I should take?'

He shook his head. 'You no fit to go anywhere. You be very sick. You shake and sweat, and you no answer when I speak.'

'I lost my hearing for a couple of minutes,' I said. 'It's back now.'

He looked at me. 'This has happen to you before?'

I felt inside my shirt pocket and pulled out the soft pack of Players. So much for my little game – the remaining cigarettes were all sodden.

'Who the hell is Samuel Johnson?' I said.

He smiled. 'Someone I know at school. It was the first name that came to my mind.'

I nodded. 'Thanks for the help back there,' I said. 'I appreciate how hard it must have been.'

There was an awkward silence. When he'd seen that I was still visible from the road, he had realized it would lead the men down the hill – to me, but also to him. So he'd run back, made me duck for cover, and it had worked. But we'd lost Senegal and Boxer as a result – and who could blame them?

Now we were resting for a moment against a large palm tree he had picked out. He had found some of its flowers in the surrounding shrubbery and squeezed them open until a string of sap had dribbled from the stems, which he had offered me. Fermented, it would have become 'palm wine', but the sweet stickiness had been welcome enough and I had gained a little strength from it. My shivering had also subsided, although my thigh still pulsed with a dull pain.

'I sorry about your girl,' said Gunner.

I crumpled the cigarette pack in my hand. The tenses in his English were sometimes hard to decipher: the present was also used for the past. Did he mean that seeing Isabelle killed had helped persuade him to come with me – or was he sympathizing generally? Perhaps both. I had a sudden memory of her sitting and smoking in her black swimsuit on the breeze blocks at the Lagos Yacht Club, when I had mistaken her for Anna. And then later that night, her body glistening with sweat as she had called out to me in the dark.

'She wasn't my girl,' I said. I considered whether or not I wanted to know the answer to my next question, and decided it might be important. 'What's the procedure for prisoners' deaths?'

He nodded. 'It depends on the importance of the prisoner. I think they will bury her and the compound reverend bless the ground. But I don't think they tell anyone about it.'

'No.'

It would probably be weeks until her office became worried enough to notify the embassy in Lagos, and then her parents – were they in France? I couldn't remember if she had said – would fly over and start trying to piece together what had happened.

'This war must end!' said Gunner suddenly, standing and spitting on the ground to emphasize the point. 'I want no more part of it.'

I wondered which part he meant – the shooting of Isabelle, or the fate of the Biafrans? Isabelle had not deserved to die, but she had chosen to be here, chosen this cause. And she had chosen, finally, to confront an armed soldier while a prisoner of war. The Biafrans, on the other hand, had had no choice, or very little. Fight for one side, fight for the other, or fight for none. Another image swam into view: their skeletal frames immobile on those flea-infested mattresses. The flies buzzing into the huge eyes of the children as they had stood in the hut. I pushed it down, as Gunner had pushed me down into the wet earth a few minutes before. Humanity coming over the hill. Don't let it spot you.

I must not make the same mistake Isabelle had, I told myself. This was not my war. Biafrans were being held prisoner across the country – so were Nigerians. Their fate wasn't my cross to bear, and there was no especial reason why I should have been concerned about the fate of a squadron of deserters, even with women and children attached. War was hell, and this one was no exception. Listening to Gunner talk about what he had seen and what he believed, I was reminded for a moment that I, too, had once been young and felt I could shake the world's foundations. Well, I hadn't done it. I wasn't sure it was even possible to do. Part of me wanted to argue against his young man's idealism, to tell him that he wasn't going to change anything by talking. But I forced myself to keep quiet: I still needed his help, and I'd soon have to persuade him all over again. I had to get to the nearest town and find transport. The scant cover that I was his prisoner was a lot more likely to get me there than going it alone.

And what would I find once I reached Udi? I wondered. From what I knew so far, it didn't look comforting. Anna was apparently not only still alive, but engaged on a mission to assassinate the British prime minister.

And yet, and yet . . . could it really be? I still had no solid proof of her guilt. There was no way I could even be completely certain about the photograph of her in Lagos: photographs could be forged. Perhaps they had found someone who looked rather like her, and Slavin's defection had been an elaborate operation to hook me in. But no, that couldn't be right. Why bother? Sasha was in touch with me whenever he needed. If they had wanted to cut me loose, they could have done so in London. But the assassination story didn't fit either . . . There were still too many unanswered questions. Had Anna really survived, and, if so, what had been her role in Father's death? How had Slavin found out about me? And how did the plot against Wilson fit into the situation?

I put these problems out of my mind — the answers lay in

Udi, and I had thirty-seven hours and twenty minutes to get there. Perhaps the thing to do was to work our way back to the road we'd come from? Would they still have men posted on it? Possibly. It wasn't worth the risk. We'd have to find another road, or intersect the same one further along . . .

I realized that Gunner had stopped talking. His face was frozen, grim, and I looked up to see what had made it so.

There were five of them. They all had black beards, fierce expressions and were pointing rifles at us. The patches on the sleeves of their uniforms bore an illustration of an orange sun dawning – or was it setting?

Biafrans. But these ones weren't starving and there were no flies in their eyes.

'Come with us,' one of them said softly. 'You come with us now.'

XIX

We were led through the palm trees to a mud track, where a battered old Land Rover was parked, camouflaged by fronds and netting. Senegal and Boxer sat in the rear, guarded by about a dozen men, all of whom looked to be armed and — always a bad sign with soldiers — bored. None of their uniforms matched, and they wore an assortment of headgear: helmets, berets, caps and what looked like beach hats. A black metal pole was attached to the front passenger window of the vehicle, holding aloft a radio transmitter, and one of the soldiers held a receiver on his lap, the announcer's voice leaking out from it in an unbroken stream. We were pushed into the back, and then the jalopy stuttered into life and we started moving slowly down the track.

Pritchard's dossier had mentioned that Biafra had a guerrilla force. I wondered what Isabelle would have made of them — how they would have fitted with her idea of the Biafrans as utterly powerless victims. Their uniforms and weaponry were tattered and piecemeal, and half of them, I now noticed, seemed to be stoned. But they had crept up on Gunner and me without either of us noticing, and had sprung their trap smoothly and efficiently. With several rifles pointed firmly in my direction, I had little choice but to stay put and watch for an opportunity to escape. I wasn't all that hopeful it would arrive – I'd faced a similar situation just a few hours ago, when Alebayo's men had driven me to Port Harcourt under a similar armed guard.

Gunner, Senegal and Boxer were seated near me, all of them staring expressionlessly ahead, lost in their own thoughts. No doubt they were repenting their decision to follow me – if it came down to it, they would probably accuse me of kidnapping them or some such story. I wasn't sure what my own story should be. My thinking was impaired, by pain, fatigue, hunger, thirst – and the nagging thought that I might lose my hearing again. The smell of the marijuana was making me even woozier, and I hadn't stopped sweating since leaving the Shell camp. Every so often, my guts gave a sudden lurch, and vomit would rise in my throat.

After a few minutes, I decided I might as well try to make an opening, and asked the soldiers seated on the bench opposite me where we were going. 'I'm ill, and I need to see a doctor. Are we anywhere near Udi? There's a hospital there.'

They stared right through me.

'If you don't shut your mouth, old man, you will soon be much more ill,' said one.

That drew our cosy little chat to an end, and I concentrated on trying to keep my innards on an even keel instead. We bumped along the track for over an hour, past glittering lagoons and mangrove swamps, all the while rending the night air with the commentary from Radio Biafra. My ears pricked up as the announcer mentioned 'perfidious Albion' and, sure enough, he began to discuss the Prime Minister's impending visit. I couldn't follow it all due to the noise of the engine and a squabble that had started between two of the men near me, but the thrust seemed to be that the visit was a gimmick designed to deflect the world's media from a sudden and brutal attack by the Nigerians.

Twenty minutes later, we stopped. The radio was switched off, and the man in the passenger seat took out a walkie-talkie and spoke rapidly into it in his language. There was a pause, followed by a reply through a sea of static. After ten long minutes of this, we started up again, but at an even slower pace. Then I caught some movement a couple of hundred yards down the path: a cluster of men in camouflage were stepping out from the long grass. As we approached, I saw that they held bottles of beer and machine guns and that they were manning a checkpoint, which consisted of a bamboo pole across the path. Simple, but effective. We slowed and our driver leaned out of the window and handed over our papers, talking rapidly in the local language. They inspected them sullenly, then waved us through and trudged back into the long grass.

We passed several such checkpoints, each following more or less the same procedure. Finally, we reached a line of hardwood trees, some of which had been felled and used to create a crude gate. Documents were once more handed over and inspected, the gate was opened and we drove down a slightly larger laterite road.

This move was apparently unforeseen, because several of the men suddenly erupted angrily. Through the din, I figured out that they were urging the driver to take another route, but he was adamant that he knew what he was doing and would reach the destination in plenty of time. This assurance was greeted by derision and much pointing at watches. I looked at mine – it was a quarter to midnight. The captain in the passenger seat, who seemed to be in charge, quickly intervened, telling everyone to stop panicking and let the man do his job; as a compromise, he also chivvied the driver along, telling him to put his foot down. This forced us too fast over the next bump in the road and we all went flying, much to the driver's delight.

About ten minutes later, we came to a wide village square, which looked like it had once been the site of a marketplace. Unlike Aba, there were functioning cars parked on the street and strips of red, black and green cloth tied around the trunks of trees and pinned to some of the buildings: Biafran flags. We drove onto a wider road that proved to be even bumpier than the one we'd been on, until we came to a standstill in front of a large, squat building, which I guessed had been the town hall or something similar. A gruesome poster pinned to the entrance advised residents how to deal with Nigerian paratroopers: 'Stake all open fields . . . leave skull-bashing to women . . . stab them to death . . .'

The atmosphere among the men had changed since they

had decided to trust the driver's timekeeping: there had been the usual end-of-journey banter and stretching of limbs, but from the tone of their voices there also seemed to be tension in the air. Were they worried they would receive a dressing down from their commanding officer, perhaps?

I was prodded out of the vehicle along with the others, and the captain ordered a quick piss break – or 'pause for bodily relief' as he put it. Once that had been taken care of – and even at gunpoint, it was a mighty relief – the captain pushed open the door of the building, and we all filed in after him. I checked my watch again: it was exactly midnight.

The hall was empty and silent, with no seating and just a bare stone floor, although I could see some marks where heavy objects had previously been placed. The windows were all boarded up and there was an acrid smell I couldn't identify – something burning?

The door clicked shut behind me, and then the lights went out, plunging us into total darkness. As my eyes tried to adjust, my scalp wriggled with incipient fear. I could hear the fast, shallow breathing of the men around me: they were scared, too. So what the hell were we doing here?

'You have come.'

The voice erupted from nowhere, and resonated in my skull. It was male, booming, commanding. A few of the men started mumbling responses, but the voice quietened them.

'Please be seated.'

Groping in the dark, I lowered myself to the floor with the others.

'Now listen,' said the voice from out of the darkness. '*Listen.*'

After a few seconds, it began to speak again, but it was now talking in an African language, and the tone was completely flat, with equal stress on all syllables. An incantation of some sort? For the first few seconds, it seemed almost comical, like something out of a Rider Haggard story. But as the voice droned on, the words merging into one endless stream of sound, it started to gather force. Although I didn't understand a word of it, part of my mind began to enter the stream and try to decipher or imagine meanings, until I was drifting along, my eyes half-glazed, my face covered in cooling sweat, transfixed by this eerie, disconnected chant. The voice seemed to be talking to me about events in my past. Yes, that was right — Anna. I remembered now. That day she kissed me back. All the world blazing in light — the future stretching ahead of us. No war now. Home to England. 'What will you do in England?' she had asked me. 'What will you do now the great dragon has been slain?' And then the direction of the voice shifted a little, and I could see myself running into the clinic, the Russian soldiers, her body on the stretcher, the red wound and the closed lids. But her face wasn't her own, it was Isabelle's and at this horrific realization the floor started shaking and I looked up and the ceiling was, too, and there was light up there, light coming from the ceiling, three sources of light, and as they came closer, drifting down, I saw that they were in the shape of bodies — that they were bodies, in fact, humans in light form, and they reached the ground and one of them leaned in, and he had a strong face, a strong African face, and he asked me what my troubles were and I started crying because I couldn't tell him, I couldn't tell him all the troubles I had because I didn't know where to begin and he took me by the arm and told me it was all right, it would be all right in a little while, but I couldn't stop crying and it was taking me over, I was heaving and my lungs were on fire, and I couldn't get the next breath out to tell him, let go of me, don't hold me, I can't breathe, my back, hit my back, I can't breathe, let me breathe, help me breathe . . .

*

It was so warm in Germany, you see. I hadn't been used to the warmth, and it had taken me some time to get used to it again. A beautiful day for vengeance. But his neck, sweating. Sweating in the sun. I was unable, I had been unable . . . The wound had been warm, and there had been something comforting about that. No more ice. No more snow. Just a seeping warmth . . .

Sound.

It jolted through me.

What was it? A stream?

No, not that. Listen.

Animals! Geese, perhaps?

No, there was more to it, it was deeper. Listen again, closer this time.

Voices. That was it. Human voices. Criss-crossing. Now changing pitch, moving deeper. Singing. They lifted, somehow, and I felt myself carried away with them, on a tide . . . Not of water. Why was I thinking of snow? The voices seemed to be drifting down like snow, drawing me into their drift. And yet I was warm. Hot, even. Strange to have snow while I sat here sweating.

But there was a breeze. Hadn't there been a breeze just now? Yes, there it was again. It felt so good. It was almost as if I could follow every atom of it wafting across my face. Now it had reached the bridge of my nose, now onto my cheek. And then it had gone again. Why? How can it have gone like that? Now I felt drier than I did before. Wait. Here it came again . . .

I opened my eyes. A man wearing a white mask was waving something at me.

A banana leaf. So that was the breeze. Yes, keep waving it, I wanted to say to him. Give it to me. Let me wave it! He didn't. Instead he stopped waving. I could see the sides of some glasses frames through the peepholes of the mask, and behind the lenses lay dark watchful eyes. The man stood suddenly and moved away from me, out of my line of vision. The singing stopped abruptly, and as it did I placed the song. The snow falling outside on the black cars. The sky darkening. Cocktails at the consulate in Helsinki, all those years ago.

I was a long way from Helsinki. I tried to sit up, but all I caught was a glimpse of the man walking away, and the room I was in. It was very narrow and low-ceilinged. The walls were white and made of some kind of stucco or wattle, propped up with logs. The man was wearing a thin white coat, and there were shelves attached to the walls with small glass objects on them.

I felt dizzy with the effort so I closed my eyes again and tried to imagine the breeze washing over my face. It didn't come, but instead a cool wetness spilled over my lips, and I opened my eyes to see the man with the mask standing over me, his arm outstretched, a white cup pressed against my mouth. As with the sitting up, the fresh experience made me aware of the old one, and I could taste vomit, and it all came back. The hall. The voice. The bodies made of light.

'Good morning,' said the man. His voice was a little muffled by the mask. I couldn't place his accent – possibly American – but he was black; I had seen a strip of arm between a sleeve and glove.

He stood and raised his arms above me. I tilted my head and saw that he was adjusting some kind of a tube – I followed it and saw that it entered my arm.

'Where am I?' I said, and was surprised at the effort it took.

'You are in a clinic run by the Red Cross,' he said. 'You are very ill.'

A clinic. Of course it was a clinic – the tubes. That smell. Those objects on the shelves were bottles, I now saw. 'The Red Cross'. That phrase was also familiar. It meant something. More than what it normally meant. It was *connected* with something. Like a player of patience, I racked my brains to match the pair.

'"Finlandia",' I said, remembering another piece of the puzzle. 'I heard a choir singing "Finlandia".'

He nodded. 'The Biafrans have taken it as their national anthem. They often play it on the radio.'

A string of pairs suddenly matched up.

'Udi,' I said. 'Are we in Udi?'

The glove stopped the calibration of the tube, and the mask looked down at me. 'No,' he said. 'But we aren't too far away.'

'I need to get there.'

The mask nodded in understanding, while the gloves went back to their task. 'You need to recover first,' he said. 'You're very ill.'

'Malaria?'

The doctor finished his work and then sat down in the chair he had been fanning me from earlier.

'That's what we thought at first,' he said. 'But now we're not so sure. Do you feel you can talk?'

I nodded, and he took out a pad of paper and a pen from his coat.

'When did you arrive in Nigeria?' he asked.

It took me a few moments. 'Monday,' I said. 'Monday evening.'

'March 24th?'

'Yes.'

He wrote it down, adjusting his peepholes a little to make it easier. 'Have you taken any anti-malarial medication since arriving?'

I started to shake my head, but suddenly remembered the pills Manning had given me on the way back from the airport. 'Yes!' I said. 'Yes, I have!'

The eyes in the mask stared back at me. 'How did you take it?'

'What do you mean? Swallowed it, of course. A glass of water in my hotel . . .'

'From the faucet — the tap?'

'Yes,' I said, hollowly. 'From the tap.'

Silence, as his pen scratched the paper. My muscles ached; my innards gurgled; my head throbbed. Was it neon they were using for the light in here?

'Have you had any other contact with unfiltered water since you arrived? Have you been in any areas containing swamps, for example?'

Only waded through one. I couldn't bring myself to tell him, so I just nodded. He scribbled it down.

'Have you been in contact with any rodents since you arrived in Nigeria?' he asked, not looking up.

I stared at him and nodded. Of course. The rat in the sink. The same sink from which I had poured the water to wash down Manning's useless bloody malaria tablet.

'What do you think it is?'

'We're not sure,' he said. 'We've tested you for everything we could think of: malaria, typhoid fever, trichinosis . . . None of them fitted. Another candidate is yellow fever, but you don't look jaundiced and if you arrived Monday the incubation is still a little too fast. It could be a new disease: there was one discovered a couple of hundred miles north of here in January, in a village called Lassa. An American nurse in a missionary hospital fell sick very quickly. Then one of the nurses treating her caught it. Nobody's sure how it's transmitted yet, but one possibility is via rodent faeces. From monitoring you and talking to others, you seem to have had some of the same symptoms as the nurses: muscle and back pain, fever, nausea . . . Have you had any retro-orbital pain?'

'Meaning?'

'Behind the eyes.'

I nodded.

'That's another.' He looked down at his pad. 'Also intermittent loss of hearing, respiratory problems, hallucinations . . .'

His outfit was starting to take on a significance I didn't like. 'What happened to the nurses?' I asked.

'They died,' he said evenly. 'But that doesn't necessarily mean anything. That disease has only just been discovered, and we're by no means certain you've contracted it. It's just an idea. We've been giving you hydroxychloroquine and tetracycline, and now I am starting you on chloramphenicol. We're doing everything we can. In the meantime, I'd be very grateful if you could make a list of all the people you have come into contact with since arriving in Nigeria. We may need to start tracing them.'

I asked him how I had arrived at the clinic, and there was a conspicuous pause before he answered. 'Some Biafran soldiers brought you in. They said they had been at a meeting with Doctor Wise when you had collapsed.'

'Doctor who?'

'Wise. He's a well-known spiritualist in these parts. Many of the Biafrans are devotees of his – some of the soldiers insist that he has the final say on whether to go ahead with military manoeuvres.' The white cotton shoulders shrugged. 'It's crazy, of course. They think he can invoke spirits from the sky.'

It didn't sound so crazy to me. As he had been talking, I had managed to raise my head enough to have another look at the room. There was something I didn't like about it — there were no doors, just a flight of steps.

'Where are the doors?' I said. 'And why are there no windows?'

The doctor shifted a little in his chair. 'Because we are underground. This is usually a theatre for emergency operations, but we've converted it into an isolation ward to treat you.'

I looked around at the dank walls and low ceiling. The prognosis didn't look too good — I had already been buried.

The doctor closed his pad, placed the top back on his pen and placed them both back in his coat. 'Even though your fever has subsided somewhat, you are still in a critical condition,' he said, pushing his chair back and standing. 'I'll be back to check on you later. In the meantime, you have a visitor.'

As if on cue, there was a clanging sound and I looked towards the end of the room, at the staircase. Black boots tucked into khaki trousers appeared, followed by stocky legs, a stockier torso and, finally, the head of an African man with a bushy beard.

He walked over and nodded to the doctor, who turned to a trestle and picked up a white coat lying there. The newcomer carefully placed this over his uniform — it was a little tight on his shoulders. The doctor offered him a mask, but he shook his head and said something I couldn't catch. The doctor nodded and walked away, disappearing up the staircase.

The African approached my bed and leaned over me. I had never met him before, but I knew who he was.

'Hello, Mister Kane,' he said in a deep velvety voice. 'Welcome to Biafra.'

XX

'A bearded Othello.' The phrase came into my mind, but I couldn't place where I'd heard it. Then I realized I hadn't – I had read it. I had been in an airport. That was it. The interview in the *Newsweek* I had bought at Heathrow.

As I watched him moving around my bed, I concurred with the journalist who had come up with the phrase. There was something of Othello about Colonel Chukwuemeka Odumegwu Ojukwu: a measure of dignified hurt, and an aura of self-importance. He was taller and broader than I would have expected; the photographs didn't get across how much space he took up. But he had a kind of lumbering elegance, a studied stillness, that seemed familiar from what I had read of him. Pritchard's briefing notes had referred to him as a 'power-hungry menace'. That, too, seemed a well-chosen phrase.

But this was all by the by. What the hell was the leader of the Biafran army doing here? And why did he want to talk to me?

After he had fidgeted with his coat a little, he sat himself on the chair vacated by the doctor, squeezing his frame into it as though it were a makeshift throne. Apart from a gloss of sweat on his forehead, he looked calm, well rested, relaxed. With one hand he stroked his massive beard. I'd read about that, too: he had grown it as a symbolic gesture after the pogroms against his tribe three years earlier, and many Biafran men had since grown their own in deference to him.

'I am sorry about your mishap,' he said. He made it sound as though I'd stubbed my toe in his swimming pool. 'My men are superstitious, you know. They had strict orders to bring you straight to me, but they didn't want to miss their rendezvous with their witch-doctor.' He smiled tolerantly at his charges' roguish ways. He struggled with his coat some more, eventually bringing out a pack of cigarettes: Three Fives. He slid one out and lit it with a worn gold lighter. 'The men responsible have been reprimanded.'

He took a puff of the cigarette. It looked like heaven from where I was sitting. He exhaled, and looked up at the low ceiling. I could sense him thinking, preparing his words.

'Do you have the message?'

I waited for him to continue, then realized that he had finished.

'What message?' I asked.

He laughed, a deep, hearty and utterly insincere bellow. It faded, and he closed his eyes and rubbed them with the palms of his hands.

'Please do not play games with me,' he said, letting out a sigh. 'Let's not go through the rigmarole of passwords. We are not children.'

'I don't have any message for you,' I said. 'I'm a journalist with *The Times.*'

His eyes snapped open and he looked at me as if for the first time. 'Is there a reason you cannot convey your message?'

'You've made a mistake,' I said. 'I have no message to give you or anyone else. Colonel Alebayo . . .'

'Alebayo?' He stood up suddenly. 'What does he have to do with this?' He leaned over the bed and stared into my face. He had very sad eyes, like a type of dog you want to adopt.

'Alebayo captured me,' I said. 'A French journalist died . . .'

'Oh,' he said, sitting down again. 'That. I know about that already. Let's not waste each other's time. Where does the Prime Minister want to meet?'

The Prime Minister? What was he talking about? Was this one of my hallucinations? I tried to block everything out and examine his words. Who did he think I was, and what did he want me to tell him? What was it he had said when he had come in? 'Hello, Mister Kane. Welcome to Biafra.' So he knew my cover name. That meant he had talked to Gunner — presumably that was how he had heard about Isabelle's death, too. But there was something else there, some clue. What was it? Why was the leader of the Biafran army in an underground hospital in the middle of the bush? He was apparently waiting for a message from the British prime minister to set up a meeting between them — presumably to talk peace.

Ojukwu was smoking, studying me.

'There is a plot to kill the Prime Minister,' I said. 'In Udi.'

He didn't react, just carried on smoking his Three Fives

cigarette. Where did he get them from, I wondered, in the middle of a war?

'This is not the message I was expecting,' he said softly.

'It's the one you're getting,' I replied. 'The Russians are planning to assassinate him at the Red Cross camp on Friday afternoon. Help me get there.'

He examined me for a moment, then slumped back as far as he could in his chair, as mystified by me as I was by him. 'But why should I do that? Your prime minister is my enemy, and so are the Russians.'

I shook my head. 'You're not thinking it through,' I said. 'Think of the *effect* of killing him. Think of what it will do to public opinion in Britain. They are already opposed to this war. There are marches, petitions, debates . . .'

He nodded slowly.

'So how do you think they will react if their prime minister is killed out here?'

He opened his hands, waiting for the answer.

'They'll be furious!' I said. 'Not only are their taxes buying arms for this horrific war that is starving innocent children — now their prime minister has been murdered here. They will demand the immediate withdrawal of any assistance to Nigeria, and they will get it. The next prime minister would immediately withdraw from this war.'

'Good,' said Ojukwu, scratching his beard. 'But this is not . . .'

'No,' I said. 'Not good. Not good for you. As soon as the British have left, the Russians will step up *their* support. They will be the Nigerians' only hope, and make no mistake, they'll capitalize on it, and fast. They will flood the Federal side with weapons, and the war will be over before you know what's hit you. Then they will have their stepping stone in Africa . . .'

'This is all very interesting, Mister Kane,' said Ojukwu curtly, mashing out his cigarette on the floor with the heel of his boot. 'But I feel that we are drifting away from the main issue.'

He was looking up at the ceiling, and without his gaze to distract me, I was free to focus on his voice. And that was when it hit me.

'Take me to Colonel Ojukwu,' I said.

His head snapped back down and his eyes opened wide.

'What did you say?'

'You heard,' I said. 'I want to see Ojukwu. You're an impostor.'

*

My reading jag in Heathrow on Monday evening had been well worthwhile. Pritchard's dossier on the war had contained extensive briefing notes on the major figures of each side, and one of the Biafrans in particular had attracted my attention. Simeon Akuji, the Commissioner for Internal Affairs, was Ojuwku's second cousin and a possible means of communication with him via a personal cipher. Although it hadn't been spelled out, I had taken it that the link was overseen by Pritchard — especially as Akuji had been educated at Fettes, Pritchard's alma mater in Edinburgh.

As I had listened to 'Ojukwu' pontificating, something had bothered me about him. That he seemed to be performing an act was in character, but then I had realized why his little welcoming speech had jarred: there had been the faintest touch of a Scottish accent to it. My guess had been that Ojukwu had pulled a Monty and had Akuji impersonate him. Judging by the reaction, I had been right. But what was the reason for the subterfuge?

The answer, surely, lay with Henry Pritchard. Akuji seemed to be expecting a message from the PM, but according to the official programme no visit to Biafra was planned. Unless his entire trip to Nigeria had secretly been about meeting Ojukwu? Pritchard had denied that there had been a negotiating element to it back in London, but why else would the Prime Minister fly out here? So he could report to Parliament that he'd seen the war with his own eyes? To deflect attention from a Nigerian attack, as Radio Biafra had alleged? A peace mission made much more sense. He had even come with HMS *Fearless*, which he had recently used, albeit without much success, to hold talks with Ian Smith over the Rhodesian problem. A peace mission, then, with Pritchard the go-between setting up the meeting with the Biafran leader? Perhaps Akuji was the deal-broker; or perhaps Ojukwu was scared of being assassinated himself.

'You British have a most amusing attachment to conspiracies,' Akuji was saying, but I didn't have time for that.

'You read history at Lincoln, Colonel. I was there a few years before you, but I imagine they still had that marvellous portrait in Hall of — ah, who was it of again?'

He opened his mouth, and for a moment I thought he was going to try to bluff me, but then he dipped his head and sighed deeply. It hadn't been the most sophisticated ruse, and I'd been at Wadham anyway, but it had been enough.

'Is that why you're not wearing a mask?' I asked. 'So I could see how similar you are to Ojukwu?'

He nodded slowly.

'Quite a risk,' I said. 'If you lose your hearing, you know where to come.'

'The doctor warned me of the dangers,' he said, somewhat sniffily. Then, his pride hurt: 'How did you realize?'

'I'll come to that,' I said, though I had no intention of doing so. 'What made you so sure I was the messenger?'

'Who else would you be? The message told me to expect someone to turn up here on Wednesday, and here you are. Granted, you were waylaid for a couple of days, but I knew the reason for that — the men told me.'

'Waylaid?' I said. 'What do you mean?'

He gestured at the walls. 'You're ill, unless you hadn't noticed!'

'Not that,' I said. 'Not that. You said I was waylaid by a couple of days. But I'm not. It's still only Wednesday morning.'

He looked at me quizzically. 'Does British intelligence now train its agents to bamboozle its allies? Today is Friday.' He looked at his watch. 'Just after ten a.m.'

The walls suddenly seemed to be melting towards me, and all I could think of was Anna, on a roof, looking down at a black car with the Prime Minister in the back seat.

It wasn't Wednesday. It was Friday, at just after ten in the morning. I ripped the sheet off the bed and sat up. Then I set about trying to find how to disconnect myself from the feed.

'What are you doing?' asked Akuji, alarmed.

'Leaving,' I said. I had just over four hours to get to Udi.

XXI

It took me less than a second to realize my mistake. Our little chat had sharpened my mind but not my body, and I hadn't made enough allowances. I had deliberately stepped onto the floor with my back facing him, calculating that my apparent helplessness would delay him for a fraction of a moment in reaching for the gun he would inevitably be carrying. As I landed, I raised my right foot so it was in front of my left kneecap, then fired the right edge of the foot out towards Akuji, aiming at his thigh.

I'd executed this manoeuvre hundreds of times, and Akuji was no match for it: he crashed into a table on wheels behind him before I'd even brought my foot to a stop. I immediately followed up with a two-finger hand to his left carotid, after which he fell to the floor with a permanent-sounding thud. But by then I was also falling, because my stomach had suddenly been engulfed by a wave of nausea so intense I thought I was going to pass out. I managed to turn back to the bed and caught hold of the iron bars that ran around it for a second

or two, but the nausea was overwhelming and I started slip-
ping to the floor, automatically hunching myself into the fetal
position as I came into contact with the concrete. My ears
started ringing, and grey blotches were floating in front of my
eyes, so I took to slapping myself in the face to stave off uncon-
sciousness.

'Four hours,' I said aloud, partly to remind myself of the
deadline, partly just to get my body and brain back on speaking
terms. It was down to the wire now, and I couldn't afford to
lose another minute. I couldn't wake up with the Prime Minister
dead and Anna having fled the country, never to be seen again.
Which would be worse, I wondered: Nigeria becoming a Soviet
state, or the Biafrans continuing to be slaughtered in a war
they could never win? Wilson dead or alive?

'Four hours.'

Akuji. You need to find him, make sure he's out, get his
gun. You need Akuji's gun to get through this, so turn now,
turn to your right . . .

If I'd had any voice then, I'd have screamed. I was practic-
ally on top of him: his eyes lolled obscenely, and blood was
leaking from his mouth. He was out, all right, and would be
for a while.

On his wrist was a slim gold watch: some fancy Swiss make.
I managed to reach out and unclasp it and held it in my palm,
staring at the second hand as it slowly made its way around
a smaller circle set within the dial. When it gets to the top,
I told myself, you must straighten your legs. I breathed in as
deeply as I could, and the ringing slowly began to subside.

The room was completely silent and I couldn't remember hearing anything since the thud of Akuji's landing, so I lifted the watch to my ear and was rewarded with a faint *tick-tick tick-tick tick-tick* . . . Another wave of nausea swept over me, and I longed to find a bathroom and shit all the bad stuff out of my system. In the shapes behind my eyelids, I suddenly saw the rat from the bathroom sink of the Palace Hotel tunnelling towards me, its claws outstretched, and the landscape it was tunnelling through was my bowels. I looked back down at the circle in the dial and saw that there were five seconds, four, three, two, move now, move your legs, and there we were, rest. Rest. Breathe. Now look at the dial again. Through the rat. Ignore the rat, look past him, there, at the hand inside the circle, concentrate on the shape of it, yet another circle at the bottom, so many circles, but this one is like a pivot, and then the arrow of the hand through it, sweeping slowly around the soft gold field. Now follow that, yes, there we are, no ignore that, ignore that feeling, just keep watching, coming down, coming down, there, now it's going up, focus, focus, not long to go, fifteen, smooth sweep, thirteen, twelve, coming up, are you ready, get ready to move your knees, now, now, shift your knees up and move your feet, both of them, a bit more, there you are, there! You're sitting. Now you are sitting. Breathe slowly, not too much at a time, and take in your surroundings.

My heart jolted as I saw the rat scuttling across the floor. So I hadn't imagined it? It was a large, dirty-looking brute with yellowish eyes and a bright red tail breaking through the coarse brown hair. It scampered over the mountain of Akuji's body, past me and over to the other side of the room.

I watched the rat, following its movements obsessively, like a seasick passenger watching the waves. It placed me in the room and it made it easier to regulate my breathing and to hold the nausea at bay.

I gave myself a threshold of ten minutes' rat-watching time — any less and I'd be out cold again, any more and I'd be whistling down the seconds until her finger squeezed the trigger and it was all over. After seven and a half minutes the rat scuttled under a bed in the corner and started biting at a dirty piece of gauze, and I felt ready.

I leaned over and gently prised the gun from Akuji's hands. It was a version of the Tokarev: unmarked, but possibly Chinese, by the look of the barrel lug. China was supporting the Biafrans, so that made some sense. I checked the pistol — fully loaded — and placed it in my waistband. Finally, my lesson from Pritchard from all those years ago in a clearing outside Frankfurt: pockets. They had nothing in them but the packet of Three Fives in his jacket, which I decided to take. I slid a cigarette out and lit it. The nicotine burned my lungs and brought some fire back into my head.

After I'd taken a few drags, I grabbed hold of the table Akuji had crashed into for leverage and pulled myself to my feet. Several bottles had been smashed and thick sharp-smelling liquids were flowing into each other across the metal tray. Taking care not to touch any of the broken glass or liquid, I examined the small bottles, turning the tops of them with my fingers so I could read the labels. Most had trade names I didn't recognize, but one I did. In bold black letters was a word that might save me: Benzedrine.

The small type on the bottle said it was 'fast-acting': I timed it as seven minutes before the tablet started to take effect. In that time, I found a white coat on one of the beds and put it on, and I was in the middle of ripping a sheet into strips so I could tie Akuji's hands together when the fatigue lifted and my senses came alive and I heard the footstep at the top of the stairs.

★

'Is he dead?' said the man in the mask as he surveyed the scene: Akuji on the ground and a half-crazed British spy shaking a pistol at him.

I took the cigarette from my mouth to answer, and promptly threw up all over my trouser-leg. There was blood in the vomit, and the man responded to his professional instincts and stepped forward. I waved the pistol at him and grunted threateningly, and he got the message and stopped, and I sorted out my throat and used some of Akuji's uniform to wipe off the stuff and then looked back at him again through stinging eyes, took another drag and tried again: 'He's just out of action for a while,' I said.

The doctor nodded. 'Please get back into bed now,' he said. I had to admire his sangfroid.

'How far is it to Udi?'

'We have all the facilities you need here . . .'

'I need to get to Udi now!' I said, banging my hand against the bed and making the bottles rattle on the shelves.

It must have come out stronger than it had in my head, because his eyes were wide now, through the slits.

'Please calm yourself,' he said. Then, slowly, reaching for the right words to pacify me: 'What medication have you taken?'

'A tablet of Benzedrine you had lying about.'

The white mask stared back at me.

'You are joking, I hope?'

'No,' I said, 'I'm not joking. Because in' — I checked Akuji's Longines — 'around three hours and forty-five minutes' time, something very bad is going to happen in Udi, and I need to be there to stop it. I need to be alert until then. After that—'

'After that you may die,' he said. 'There's no telling what Benzedrine could do to your system right now. And please put the gun away — soldiers threaten us all the time, and we're accustomed to standing our ground. You can threaten me all you want, but I can't let you leave here. It's just not safe.'

I started laughing then. 'Safe?' I spat at him. 'Half an hour ago you told me I might have caught this disease from rat shit, and there are rats in *here*, for Christ's sake!'

'I know. Unfortunately, they were here when we arrived. They were attracted by the smell of amputated limbs. But I didn't mean safe for you — I meant for everyone else. Your condition is probably highly contagious.'

'Yes,' I said. 'I didn't think you just liked masks.'

I walked towards him and pulled it down. A neat beard failed to hide that he was barely out of his teens.

'What's your name?' I asked.

'David.'

'David what?'

'David Kanu.'

'Born here and educated in the States, I presume? Wanted to come back to help out?'

He nodded. A trickle of sweat travelled down his left cheek.

'Can you drive, David? Do you have access to a car?'

'Why?'

I gestured to the body lying on the bed. 'Do you know this man?'

'No,' he said. 'He turned up in his car and asked if I had a British patient here. I said I had and he—'

'I mean do you know who he is?'

'Yes, of course.'

I waited for him.

'Colonel Ojukwu. The head of the Biafran army.'

'Wrong,' I said. 'He's an impersonator, name of Akuji. And, like me, he's a British agent. How far are we from Udi?'

'Sixty or seventy miles.'

'Right. Well, sixty or seventy miles from here, in a very short time, someone is going to try to kill the British prime minister. Do you understand?'

'We have a telephone,' he said. 'You could call your embassy.'

'They already know about it. But they might not get there in time.'

283

'You can't leave,' he said firmly. 'You might cause an epidemic. I can phone someone at the clinic in Udi. I have some connections with the American government.'

'Do you, now?' I said. 'That's interesting. But no, thank you. As for an epidemic, I may not be fit to pass a company medical but I'm not about to die either, and if I understood our conversation earlier the other people who caught the disease you think I have *did* die, and very quickly.'

'You've taken medication—'

'I've taken a tablet of amphetamine, which you've just told me should make me even more ill. So how is it that I am standing here talking to you about all the rats there are going to be scuttling around here if you don't help me?'

'What do you mean?'

'If the Prime Minister is killed,' I said, 'his replacement may decide to start providing arms to the Biafrans instead of the Nigerians.'

'Good for them,' he said, folding his arms.

'I thought the Red Cross were meant to be neutral.'

'We are,' he said, clenching his jaw. 'As much as it's possible to be.'

'I see,' I said. 'But it's not as simple as that. Strengthening the Biafrans may simply mean that neither side will be able to deliver the knockout blow. The war could last months, perhaps even years longer. In which case, you'll be treating a lot more amputees, and the rats will be the only ones happy about it.'

He considered this, and I tried to ignore the ticking of Akuji's watch.

'From what I hear,' he said, 'this war is very unpopular in Britain. If there is a new government, it might decide not to supply either side with arms, and that could lead to a cease-fire coming sooner rather than later.'

It was the same argument I had used on both Pritchard and Akuji, and the one I personally thought was the most likely to happen. I made a note that David Kanu was not as green as he appeared, and tried again.

'That may be the case,' I said. 'But I wouldn't like to have it on my conscience if it weren't.'

'You don't strike me as a man whose conscience often troubles him.'

'Perhaps not,' I said. 'But I think yours does. So, David, do you want to be kept awake at night because you have helped prolong the bloodshed among your fellow men or do you want to give me a lift and save a respected world leader from being murdered in cold blood by the Russians?'

He stared at me with hatred in his eyes, and I knew I had him.

XXII

Friday, 28 March 1969, Biafra, 11.30 a.m.

Emerging above ground, my eyeballs throbbed as they adjusted
to the glare of the sun. We were in a small clearing surrounded
by dense forest, deserted except for two vehicles: a dirt-
spattered Land Rover with a large red cross on its side and a
white Mercedes estate in which were seated several heavily
armed soldiers, all of whom were watching us keenly.

'Akuji's men?'

David nodded.

I got him to hand over the keys to the Land Rover and told
him to wait for me.

There were six of them, all seated in varying postures designed
to intimidate, all in crisp uniforms with the Biafran sun on their
shirtsleeves and berets sitting on their heads at the correct angle.

'Hello,' I said. 'I'm Doctor Foster.'

'Where is the Colonel?' said one of the men, his thumb toying
with the trigger of his machine gun.

'He's still downstairs,' I said. 'He wants to talk to the patient some more. Doctor Kanu and I are needed elsewhere, so he asked me to tell you to wait here for him.'

A few of the men sighed or rolled their eyes.

'I'm sorry,' I said. 'He should be up in about half an hour.'

David had told me that all the patients below ground had been moved to another clinic on my arrival. But they didn't know that, and I reckoned it would be at least another hour before they ventured downstairs to check up on Akuji. I turned to walk away.

'Doctor Foster!' one of them called out. I turned to face him and smiled through clenched teeth. 'Are you from Gloucester?' he asked.

A couple of the others broke into laughter, no doubt remembering the rhyme from childhood. Careless, Dark: you may be in the middle of the bush, but it's also a former British colony. If you're going to make this cover work, you're going to have to use your head a bit more.

I smiled wearily. 'Very funny,' I said. 'I've never heard that one before.'

Their cackles followed me back to the Land Rover. David was already behind the wheel, so I climbed in and handed him the key. As he started the ignition, he gestured at a small plastic container on the dashboard, which looked to be filled with yellow mush.

'*Garri*,' he said. 'Crushed cassava.'

I told him I wasn't hungry.

'That's because Benzedrine suppresses the appetite. But your body needs this. Eat.'

I did as I was told. The taste was coarse and bitter, but I was soon using my fingers to scoop out the last of it. When there was none left, I laid my head against the window and watched the landscape judder by.

I still had no idea why Akuji had been impersonating Ojukwu, but with an armed guard and a swish car, it seemed he had some pretty powerful backing. I had told both him and David that the PM's death would lead to Britain switching allegiance in this war, but that was because I thought it would persuade them to help me. I wasn't sure what the game was. Pritchard was still nagging at me: what was the message he had wanted to pass to Akuji?

I turned my head and was startled to see a man staring back at me from the road: sunken eyes, a few days' beard and a bloodstained white coat. It took me a fraction of a moment to recognize myself in the wing mirror, which was hanging at an odd angle. I felt light-headed and exhausted, but I couldn't sleep, not now. I caught David glancing at me, and I lifted my gun fractionally and met his gaze. He looked away and pushed his foot down.

*

Within twenty minutes of leaving the clinic we reached our first checkpoint. It was a distinctly unofficial-looking one, consisting of a gang of youths in unidentifiable uniforms and a few cleverly positioned oil drums. I had hoped that the large red cross painted across the side of our vehicle might speed us through such situations, but they signalled us to stop nevertheless, and I quickly slipped the gun into my waistband and covered it with my shirt. David pretended to brush some mosquitoes from the windscreen and in the same gesture brushed the *garri* container to the floor. 'They're looking for food,' he said. Sure enough, as we came to a standstill the group immediately headed towards the back of the Land Rover to investigate our cargo. Without turning my head, I tried to calculate the odds of survival if I had to make a run for it, but presumably there were no edible supplies under the tarpaulin because they quickly sauntered back and waved us through with their sticks and machetes. We passed two more similar checkpoints before reaching our first back in Federal-occupied territory, but apart from flicking through David's identity papers, which the boy held upside down, they were no more interested in us.

I was nevertheless getting anxious. I had to be there by half past two at the latest; it was now twenty to, so I asked David for an estimate of how far away we were. He pointed ahead, and as the haze lifted, I saw the concrete barriers, machine guns and ring of barbed wire reinforcing a solid perimeter fence.

'We're there,' he said.

Udi.

*

'Can I help you?' said the man in the uniform of the British military police, but his tone of voice suggested he couldn't.

'We're from the clinic over in Awo Omamma,' I said cheerfully. 'We were asked to bring over some supplies.'

The Benzedrine was really kicking in now: every pore on the Snowdrop's face was in focus and my fatigue had miraculously vanished.

He stepped back from the window and took a small notepad from his belt.

'Name?'

My stomach tightened, and a fresh supply of sweat broke across my neck and back.

'We probably won't be on there,' I said, lowering my voice. 'Has Pritchard arrived yet? I'm with his group.'

He looked at me.

'And you are . . .?'

'Paul Dark. Government liaison.'

He frowned, and I knew why. Never change your story. I had started by saying I was with the Red Cross, before suddenly claiming to be a British government agent. I'd had to, because he had a list of authorized personnel and I wasn't on it and I didn't have time for the inevitable runaround that path would have led to: Snowdrop disappearing to fetch someone higher up the chain, bluster about phone calls received from people whose names I couldn't quite remember, and so on. No choice but to switch horses quickly and hope that the hint of top-secret hooha carried enough authority to sway him – and that Pritchard was curious enough to come out and get me, despite apparently warning every soldier in the country to lock me up on sight. I cursed myself for letting the local roadblocks lull me into complacency. The British prime minister was visiting – of *course* they would have something professional in place.

'Can't say I know of anyone by that name, sir,' said Snowdrop, and put his pad away. 'I'm afraid I cannot allow you to come through here—'

'Oh for Christ's sake, stop mucking me around!' I said. 'It's vitally important I get through before the PM arrives. Find Henry Pritchard and tell him . . .'

I trailed off. A man with a jovial red face and a Saint George bow tie had made his way through the checkpoint and was striding towards us.

*

'Gosh — you have been in the wars, haven't you? So to speak.' He chuckled into his chins.

'Yes,' I said. 'I've caught some rare new disease, apparently.'

His eyes widened. 'Contagious?'

'Could be.'

He wiped his brow with a dirty-looking handkerchief. 'Best keep out of your way, then!' He squinted into the sun, which was almost directly above us. 'Mad dogs and Englishmen, eh?'

David had gone off with Snowdrop to park the Land Rover, and Manning was leading me through the compound's main courtyard. All the usual pageantry and pomp of a state visit had been rolled out: Union Jacks hung from every available flagpole and a banner welcomed the British prime minister in foot-high letters above the main gate. Shirtsleeved photographers circled each other trying to find innovative angles to shoot it, while doctors in spotless white coats muttered abstractedly to journalists as they glanced anxiously at the wards that wrapped around the place like a quad.

It was easy to take the scene for granted, but I knew it could all change in an instant. I mentally replaced the Union Jacks with Hammer and Sickles and the black Rovers with Ziks: one squeeze of a trigger and that could be the next state visit this place saw. So where could she be? The wards were very low-ceilinged, but there were three floors, so it wasn't possible to see into them all. Especially the corners . . . Manning was babbling something next to me, and I interrupted to ask him if he had heard from Pritchard yet.

'Yes, he arrived with Smale a few hours ago.'

'Smale? What's that little prick doing here?'

Manning looked offended. 'I thought he was rather a nice chap, actually. He's over there.' He pointed to a group of whey-faced men in suits standing by an armoured car at the other end of the courtyard. One of them seemed vaguely familiar, and I asked Manning who he was.

'Sandy Montcrieff,' he said. 'You met him at the Yacht Club, remember?'

I remembered: the ghostly figure in the nightshirt. Ex-BBC *Mirror* man.

'What's he doing here?' I asked. 'And Smale?'

'They're both with the PM's advance party. Making sure of security with Henry.'

'And where's he?'

'Oh, Christ knows. Last time I saw him he was about to head off to check the wards. Lord knows why he's so anxious: I'd have thought he'd have been used to this sort of thing, what with his connections.'

I stopped walking. 'What connections?' It sounded odd coming from Geoffrey: he was also a spook.

Manning turned to me, his piggy little eyes looking a little forlorn. 'Well, you know . . .'

'No, I don't know. Tell me: it could be important.'

'Ah,' said Manning. 'Did I not mention that Henry is Marjorie's brother?'

'No,' I said. 'You didn't.' It explained how the old fool was still working, though. 'So Henry is an aristocrat, is that it?'

'Well, yes — but not just any old Scottish aristocracy, old boy! They're second cousins to the Queen. I just thought with the number of state functions Henry's been to, he must be used to—'

I didn't hear the rest. I had already started running in the direction of the wards.

XXIII

'Hello, Henry,' I said. The sweat was pouring off my right hand, the one clutching the pistol.

Pritchard turned and smiled at me. *Actually smiled.*

'Paul,' he said. 'I wondered when you might turn up.' He looked back at the window. As I had suspected, it was one of the corner rooms. 'Game's up, is it?'

'I'm afraid so.'

'"No sudden movements?"'

'That's the drill.'

It was dark in here: it seemed to be some sort of office-cum-storeroom, with filing cabinets and shelves of medical supplies. I mustered all the concentration I could to follow his arm as he dropped to his knees and placed the rifle on the floor.

'When did you find out?' said Pritchard, standing again, still affecting the absurdly casual tone, as though I'd walked in on him searching my drawers or reading my diary rather than preparing to shoot the prime minister.

'Just now,' I replied. 'Manning mentioned you were related to the Queen, and I wondered why I'd never heard that before. Where's Anna?'

Pritchard looked at me for a moment, then tipped his head back and gave a slightly deranged laugh. 'Oh, Paul!' he said when he'd managed to pull himself together. 'I thought you'd got a little further than that.' He adjusted his spectacles primly. 'Anna's dead.'

Something broke inside me. I don't know why, as it was what I had believed for nearly twenty-five years. But I had wanted to see her, just one more time. To hear her voice, just one more time.

'The photograph,' I said with the part of my brain that wanted all the details accounted for. 'In the marketplace . . .'

'Faked,' said Pritchard. 'Rather a good job, considering the time we had to put it together.'

'So Geoffrey is working for you?'

'Sometimes,' he said. 'He's not aware of the full ramifications, one might say.'

'Did you kill her?'

He dipped his head. 'In '45? No, that was also faked. Sorry, old boy. Anna changed her name and moved to Tunisia, where she died in '57. Lung cancer. Those unfiltered cigarettes she liked, do you remember?'

I remembered. 'So you and she . . .?'

He nodded. 'Always. Yes, I was her one true love.' He saw the look on my face. 'You're lost, I know. I have a lot I need to tell you.'

I leaned against the wall. 'You can start with this' – I gestured at the rifle. 'Why kill Wilson? And why send a plant to London?'

He shook his head. 'I didn't send Slavin. Do you think I'd have given him my code-name?'

'What then?'

'Think, Paul. I'm no sniper – the chap you strangled on the golf course was meant to do the job. So why did I fly out here?'

'To protect yourself,' I guessed. 'To make sure Slavin didn't have anything else that could point to you being Radnya.' But even as I said it I knew I was wrong.

'To protect *us*,' he said.

So he knew about me. All right. Let that sink in for a moment.

'Slavin didn't know the double's name,' I said. 'So that meant either one of us could be blown.'

The corners of his mouth twitched. 'Well, you certainly seemed worried about the possibility. I must say I wasn't expecting you to kill poor old Chief. That's made life rather tricky for us, I think.'

'I had to,' I said, then stopped. I wasn't going to justify myself to Pritchard. 'So . . . Slavin was a genuine defector.'

Pritchard shook his head slowly from side to side.

'But why would Moscow want to expose a long-running double agent?' I asked. 'Possibly even two.'

'Moscow's a large city,' he said. My skin was prickling, but I didn't yet know why. 'Whom do we work for?' said Pritchard, and his pale blue eyes searched my face for a reaction. I realized that although he knew it was the end of the road, he was enjoying revealing the plot to me, like a conjuror finally able to show his audience how clever he had been. 'It's a simple enough question,' he said. 'Whom do we work for?'

'The KGB,' I replied, and winced; it sounded so childish suddenly, so cops and robbers.

'No, Paul,' said Pritchard. 'We don't. When Anna recruited me, it was into *Glavnoe Razvedyvatel'noe Upravlenie*: military intelligence. She had been persuaded of my good intentions by another of her agents – your father.'

He was lying. He had to be lying.

I knew he wasn't lying.

A dozen images flew through my head, but above them all I could see my father's body sprawled across the bed at the farmhouse, one half of his head a ruin.

'Did you . . .' My mouth was sewn up. 'Did you kill him?'

'But it was I who persuaded Anna to recruit you,' Pritchard went on, as though I hadn't spoken. 'Larry hated the idea – he felt you were too young. He always said that successful recruitment depended on the subject having a firm ideology. I thought you were at precisely the right age to foster that. I proposed we give you the ideology – through Anna.'

It was like listening to some macabre joke. The man whose views he was blithely referring to was unrecognizable to me – and yet, recognizable, too.

'Larry still wasn't satisfied,' said Pritchard. 'He desperately didn't want you spoiled by betrayal, as he felt he had been. He didn't want that life for you. In the end, he had no choice, though: Moscow demanded it. And Larry always obeyed Moscow. I never left for Gaggenau, of course – I was with Anna then. We knew it was only a matter of time before you were injured in one way or other. That cut you got wasn't much more than a scratch, really. Anna made certain you were isolated, and took care of your treatment. And you walked right into it, of course. Who wouldn't? She was young, beautiful, good in bed . . .'

I ran towards him then and hit him, smashing my fist into his mouth. He barely even flinched, just dipped his head a little, and I slouched to my knees, my hands falling uselessly into my stomach, where I clutched myself as though I were the one who had been hit.

I tried to stand up, failed, tried again. 'Finish the story,' I said, steadying myself by leaning against the wall.

Pritchard wiped the blood from his lip and smiled at me mock-affectionately. 'You always were too emotional,' he said. 'But the problem was you were stubborn, too – you refused to be swayed. You had your precious principles. So we came up with the idea of Anna's death, and that did the trick, finally, didn't it? You ran into our arms. Anna was taken out of the country. Larry . . . well, Larry didn't take it well. He could never really handle the hard decisions. He was weak.'

So well-spoken, this Scottish aristocrat. It was hard to believe that monsters dwelt inside him.

'So you killed him.'

He looked genuinely surprised. 'No, no. When he received your note about Anna, he immediately ran to his old friend Colin Templeton in Lübeck and asked him to take her away from the scene. But Chief and his men were too slow. When the soldiers brought Anna back to the safe house in her coma-tose state, Larry saw that he had failed and went, quite literally, mad. Said he couldn't live with the choice between betraying you or Moscow, so he was going to take the only way out he knew. He already had the gun — there was nothing I could do.'

He could have been lying — I was pointing a gun at him, after all, and confessing to killing Father might make me pull the trigger more readily. But somehow I knew he was telling the truth.

'And Churchill authorizing the mission personally — all a complete hoax.' I laughed at my own naivety.

'Yes — we were working to Beria's orders, in fact. All those men were traitors to the Soviet Union.'

'It's 1969,' I said. 'Tell me you don't still believe in all this.'

'Yes,' he said simply. 'I've always been a believer, ever since I read Marx at school. I'm still a believer, even with all this.'

'All what?'

'After the war, the foreign intelligence arms of the GRU and the Ministry for State Security merged. The new organization was called *Komitet Informatsii* — the Committee of Information.'

I nodded dumbly. KI. I knew it from a hundred dossiers: Molotov had been appointed chairman. 'It didn't last long,' I said.

'Indeed not. A couple of years later it was wound up and the GRU was once again an independent intelligence agency. So, what can we deduce?'

'That while the two organizations were merged, someone found out about you.'

'Bravo, that man! Yes, someone discovered that the GRU had recruited a British agent in Germany at the end of the war and given him the code-name Radnya. They didn't have my real name, but it was enough. They stored away this information – perhaps they had an inkling that the KI wouldn't last long. Then, a couple of decades later, as this same fellow sat at the head of some nasty little division of the KGB, he decided that Radnya would make the perfect ingredient for a grand plot against his counterparts in London.'

So I had been right about Slavin being a plant – albeit a very unusual one. Plants had to have a few secrets to hand over or nobody would believe they were genuine defectors. But that information couldn't be too valuable, or it would defeat the purpose. So you gave them lots of pieces of genuine but not very important information that you knew or suspected the other side already had. Barium, we called it: chicken-feed. But it had got trickier. With the paranoia over plants, all would-be defectors had come under pressure to produce much more than barium. The KGB officer handling Slavin had calculated that the details about a double being recruited in the British Zone in 1945 would be enough for the Service to unmask Radnya's identity on their own steam, thereby cementing Slavin's credentials and simultaneously sinking the British into a morass of recriminations over yet another traitor in their ranks. Slavin would then have been able to concoct the most outrageous untruths and have everyone hanging on his every word. At the same time, a body blow would have been dealt to the KGB's old rivals, the GRU, who wouldn't have known what had hit them.

It was a brilliant ploy. The only problem with it had been
... me. The KGB hadn't known that the GRU had, in fact,
recruited *two* British double agents in the same part of Germany
at the end of the war, and that both of them – the Russian
practice being not to tell agents their own code-names – would
presume they were under threat of imminent exposure.

'Where does the PM come into this?' I asked.

'Ah, that,' said Pritchard, making it sound like a trifling
affair. 'It's a long story.'

'We have time,' I said.

He smiled. I didn't like the smile, and it set alarm bells off
in my head.

'Anna's here, isn't she?'

'No, Paul. Please let go of that idea. I told you: Anna died a
long time ago.'

I could sense a false note somewhere. The eyes. His eyes
didn't move – they were fixed on me. Because he was fighting
the urge to look elsewhere. The window? Was it my imagination or was there some noise coming from that direction?
What was it – cheering?

I glanced down at my watch. I managed to register that it
was twenty-five past before I picked up the movement in my
peripheral vision and looked back up to see Pritchard leaping
towards me, his hands outstretched like claws. I pulled the
trigger without even willing it to happen, and watched as
the bullet ripped through his jacket and forced him back
onto the floor.

'Where is she?' I screamed. 'Which corner?'

He whispered a word, and then was silent. His voice had been hoarse, and the word hadn't come out clearly, but I knew what it was instantly: 'Pockets,' he had said.

I searched them, and then headed downstairs and into the courtyard. A long black car was slowly approaching the gates, and somewhere above me was Anna with one eye glued to her sniper sight, waiting for it.

XXIV

The courtyard was packed and noisy, with the crowd jostling against the ropes to catch a glimpse of the car that was now edging through the gates one yard at a time, presumably so the PM could wave at everyone. One of the Snowdrops saw me and started racing over, so I dropped back to a brisk walk and made as though I were calling out to someone on the other side of the ropes. Manning had also spotted me and was heading in my direction, but I was just a few yards away from the next corner, and yes, there was the staircase. I took the steps three at a time, my ears hot and pulsing and my chest constricting. Then I was on the landing.

I took out the Tokarev and uncocked the safety. As there had been with the other staircases, two large open wards faced each other. All the patients who could move had thronged into the one facing the courtyard and were gathered around the windows peering down. All but one, a young boy with an artificial leg, who was leaning against the wall, watching me with large eyes. I had a sudden memory of a German boy of about the same age who had once looked at me like that, a lifetime ago.

At the far end of the landing was a door. If this staircase followed the pattern of the others, which it seemed to, it should lead me to a storage-room-cum-office. This was the door I'd travelled thousands of miles to open: behind it, almost certainly, lay the answers I was looking for. I grabbed the handle.

Locked.

I smashed my foot into the lower half of the door. A couple of splinters flew up, and after a couple more kicks the whole thing fell in.

The gun was the first thing I saw, a dark snake pointing out at me, the barrel gleaming. Then the figure in white behind it.

'Drop your weapon!' she hissed, and there was such danger in her voice that I immediately leaned down and placed my pistol on the floor, then kicked it towards her.

She picked it up and pocketed it, then backed away from me to the window. Thin bars of sunlight glowed through the shutters but much of the room was in darkness and it took my eyes a moment to decipher some of the objects. A mop and bucket leaned against one corner, a duffel bag on the floor nearby. On the window sill, a tripod had been mounted. It wasn't until she started placing the rifle onto this that I got a good look at her.

She had changed. There was still the dark soulfulness in her eyes, the wide jaw, the wave of hair swept back. But the mouth that had been full and sensual was now thin and hard, and her skin was also somehow different: still bronzed, but now a little leathery. Perhaps Pritchard hadn't been lying about her having lived in Tunisia. She turned to look at me then, and it was almost as if her skin tautened under my gaze, until, like the surface of a painting being scratched away, the ghost portrait that had been hiding beneath was revealed.

It was her. Nearly twenty-five years after I had last seen her, here she was again, still in a nurse's uniform, and this time she was clutching a sniper rifle. I looked back at the duffel bag and saw the small white cap with a red cross on it peeking out of the top. It was just like the one I'd seen at the Afrospot. Or close enough: I noticed that the thread was slightly the wrong shade, and guessed she had taken the outfit from one of the Nigerian clinics and adapted it.

'Hello, Paul,' she said, and then she turned from me and lowered herself into position, crouching down on one knee and screwing her eye into the rifle sight.

*

I closed my eyes and swallowed the vomit that had risen in the back of my throat.

'I thought you were dead,' I said.

'You were wrong.'

I laughed involuntarily, though it came out more as a whimper. 'I was . . . Is that . . .' My breathing failed again and my legs nearly gave out from under me. Come on, get the words out! 'Is that the best you can come up with?' I said. '*I was wrong?*'

'We can discuss this later. Did you see Henry?'

I didn't say anything, mainly because my right thigh was jerking and I was trying to keep it under control with my arms, but she misinterpreted the silence.

'Did you see him, Paul?'

Her voice had a coldness that cut right through me. Even with everything that was happening, something told me not to let her know he was dead, and I shook my head, then answered, 'No' aloud when I realized that she still wasn't looking at me, but remained fixed in her position at the window. *With them that walk against me, is my sun.* Only she wasn't walking: she was staying put, waiting for the PM.

'Don't tell me you still intend to go through with this,' I said. She didn't reply, just kept on looking through the sight. I wanted to lunge across the room and rip her away from it, force her to stand and face me and answer me. But I was too weak, so instead I just stood there, clutching my leg uselessly. More seconds passed. What was going on down there? Had the car stopped?

There was too much flooding through me, and I couldn't slow it down or order it.

'How did you do it?' I asked, finally. 'Make-up and something to stop your pulse?' I had no idea what part of my mind had come up with the question, but another part approved. Keep her talking, get some answers, distract her. Distract yourself.

'Yes,' she said. 'Something like that. I was one of the first — they have done it many times since.'

'*Why*, Anna?' Here was the question. Here, finally, was the question I had wanted her to answer.

She didn't say anything for a while, and I wondered if she had heard me. Then she answered. 'Love,' she said simply. 'Love of my cause.' She lifted her head a fraction and glanced across at me, and the Anna I had known all those years ago receded once again. I searched her face desperately for the glimpse I'd had just moments before, but it was no use. 'I am sorry I hurt you,' she said, still talking in the same calm slow way. 'I didn't want to. But I knew you were one of us the first time I saw you. I could sense that you wanted to do good, that you would be a strong soldier for us. Are you still a strong soldier for us, Paul? Can you keep fighting a little longer for me?'

The anger welled in my stomach. *Did she think I was a bloody child?* My legs started to spasm, and I fought back the dizziness. Please don't let me lose my hearing now! I closed my eyes for a moment and tried to find some stillness and regulate my breathing, but all I could see were dozens of tiny bursts of light, darting here and there, trying to make connections with each other. I placed a hand behind me and let myself slump slowly to the floor, leaning my head against the jamb. It was more comfortable here and, after all, it was where I belonged. How did the next line run? *The wheel is turned*, that was it: '*The wheel is turn'd; I hold the lowest place*'.

'I have paid a price, too,' Anna was saying, and I woke from my dreams of poetry in a distant classroom and strained my ears to make sure I heard her right. I wanted to catch every word of this extraordinary confession, wanted very much to know how she had paid a price for betraying me. 'I have sacrificed my career and a good part of my life to protect you,' she said. 'Because if anyone ever found out I was alive, that might have exposed you.'

Ah, well: that wasn't bad. One had to admit that that wasn't bad. So that was why she hadn't shot me yet – because of my value as an agent?

'But Slavin found out,' I said.

'Yes, that was unfortunate. Vladimir Mikhailovich had been out here too long – he was lonely. He became obsessed with me. I told him there was someone else. That was a mistake. I have spent much of my time away from Lagos in recent weeks, and on one occasion he must have broken into my quarters and found some letters I had never sent Henry. I had kept them – a weakness. I suppose he sent photographs of them to Moscow and someone in the KGB realized who I was. But he's gone now.' She smiled tersely. 'Nobody knows.'

'You're still a believer, then?' I said. A phrase she had often used in Germany came back to me. 'In the brotherhood of man?'

Her mouth tightened. 'Of course. Why not?'

I clawed my way up to a sitting position, but she heard me and lifted the rifle an inch so I stopped and she replaced it again.

'I don't know,' I said, as though nothing had happened. 'The gulags, the mock trials, the tanks in the streets? The use of assassination to sustain a civil war in Africa until you can install a puppet leader to further your own aims?'

The car must have stopped because she moved her eye away from the sight and turned to look at me. 'Henry warned me you might have lost your nerve,' she said. 'I didn't believe him. You've worked for us for over twenty years, Paul.'

'Based on what, though?' I said.

She went back to her previous position.

'I never lied to you about the big things. And you're hardly in a position to lecture me about sustaining a civil war. Your government—'

'My government. Not me.'

'So whose side are you on then?' she said, and the false politeness vanished for a moment.

'My own,' I said.

'I see. Just a neutral bystander, condemning everyone else from your position of complete superiority . . . and inactivity?'

'You're all as bad as each other,' I said. 'I refuse to take sides any longer.'

'But you must, Paul! Don't you see? You must! There's no room for sitting on the fence in this world. One side will win, and it will change how millions of people live. You have to take sides, and act on your beliefs. And I believe we will help this country.'

There was a mad glare in her eyes. I didn't want to hear how killing the PM was going to help – no doubt she had her answers. She'd always been good with the abstracts. 'So that's it?' I said. 'The cause above all, and screw anyone who gets in the way?' I forced myself onto my feet and began trudging across the room towards her. She didn't even flinch.

'What's to stop me from killing you?' I asked.

She looked up, surprised, then calmly put her eye back to the sight as though I were a child.

'Because you loved me,' she said. 'Perhaps you still do, in some way. I am what *you* have believed in for most of your life, and you can't destroy me. You will watch me finish this and then you will leave here, and we will never speak again. You will continue your work in London with Sasha.'

'No!' I said. 'I won't be—'

There was a sudden lift in the noise of the crowd outside.

'Here's the test, Paul,' she said. 'Here it is now. Which side will you take?'

I lunged forward, hitting her in the back. My pistol clattered onto the floor, out of reach, and Anna turned and lashed out at me, scratching at my face, but I managed to hook my arm around her right shoulder and brought her weight back and slipped the other arm around her neck and squeezed as hard as I could, trying to block out the pain, the sounds, everything. My hands were tingling and I looked down and saw that blood was flowing from the palms and I saw her face, her eyes fixed open, no drugs now, no clever injections, and I kept squeezing her even though I knew it was too late, because I could still hear the echo of the shot, and then I thought a flock of seagulls swept over the courtyard, but it wasn't seagulls, of course, it was humans, screaming. What a strange sound, I thought.

I looked down. I could see everything perfectly – the black car surrounded by a swarm of people, their shadows making everything seem to lean to one side: the black man in the peaked cap kneeling beside the body of the white man in the summer suit whose head didn't seem to be there any more. I let go of Anna, and she slumped to the floor. Releasing her seemed to do something to my breathing, because I started heaving uncontrollably.

There was a scraping noise and I looked up to see a small crowd of people tumbling into the room. I registered Smale first, then David the doctor behind him, and finally Manning, lobster-red in his tropical suit, his handkerchief the size of a windsail fluttering above the scene. Smale slapped me and screamed something I couldn't understand, and when I didn't answer he started shaking me. I wanted to tell him it was useless, he was wasting his time, I didn't have long to go. 'Murder!' he was shouting, and I realized it was directed at me. 'I am arresting you for murder!' It seemed like the wrong thing to say and I started counting aloud, for some reason. There was a lot of movement, a lot of panic, but I was perfectly conscious of it all, right until the last moment, the last breath. I was watching it all, right up until I died.

XXV

Nobody tells you you're dead — you have to figure it out yourself. It took me rather a long time. In fact, it was the presence of time that held me back. At the start, the idea didn't even occur to me. I seemed to be surrounded by an endless grey landscape, but that didn't mean death, surely: I was simply unconscious.

Only I wasn't. I could vividly remember everything, right up until when Smale had shaken me and I had stopped breathing. But still, the fact that I was thinking meant I was alive: probably in a hospital somewhere, recovering.

I clung on to that idea for a very long time. I thought it must have been at least a few months since I'd 'gone' and ended up . . . wherever I was. That was when it occurred to me that perhaps death wasn't what I had always thought it would be, but that it was a limbo state in which you had all eternity to reflect on the life you'd had, without being able to return to it.

My considerations of death were briefly interrupted by a

series of extremely vivid hallucinations. One of these involved a tie I'd owned when I was a boy, a dark green silk tie with tiny red spots my father had bought me from Gieves when I'd turned sixteen, my last birthday in London before the war. The silk had been so thick and smooth it was like a river, and now it became just that and I dove deep into its comfort, luxuriating in its coolness and wishing I could stay there for ever, breathing bubbles up to the green, red-spotted surface. And then others started diving in after me, like the bodies in the ceremony I'd been at in Biafra, spirit bodies that cut through me and around me and seemed to keep diving further and further but never got any smaller or changed shape. And I wanted to climb up to the surface but I couldn't, because it was blocked by loose threads of silk, white and sticky, and I couldn't struggle past them and again I felt the weight on my chest and the trouble breathing, until I opened my eyes and saw a pair of disembodied eyes staring down at me from deep within a ball of white silk . . .

*

The lamps, though dimmed, had an unpleasant glare to them, and the walls a greenish tinge. I *was* in a hospital somewhere, but it was almost as bad as whatever I'd woken from. My food and drink were passed to me through a network of tubes, and I sat there, alone, imagining the fluid pumping into me and thinking back to what had happened, and what might happen next. I was in England, I knew, because the place smelled unmistakably of Dettol and every so often there was a hollow clanging, which I eventually realized was a radiator that was out of my line of sight.

I still couldn't move. There was a window, but like every-thing else it only changed from white to grey to black and back again. But I was in a hospital in England, recovering. Of that I was sure.

*

The disembodied eyes returned one day: now I saw they were attached to a man in a white coat, white gauze mask, white hood, white gloves. I couldn't speak to him, and he didn't say anything to me – just checked my tubes and wrote things down on a white pad. I thought that my hearing must have gone again at some point, because every sound was amplified. When he moved his foot on the linoleum, it was like a coin dropping in a well.

I no longer felt pain – physical pain, that is. I thought about Anna every day, every hour. And grieved for myself, and the life I'd wasted.

*

Another man came to see me after that, wearing the same garb. It was Smale.

'You survived,' he said. 'They didn't think you would.'

I watched his eyes. Narrow and slanted, they seemed to me to be the kind of eyes that would belong to a small ugly grey fish. I tried to imagine the face of such a fish, and fitted it behind his mask.

'You were extremely lucky,' said the fish. 'You were in a medical facility when it happened. You were out for a minute and a half – your heart even stopped beating. The wog doctor you came with declared you dead. But then you came to – almost as if you had heard us and weren't willing to go.'

The fish paused. 'Of course, a lot of people have been hoping you wouldn't make it.' He looked away contemplatively. 'Not me, though. We'd lose so much valuable information.' He pushed his chair back. 'Let's get your clothes sent up, shall we? We've an important meeting to get to.'

*

London looked exactly the same: office workers jumped around puddles and struggled with umbrellas. We sploshed through the streets in the black Bentley. I sat in the back in my old suit, my hands cuffed to two soldiers sitting either side of me. Smale was up in front. Near Piccadilly Circus Underground, we stopped at some lights and I glimpsed the headlines at a newspaper kiosk. 'THE PRIME MINISTER AND MOSCOW: LATEST REVE-LATIONS!' blared the poster for *The Times*, while *The Telegraph* had the more subdued: 'MOUNTBATTEN SUSPENDS ARMS TO NIGERIA'.

'Mountbatten?'

Smale turned back to look at me, his eyes dead. 'He formed a government a couple of weeks ago.'

I couldn't think what to say. 'Wilson wasn't KGB' was what eventually came out.

'Really?' Smale replied, with a smile soaked in aspic. 'Did you believe everything your handler told you?' Then he turned away again and told the driver to take a right at the next junction.

*

They blindfolded me soon after that, and about twenty minutes later I was bundled out of the car and marched down a steep stairway. The room was cold and there was a slightly dank smell. Pipes gurgled in the background. Someone took the blindfold off. The two soldiers turned on their heels and took up station outside the door; Smale pushed me inside.

It was a familiar scene, right down to the naked bulb hanging from a coat-hanger. Beneath it, three men were seated behind a large desk that looked as though it were made from a solid block of steel. Two of the men were no surprise: Farraday and Osborne. The man sitting between them gave me more food for thought: Sandy Montcrieff, the *Mirror* reporter I'd met at the Lagos Yacht Club, and whom I'd later seen with Smale at the clinic in Udi.

We were in the 'rubber room', a space reserved for the interrogation of suspected double agents and other such undesirables; I'd sat in on a couple of sessions here before, during the renewed round of vettings after Philby had made a run for it. This gave me an advantage, of course. The bulb was burning through my eyes, but I knew it was a trick: it had been especially made by a company in Vauxhall to burn that bright, and the things were a devil to get replaced. Apart from the lamp, desk, chairs and a plastic bucket filled with dirty-looking water on the floor, the room was unfurnished, so as to enhance the

316

subject's isolation and disorientation – but I knew that we were in the soundproofed basement of one of the smarter hotels in West Kensington.

Despite all of this, I was much more afraid than the poor souls I'd seen interviewed here before. Because I was guilty.

Osborne asked me to take a seat, which I did. The chair was cold and too low. I mentally stripped the three of them, visualizing Montcrieff's pale and bony legs, Osborne with his gut hanging over his belt and Farraday with unsightly moles across his back. It didn't help much.

'What's this about?' I said, selecting a tone somewhere between irritation and puzzlement. Might as well kick off proceedings. 'Are you holding me responsible for Wilson's death? I did everything I—'

'I'm sure you did,' said Montcrieff. 'Thankfully, it wasn't enough. But that's just between ourselves. If you don't tell us what we want to know, we'll announce that you were the assassin.'

The other two didn't flinch.

Montcrieff adjusted his cuffs and smiled innocently. 'What we want to know,' he went on, 'is how long you thought you could get away with playing us all for fools.'

'"Us"?' I said. 'Sorry, who the fuck are you again?' I turned to Osborne: 'William, I thought this was Service business.'

Osborne was stony-faced. 'Sandy's been with Five for years,' he said. 'And he was appointed Foreign Secretary two weeks ago.'

So. Not just a *Mirror* hack, then, but one of Cecil King's men

in Five, and these two – along with Pritchard – had been plotting with him from the beginning. It was a repeat of King's
coup attempt from last year, only this time the idea had been
to have Wilson assassinated and then exposed as a Russian agent
– and this time they had succeeded. Mountbatten was merely
the figurehead: these three and a handful of other right-wing
crackpots were in power now. No swastikas waving over The
Mall – just a few desks moved. I imagined Chief would have
been given the option of carrying on under the new regime
or being shunted into retirement.

'You know I didn't kill Wilson,' I said. 'The Grigorieva woman
pulled the trigger before I got to her.'

'We only have your word for that. According to Smale, you
were holding the gun when he came in.'

'And he's willing to testify to that, is he?'

Montcrieff laughed. 'I don't think you fully understand
the situation,' he said. 'We don't need to *try* you. The public
are distraught, and crying out for revenge. We could have
you hanged in Wembley stadium and sell tickets if we wanted.'
He leaned down and took a rolled-up *Standard* from a briefcase by his legs. He slapped it onto the table and pointed to
the headline: 'BRITAIN BACKS UNITY GOVERNMENT'. It was the
twenty-eighth of April, I noticed – exactly a month since
Udi.

'What do you want?' I asked, though I had a fair idea.

'We found Templeton's body,' said Osborne, referring to Chief
by his surname; presumably he had the title now. 'Washed up
near Limehouse.' He threw some photographs onto the desk.

I picked them up and forced myself to look at them. They were as grim as could be expected.

'Well?' I said. 'It's obvious, isn't it? Henry killed him.'

'And why would he do something like that?'

'Because he was Radnya, of course.'

'We also found this in the clinic in Udi,' said Osborne, making the recommended sudden leap of subject to disorient me. He placed the Tokarev on the table; it spun for a moment on the surface before coming to a stop. 'Do you usually favour Soviet weaponry?'

'That's not mine,' I said. 'It belonged to a man called Akuji.'

'Yes, we know about him – Henry's contact with Ojukwu. We received his report a few days ago. He has shown no signs of developing the disease you had, thankfully.' He nodded at the gun. 'So what do you normally use, then? Henry told us you shot someone on a golf course.'

'I didn't shoot him,' I said. 'He took a pill.'

Osborne turned down the corners of his mouth. 'What weapon do you use?'

They had me. They must have searched my flat, found the safe, cracked it open.

'A Luger P08,' I said. 'As I presume you already know.'

'Indeed,' said Farraday, and he took it out and placed it next to the Tokarev. 'Did you get a chit from Armoury for this? Because I wasn't aware we kept a stock of antique German pistols.'

I smiled tolerantly. 'You haven't brought me here for carrying a non-regulation weapon. Presumably you're about to tell me that Chief's bullet-wound is consistent with it being fired from this gun.'

'Bingo,' said Montcrieff.

'Most officers have their own weapons,' I said. 'No doubt you all have your own, somewhere, in case of emergencies.' None of them reacted, so I went on. 'These little things' — I gestured airily at the Luger — 'were highly prized in their day, and are still very efficient. It wouldn't surprise me in the least if Pritchard also had one.'

'So where is it?' said Farraday.

'How the hell should I know?' I asked. 'Have you tried searching *his* home? It's interesting that he told you about Akuji, though. "Henry's contact with the Biafrans", my arse — don't you remember Henry told us we didn't *have* any contacts on the Biafran side? That's because we don't: the KGB does. Akuji is a Moscow man. He's closely related to and physically resembles Ojukwu. His role was to pose as Ojukwu to any British representatives sent to try to arrange peace talks with the Biafrans — I suspect Geoffrey Manning had just such a meeting arranged on the day I met him. My guess is that Akuji was to agree to whatever Manning proposed regarding talks, naturally without informing Ojukwu or anyone else in the Biafran hierarchy about it. Then whoever from the PM's party had gone along to meet him would either have found themselves stood up or wasting a lot of time trying to negotiate peace with an impostor — all of which would have drawn away vital resources and attention from the security arrangements for the visit to Udi.'

They just stared at me, and I kept looking from one to the other.

'For Christ's sake!' I said. 'I'm not the double. Look, it's obvious, isn't it? Chief must have called Henry out to Swanwick to discuss Slavin, and during their conversation twigged that he was Radnya. So Henry shot him, took a few of his clothes, dumped his body and pretended he'd gone missing.'

Osborne sighed. 'No. That is precisely what *you* did.'

It was my turn to stare. He sounded certain of it.

'As well as the gun, we have three witnesses. The firmest is a local solicitor, who lives in the village and was passing on the way into town. But all three described a black sports car very much like your little toy.'

'Impossible,' I said. 'It was in my garage. Did they get a licence plate?'

Osborne spread his hands on the desk.

'Well, then!'

'But they did identify the car in other ways. Our solicitor friend told us that it had no boot. There are very few models with that feature. Yours is one.'

'Who questioned him?'

'That is immaterial.'

'No,' I said, 'It's not. I'll wager that whoever questioned him had already come up with the theory that the car was mine, and the solicitor was just doing his best to give the answers he thought would satisfy the man from London. It's a classic investigative error.'

'Don't be so bloody patronizing,' said Osborne, and I knew

he'd done the interview. Farraday's scornful glance in his direction confirmed it.

'Henry admitted to going out there — and admitted to the timing of the witnesses, if I remember rightly,' I said. 'It was also in the middle of the night, so anyone who saw a black car would have had to have been looking very closely. And as none of your "witnesses" took a number down, that seems unlikely.'

'Then,' said Osborne softly, 'there are the fingerprints. We took yours when you were in your coma. And then we compared them to all the sets we found in Templeton's house. Care to hazard a guess at what we discovered?'

'That some of them matched. Bravo — I've probably visited that house fifty times in the last three years. I was there the weekend before Chief disappeared.'

'Can you prove that?'

'I don't have to. You have to prove I wasn't.'

He raised his arm and for a moment I thought he was going to try to punch me, but he brought the palm of his hand down on a small bell on the table, the kind you see in hotel receptions, and a few seconds later the soldiers marched in. They aimed truncheons at my solar plexus, sending a jolt of pain through me and making me vomit. I tried to reach Montcrieff's shoes but he was too far away.

'Get him a towel or something,' said Farraday. I wondered what his reward had been — one of the more important ministries, no doubt. I remembered his little spat with Osborne over whether Pritchard or I should be allowed to go out to Lagos. They'd played it well, the three of them. If the coup hadn't come off perhaps they could have set up a small theatrical company.

I raised my head. Osborne was consulting a small leather-backed notebook. 'You hadn't visited Templeton in months,' he said. 'According to his daughter.'

I wiped my mouth with the cloth that had been handed me. 'How would she know?' I said.

'Well, you were sleeping with her, weren't you?'

'Where do you get these absurd—'

'She told us all about it,' said Farraday, chipping in.

'I hardly know her. She isn't my type.'

'Very suave,' said Montcrieff. He pushed forward another set of photographs. 'How do you explain these, then?'

In the car, rehearsing all the possible questions they could ask me, traps they could set, paths I could and could not take, this was one eventuality I hadn't envisaged.

She'd hanged herself, the poor cow. Her final few hours must have been hell. I remembered the look on her face as she had stood on the steps of her flat. Sorrow and despair. I had known it — and done nothing, too wrapped up in my own problems.

'Did she leave a note?' I asked, my lips tight.

Osborne nodded solemnly. 'Something about not being able to live with the fact that her boyfriend had killed her father.'

I leapt towards him, something like a scream coming from deep down in my throat, but I hadn't even reached the desk before I felt the thump. The soldier helped me back into my seat.

'So you *were* sleeping with her,' said Osborne, taking the cap off his fountain pen and noting it down neatly in his book.

'You really are a shit, Osborne,' I said, once I'd got my breath back again. 'Did you know that?'

He didn't look up from his writing. 'Murder and treason are more serious crimes.'

'Indeed,' I said. 'Conspiring to kill the prime minister is about as serious as it gets.'

That hit something. He pushed back his chair and stood up: his body may have been encased in finest Savile Row wool, but it did little to hide his bulk. He walked over to the plastic bucket and pushed it across the floor with a pointed little shoe, until it was just by my chair.

He yanked my head back by the forelock and brought his face up to mine. 'Did I ever tell you what we used to do with the Yids in Palestine back in '47?' he said, his eyes glazed over. 'The ones who wouldn't talk?'

He gestured at the soldiers again, and they stepped forward, took me crisply by the arms and shoved my face into the water, holding me down. I'd counted to twenty and was starting to panic when they jerked me out and dumped me back in the chair.

'Could we get some sandwiches or something?' said Montcrieff. 'I'm starving.'

'Yes, good idea,' said Osborne, whose face was flushed. He turned to one of the soldiers. 'Anderson, see if they have any decent food they can send down. Sandwiches or something.'

'Sir!' The soldier saluted and he and the others turned on their heels and left the room.

There was silence for a moment, then Farraday cleared his

throat. 'Listen, Paul,' he said reasonably. 'We don't want to spend all day on this. We know you're working for the Russians. We just want the details. The name of your handler, where you meet him, how often. What information you've passed over. You know the drill. I can't guarantee immunity, but if you cooperate now it will be a lot better for you.'

I'd got my breathing back now, and I summoned up my energy to look up at him. He was busy adjusting one of his shirt-cuffs, which had unpardonably jutted against the bevel of his wristwatch. It was twenty past one. So I could at least place myself: it was twenty past one on the twenty-eighth of April.

'The smoked salmon and cucumber ones are good here,' I said. 'Could we have some tea as well?'

'This isn't funny, Dark,' said Osborne. He held out his hand in a fist and then opened it, like a child playing a game. 'Do you recognize this?' he said. It was a small green booklet about the size of a box of matches. He flipped it open, revealing a string of numbers and other figures. 'A one-time pad. To be used in conjunction with a radio transmitter. Care to explain?'

I was still catching up with a thought I'd had a few seconds earlier. I wasn't certain of it, but I played it anyway.

'By all means,' I said. 'But before I do, perhaps you can all answer one question that has been troubling me. Who was the poor chap who had his head shot off in Udi – one of the PM's bodyguards? I presume there's a D-notice on it.'

Osborne made to stand up, but Montcrieff gestured at him to stay seated.

'What are you talking about?' he said.

'It was bloody good,' I said. 'I'll give you that. The posters at the traffic lights were a nice touch. How long did that take you to put into place? Was it just the one kiosk, or did you set up several along the route between here and the hospital?'

None of them answered.

'It was this that gave it away,' I said, tapping the copy of the *Standard* on the desk. 'You're a newspaperman, Sandy, so I'm a little disappointed. I'm sure all the details in it are perfect, but you over-egged the pudding making it today's West End Final. That edition doesn't come off the presses until two o'clock, and according to John's watch we're a good half-hour away from then. Careless, really – yesterday's edition would have done the trick just as well.'

They stared at me for a moment, and I savoured it.

'Fuck you, Dark!' spat Montcrieff, the first time I had seen him angry. 'This doesn't change that you're a traitor. Confess now and . . .'

'And what? You won't arrange my hanging at Wembley? Something tells me the PM might not be too keen to sign the chit for that whatever I say, and even if it were signed by the real Foreign Secretary.' I turned the screw. 'Perhaps he'd be more interested in hearing how you planned to kill him. I bet you all loved it when Henry proposed the idea – it was Henry's idea, wasn't it? Kill Wilson, then pin the blame on Moscow and claim he had double-crossed his masters at the KGB. Masterful. Did he tell you an actual KGB agent would do the job, though?' They didn't respond. 'How do you think he got her to do that?

Did it not occur to you that his more-fascist-than-thou act might have been just that — an act — and that he was, in fact, leading you straight into a position in which the KGB could send a sniper to assassinate our prime minister?'

I let it sink in for a moment. Osborne rallied from the shock of me discovering their little subterfuge and waved the one-time pad at me. 'This was found in your pockets when we searched you . . .'

'And I took it from Henry's pockets moments after I discovered he was Radnya and shot him,' I said. 'Radnya means "related" in Russian, and just as you were all delighted Henry had access to the Queen — who you would need to form a government — so were the KGB. What could be more precious than a double agent with blood ties to the throne?' Their faces were turning white, so I closed in for the kill. 'I suggest you send a team to Henry's house and search the basement. Once you've found his transmitter, perhaps we can stop this charade and get down to the serious business of trying to assess just how much the bastard has compromised over the last twenty-five years.'

*

He was wearing a green tweed coat and a polka-dot bow tie. It had taken me four and a half hours to get to the meeting, and he'd turned up in an outfit a child could describe.

I wasn't in the best of moods. I'd spent most of the day with a team from Five, searching every inch of Pritchard's enormous flat in Belgravia. He'd made me sweat — for several hours I had seriously wondered if I might still be looking at the rope. In the end, it hadn't been in the basement, or the attic, or under the floorboards, but in a compartment concealed in one of the bookshelves.

'I want out,' I said to Sasha. 'I mean it.' But it sounded weak, even to my ears.

He leaned over and placed a hand on my arm. 'Please, Paul,' he said. 'Is that any way to greet an old friend?' We were in the Mayflower in Rotherhithe, which he had once confided in me was his favourite meeting-place. I assumed it wasn't for the beer or because you could visit the stairs where the Pilgrim Fathers boarded the ship, but because it was dark and cosy. The place was about half-full, with a good deal of background noise, and we were seated at a remote corner table, next to a mantelshelf filled with the usual assortment of books gathering dust: Lloyd's *Shipping Register* for 1930, *Bernard Spilsbury — His Life and Cases*, Foote's *Handbook for Spies* . . .

On the way over, between checking for tails and hopping on and off buses, I'd bought a paper — a real one — and seen that de Gaulle had resigned over a referendum on the Senate: it looked like the events in Paris the previous year had finally caught up with him. The editorial on page nine opined that his 'ideas and presence would nevertheless continue to play a part in French affairs', while the item beneath it discussed the fall of Biafra's stronghold, Umuahia. Would his idea of supporting the Biafrans continue, too? I'd thought of the deserters and their families huddled in the hut in Aba; and of Gunner, ranting in the field at the futility of it all.

'I'm no use to you any more,' I said. 'I don't believe any of it.' And too many people were dead, I could have added – most of them because of me.

He pursed his lips, then placed his forefinger and thumb either side of his mouth and stroked his beard. It meant he was thinking.

'They have questioned you?' he said, drawing his head a little closer to me. I gave him a look. 'What did you tell them?'

'I thought of something.'

He stopped stroking his beard. 'What?'

I took a sip of my pint. 'I blew Henry's cover,' I said. 'And I don't care what you say, it won't scare me. Trust me, nothing you can say will scare me.'

He didn't move for some time, and then he suddenly leaned back in his seat and started laughing. I asked him if he would mind explaining the joke.

He slowly wound down the merriment. 'You were worried about how I might react?'

I shrugged.

'This was foreseen, Paul,' he said pompously. 'This was always the endgame.'

'What was?' I asked. 'For me to blow Henry's cover?'

'Of course. If he was not going to survive, you had to remain protected at all costs. It does not matter that you have exposed him now. They can't question him, and you are clean.' He frowned. 'You told them about Anna also, I presume? I mean, that she was . . . working with Henry?'

I noted the hesitation and tried not to hate him too much

for it. 'Yes,' I said. 'Was that also part of the endgame?'

Sasha raised his hands in a very Russian gesture. 'Perhaps. It is possible. I was never in contact with her. It was always Henry.'

It was always Henry. 'So Pritchard was running you?' I asked. He nodded. That explained a lot — why he'd had the transmitter, for a start. He had run Anna, he had run Sasha and, although I hadn't known it, he had run me. That night he'd left Vanessa's table at Ronnie Scott's — he hadn't gone home. He'd gone to meet Sasha and *then* home, where he had sent a message to Anna in Lagos. She had immediately upped sticks for Udi, telling her back-up man to find Slavin and kill him — and me if I tried to get anywhere near? Yes, that was how it must have been, or something like it.

I shivered inwardly and turned back to Sasha. 'If Henry was Radnya,' I said, 'what was my code-name?'

He pretended not to hear the tense I'd used. 'You really want to know?' he said. 'It's an ugly one. "Nezavisimyj".'

'"Independent" — why that?'

'Because we had to keep you separate from the rest of the cell, for . . .' — he looked around for a suitable phrase — 'personal reasons.'

'You mean because if I had discovered that Anna was alive, Henry had pimped her to me and Father had shot himself over the whole affair, I might not have been so cooperative.'

He smiled tolerantly. 'If you prefer. But from the start you were seen as an independent operator. A free agent. Someone who had to be nurtured, but who was his own man.'

'And now?'

He leaned over and grabbed a handful of peanuts out of a tinted glass bowl I hadn't noticed on the table between us, and dropped a few into his mouth.

'Now we need you more than ever,' he said, and crunched a few of them down noisily.

'Not interested,' I said.

'Paul, listen. I understand you are no longer a Communist. In truth, I sometimes wonder if I am either.' He caught my look. 'It is the truth. But times and circumstances change. Look at what you distrust about us. About me, if you wish. Do you really believe I am a worse master than the men now running your country?'

'The coup failed,' I said. 'They're not running it any more than they were last month.'

He tilted his head a little. 'No? With your old Chief gone, I think you will see some changes. These men have a lot of ambition, Paul. That is why Henry thought of the coup: he felt it would be less dangerous in the long term to let them into the open, with the illusion of victory, than to continue their games behind the scenes. The plan was for him to control them from the inside — and in doing so slowly immobilize them.'

'Hell of a risky plan.'

He shrugged: he could wear as much tweed as he wanted, but his shrugs were more Russian than vodka. 'I think it was well calculated. Britain would have been in a state of shock — look at what happened with the Americans — and a traumatized enemy would have suited us well. But, as you say, the coup failed. And Henry is dead. The faction is in a more powerful position than ever, however: far from being under suspicion for the attempt on the Prime Minister's life, they have used it to call for more financial support, which I think they will receive. They have a hold of the reins, and we need a way to control them.'

'Did I mention that they offered me Deputy Chief?' I said. 'Same as Pritchard would have got — isn't that funny?'

Sasha swallowed his peanuts. Very slowly, he let out a wide, car salesman's beam. Then there was the faintest quiver in his lower lip.

'You accepted, naturally.'

'I told you,' I said. 'I'm retiring.'

His face froze for a moment, but almost at once he decided I was joking. 'You can't *retire*! You are finally coming to fruition!'

I didn't like it — being talked about as though I were a wine.

'I'm going to teach English at a prep school in Berkshire,' I said. 'Read Bulldog Drummond to the boys before lights out and learn to smoke a pipe.'

He gazed at me with puzzlement. 'I've lived here nearly twenty years and I still don't understand your sense of humour,' he said. And then he reached inside his coat and took out a slim leather wallet, from which he removed a group of postage stamps. He placed them on the table, taking care to hold the corners down with the tips of his fingers. 'But just in case you have misunderstood the situation . . .' he said, inviting me to lean across for a closer look. As I did, I realized that they weren't stamps, but negatives. He held one up to the bulb for me, but I could already see what it was.

I had been wrong. He could still scare me.

*

Outside, I lit a cigarette and thought about the arrangement we had made. Arrangement is perhaps the wrong word: I hadn't had any say in the matter. The photographs of Anna and me covered every conceivable angle. I wondered who had taken them – Father? Pritchard? Well, it hardly mattered now.

I wandered down the street, looking for a cab but not seeing any. It was getting late, and I was on the wrong side of the river. A free agent, I thought bitterly, as I buttoned my coat.

Far from it.

Author's Note

The background to this novel is real. The Nigerian civil war took the lives of hundreds of thousands of people, and was a superpower conflict by proxy. It was waged for over two and a half years, until Biafra finally fell in January 1970. The British Prime Minister, Harold Wilson, was vilified as a result of his government's support for the Federal side, and did visit Nigeria in March 1969. I am grateful to the National Archives of the United Kingdom for providing me with copies of several Cabinet Office records related to his visit, including the programme (reference CAB 164/409 105669), an excerpt of which is quoted on pages 186–7.

There is no record of an assassination attempt against Harold Wilson in Nigeria, but there were extensive and bizarre conspiracies against him, and by members of the British establishment and intelligence community. I am indebted to the work of Stephen Dorril and Robin Ramsay, whose *Smear! Wilson and the Secret State* is an impeccably sourced primer on that subject.

Cecil King did meet with Louis Mountbatten and others in May 1968 to discuss a coup against the Wilson government.

Stephen Dorril is also the author of an excellent history of Britain's Secret Intelligence Service, which led me to many other works, and I am particularly grateful to him for his advice on Nigeria at an early stage. The atmosphere and details of life within SIS during the late Sixties were drawn from many sources, but chief among them was Tom Bower's biography of Dick White, *The Perfect English Spy*. Regarding Soviet intelligence, my starting point was *My Silent War*, the autobiography of Kim Philby, which was first published in 1968. It gave me few easy answers regarding the motivations of double agents, and even fewer details of tradecraft – although he does describe taking almost an entire day to meet his handler at one point! It is a frustrating but compelling book – I returned to it often. Robert Cecil's biography of Donald Maclean was similarly stimulating, as were several other books on the known double agents of this era. Christopher Andrew and Vasili Mitrokhin's works on the history of the KGB were also crucial stepping-stones for my research into Soviet espionage.

The SAS and others did search for Nazi war criminals in Germany in 1945; they did not engage in the nefarious work I have ascribed to my fictional trio, but I used their real working methods as a basis. Anthony Kemp's *The Secret Hunters* was my main source on that subject, but I was also lucky enough to interview veterans of 5 SAS who were involved in war crimes investigations – for which, sincere thanks. Some of the details regarding the Thompson-Bolas were inspired by the lives of Fela Anikulapo-Kuti and his mother but, again, I hasten to add that none of that family was ever engaged in the activities described in this novel. Thanks to Michael Veal for his advice on the intricacies of Nigeria's music scene during this time. I have relocated the Afrospot to a different suburb of Lagos, but kept its name – it is not meant to be an accurate representation of the real club at that time.

I read many accounts of the war in Nigeria, by soldiers, spies, doctors, priests, journalists and others, but I was probably most inspired by *The Nigerian Civil War* by John de St Jorre, which I remembered seeing on my parents' bookshelves as a child. I am honoured and grateful that John agreed to read various drafts of this book, and for his encouragement and advice on it.

Many details in the book may seem incorrect at first sight, but prove not to be on closer examination. For example, Lagos is usually one hour ahead of London, but between 1968 and 1971 Britain experimented with something called British Standard Time, whereby the country remained one hour ahead of Greenwich Mean Time all year round. But any factual errors in the book are mine alone.

I would also like to thank William Boyd, John Boyle, Ajay Chowdhury, Jeannette Cook, Vincent Eaton, Lucy Elliott,

Kathrin Hagmaier, John Hellon, Kim Hutchings, Alice Jolly, Renata Mikolajczyk, Iwan and Margareta Morelius, K. V. Ramesh, Andrea Rees, Marika Sandell, Loretta Stanley, Tim Stevens and Martin Westlake for their advice on various drafts; Dr Evelyn Depoortere for her guidance on Lassa fever; David Powell for information on snipers; Alex Haw for his twenty years of friendship and keen questioning; my parents and parents-in-law for their advice, stories and contemporary material; my agent, Antony Topping, for his wonderfully astute reading of the manuscript and able guidance through this process; my editor, Kathryn Court, and everyone at Viking, for their encouragement and advice; and finally, my wife, Johanna, for her honest opinions, steadfast support and belief in this project, and my children for going to bed on time, occasionally.

Select Bibliography

Chinua Achebe, *No Longer At Ease* (Heinemann, 1960)

Chinua Achebe, et al., *The Insider: Stories of War and Peace from Nigeria* (Nwankwo-Ifejeka, 1971)

A. B. Aderibigbe (ed.), *Lagos: The Development of an African City* (Longman Nigeria, 1975)

Kunle Akinsemoyin and Alan Vaughan-Richards, *Building Lagos* (Pengrail, 1977)

N. U. Akpan, *The Struggle for Secession, 1966–1970* (Routledge, 2004)

Christopher Andrew and Vasili Mitrokhin, *The Sword and the Shield: The Mitrokhin Archive and the Secret History of the KGB* (Basic Books, 1999)

Christopher Andrew and Vasili Mitrokhin, *The Mitrokhin Archive II: The KGB and the World* (Allen Lane, 2005)

I. A. Atigbi, *Nigeria Tourist Guide* (Nigerian Tourist Association, 1969)

John Barron, *KGB: The Secret Work of Soviet Secret Agents* (Bantam, 1974)

Saburi O. Biobaku (ed.), *The Living Culture of Nigeria* (Thomas Nelson, Nigeria, 1976)

Tom Bower, *The Perfect English Spy* (Mandarin, 1996)

Andrew Boyle, *The Climate of Treason: Five Who Spied for Russia* (Hutchinson, 1979)

Jean Buhler, *Tuez-les Tous! Guerre de Sécession au Biafra* (Flammarion, 1968)

Robert Cecil, *A Divided Life: A Biography of Donald Maclean* (Coronet, 1990)

John Collins, *Musicmakers of West Africa* (Three Continents Press, 1985)

John de St Jorre, *The Nigerian Civil War* (Hodder and Stoughton, 1972)

Pierre de Villemarest, *GRU: Le plus secret des services soviétiques, 1918–1988* (Stock, 1988)

Len Deighton (ed.), *London Dossier* (Penguin, 1967)

Stephen Dorril, *MI6: Inside the Covert World of Her Majesty's Secret Intelligence Service* (Touchstone, 2000)

Stephen Dorril and Robin Ramsay, *Smear! Wilson and the Secret State* (Grafton, 1992)

Peter Enahoro, *How to Be a Nigerian* (Spectrum, 1998)

Sam Eppele, *The Promise of Nigeria* (Pan, 1960)

William Fagg (ed.), *The Living Arts of Nigeria* (Studio Vista, 1976)

M. R. D. Foot, *SOE: The Special Operations Executive, 1940–1946* (BBC, 1984)

Frederick Forsyth, *The Biafra Story* (Leo Cooper, 2001)

Henry Louis Gates, et al., *The Anniversary Issue: Selections from Transition, 1961–1976* (Duke University Press, 1999)

Mike Hoare, *Mercenary* (Corgi, 1982)

Ian V. Hogg and John Weeks, *Military Small Arms of the Twentieth Century* (DBI Books, 1985)

Madeleine G. Kalb, *The Congo Cables: The Cold War in Africa – from Eisenhower to Kennedy* (Macmillan, 1982)

Anthony Kemp, *The Secret Hunters* (Michael O'Mara Books, 1986)

A. H. M. Kirk-Greene, *Crisis and Conflict in Nigeria: A Documentary Sourcebook* (Oxford University Press, 1971)

Phillip Knightley, *Philby: KGB Masterspy* (Pan, 1988)

Phillip Knightley, *The Second Oldest Profession* (Penguin, 1988)

John Le Carré, *To Russia, with Greetings (An Open Letter to the Moscow Literary Gazette)* (Encounter, May 1966)

Colin Legum (ed.), *Africa Handbook* (Penguin Reference Books, 1969)

Akin L. Mabogunje, *Urbanization in Nigeria* (University of London Press, 1968)

Alexander Madiebo, *The Nigerian Revolution and the Biafran War* (Fourth Dimension, 2002)

Jim Malia, *Biafra: The Memory of the Music* (Melrose Books, 2007)

Peter Mason, *Official Assassin* (Phillips Publications, 1998)

Martin Meredith, *The State of Africa* (The Free Press, 2005)

Bernard Odogwu, *No Place to Hide: Crises and Conflicts Inside Nigeria* (Fourth Dimension, 2002)

Bruce Paige, David Leitch and Phillip Knightley, *Philby: The Spy Who Betrayed a Generation* (Sphere, 1977)

Kim Philby, *My Silent War* (Grafton, 1989)

AI Romanov, *Nights Are Longest There: Smersh from the Inside* (Hutchinson, 1972)

Ken Saro-Wiwa, *On a Darkling Plain* (Saros International Publishers, 1989)

Ken Saro-Wiwa, *Sozaboy* (Longman, 2006)

Julian Semyonov, *TASS Is Authorized to Announce* (John Calder, 1987)

Kate Simon, *London: Places and Pleasures* (MacGibbon and Kee, 1969)

Wole Soyinka, *Ibadan: The Penkelemes Years* (Methuen, 1994)

Gordon Stevens, *The Originals: The Secret History of the Birth of the SAS in Their Own Words* (Ebury Press, 2005)

Viktor Suvorov, *Aquarium: The Career and Defection of a Soviet Military Spy* (Hamish Hamilton, 1985)

Raph Uwechue, *Looking Back on the Nigerian Civil War* (in *Africa 71*, Jeune Afrique, 1971)

Michael E. Veal, *Fela: The Life and Times of an African Musical Icon* (Temple University Press, 2000)

Philip Warner, *The SAS: The Official History* (Sphere, 1983)

Auberon Waugh and Suzanna Cronjé, *Biafra: Britain's Shame* (Michael Joseph, 1969)

Olivier Weber, *French Doctors* (Sélection du Reader's Digest, 1996)

Nigel West, *A Matter of Trust: M.I.5. 1945–72* (Coronet, 1983)

Nigel West, *The Illegals* (Coronet, 1994)

Nigel West and Oleg Tsarev, *The Crown Jewels* (HarperCollins, 1999)

Terry White, *Swords of Lightning: Special Forces and the Changing Faces of Warfare* (BPCC Wheatons, 1992)